GOD BLESS YOU, MR. TRUMP

INDIGORIVER
PUBLISHING

GOD BLESS YOU, MR. TRUMP

A NOVEL

JESSE THOEMING

God Bless You, Mr. Trump

Editors: David Remy, Noëlla Simmons
Cover Art: Clarissa Koch

Indigo River Publishing
3 West Garden Street, Ste. 718
Pensacola, FL 32502

www.indigoriverpublishing.com

Ordering Information:

Quantity Sales: Special discounts are available on quantity purchases by corporations, associations, and others. For details, contact the publisher at the address above.

Orders by US trade bookstores and wholesalers: Please contact the publisher at the address above.

Printed in the United States of America

Library of Congress Control Number: 2026901458
ISBN: 978-1-969935-16-9 (paperback) 978-1-969935-17-6 (ebook)

First Edition

For both Carl Sagan and Sam Harris—
thanks for turning the lights on

CHAPTER ONE

ONLY ADVANCE

She's seventy going on forty. If properly motivated, she could pull off thirty-five and effectively halve her age—a dangerous thought she keeps in her back pocket for nights when the lights are low, and the mirrors are forgiving. Samantha Ravensby studies her reflection in the polished pane of glass above her workstation. Her eyes, sharp and calculating, drink in the taut skin, the smoothed contours of her face. The latest CRISPR therapy coursing through her cells is working overtime. This evening, she looks like someone she hasn't seen in years—herself, circa the Terrible Twenties. The irony is not lost on her: a rejuvenated face, but the mind of a tactician sharpened by decades of maneuvering.

The energy of the Golden Gate Nexus vibrates faintly beneath her feet, a constant reminder of the empire she's building. This temporary office, deep within the hub of the HyperLoop's west coast operations, feels more like a bunker than a workplace. The walls, sterile and angular, emanate a faint light—an echo of San Francisco's heartbeat outside. Samantha likes it this way. Isolation fuels her focus. From here, she orchestrated the integration of Loopd>In into the HyperLoop's travel pods, a milestone that will come to fruition in a matter of weeks. She glances at the schematics displayed on her brand-new retinal Leaf—a near invisible interface embedded beneath the skin, integrating with her vision almost like a second layer of sight. She closes her eyes and quiets her mind. A soft overlay appears as soon as she reopens them. The Leaf renders traditional screens nearly obsolete, allowing users to engage with the digital world without ever looking down. No distractions, no endless scrolling—just instant information woven into reality. She recognizes that, much like the innovations of the Digital Revolution of her youth, the Leaf is a collaborative effort of brilliant minds, a fusion of digitization and life sciences, akin to her very own, Loopd>In. The blueprints she reviews are a symphony of data and design that only she truly understands. Loopd>In isn't software. It's salvation.

Or so she tells herself.

Her desk, a relic in this space of gleaming technology, is a battlefield of papers, dossiers, and tactile remnants of a world she still values. Her hand hovers over the folders lining the edge, fingers grazing each one until she finds it. Dust clings to the edges of the manuscript, and Samantha's heart rate quickens. With a flick of her wrist, she brushes it clean and opens past the cover page and to the manuscript's opening chapter: *Time & Space on a Gravel Road* by Philipp Largo.

All of it unpublished. Mostly forgotten. Effectively suppressed. All by her hand.

The thought makes her smile—a wicked curve of her lips as she settles into her chair. Largo's brilliance was unmatched, his naivety even more so. He had truly believed that enlightenment could be the answer, that an awakened generation of so-called UnPluggers could steer humanity toward a harmonious future.

Samantha admired him for that, even loved him in her own way. But she didn't share his optimism. After his death—his grisly, public, headline-grabbing death—she acted swiftly. His legacy, his ideas, his influence—all buried.

I did that, she thinks, the smile widening. He was hers to remember, hers to study, hers to keep. The world didn't deserve him, and she certainly didn't want to share him.

Flipping through the pages, she lands on her favorite passage that she never tires of rereading:

> *The Great Filter presents a potential explanation for Fermi's Paradox—the absence of detectable civilizations in our universe. We teeter on a precipice, poised between self-destruction and transcendence. Technology offers liberation, but it also brings peril. To navigate this knife-edge requires enlightened leaders and a unified society. The question is: Who will guide us? Who will lead us across this fragile threshold?*

Samantha snaps the book shut and exhales sharply. Largo's words, as always, stir something deep within her—remnants of guilt, a sliver of doubt. But they're quickly extinguished. Oh, Philipp Largo—was there ever a more naively brilliant man? He knew the score better than anyone, but he foolishly believed that attempting to enlighten the youth of America would help solve our society's ills. And while these so-called UnPluggers might have a few admirable traits as a collective whole, it's nowhere near enough. Not if we're to truly evolve, escape the 'Great Filter,' and spread out through the cosmos. With nuclear fusion now powering the globe, the ability to make gargantuan leaps in space travel is right around the corner. Samantha Ravensby, more than anyone or anything, knows the masses will need controlling, kept fully occupied if the necessary moves are to be made. Yes, control is most assuredly the answer.

Not enlightenment. And the time is now. She has the fortitude and the resources to make it happen. Starting with Loopd>In—the first big domino in her grand design that needs to be pushed forward. But the rug could still be pulled out from beneath her. She knows everything could unravel with a single misstep, most especially if all loose ends aren't effectively dealt with.

"Hey there!" some stumpy bald guy calls out from the hall. Clad in standard HyperLoop attire—a silver and black jumpsuit from top to bottom with black boots and a white hard hat. He looks like George Costanza dressed up as an astronaut going out for a night on the town.

"Yes, how can I help you?" Samantha says, moving toward her doorway. Just when she thought she had this level all to herself for the night.

"Oh no, no help. I'm here to ensure you're okay. I'm Al's helper, you see, and he thought it would be wise to make sure everything was good in your office and with everything else. You're the only one onsite who's not an official HyperLoop employee."

His aw-shucks attitude and demeanor ooze from his every movement and utterance. *How'd this guy get anything more than a janitor job at a place like this.* "Everything's great here. Can't complain about a thing," Samantha says. "Is Al your boss?"

"Oh no, well, kinda, I suppose. Al is what we call the AI that serves as this place's central nervous system. I'm an AI-helper." He snorts a laugh and smiles like a fool.

An AI-helper? This guy is fortunate to not be a paperclip. Thankfully for him, people like me are far more tolerant and empathetic. "Okay then. Well, please tell Al we're quite excited to be a part of the launch. All systems go!" She feigns a laugh and gives the man a playful wink.

"And you're that gaming or entertainment system, right?" He takes his hard hat off and wipes his bald, sweaty head with a cloth from his pocket as if he's trying to solve some great problem.

"Yes, something like that," Samantha says. "Be sure to try it the first chance you get."

"Me? No way! I can't even do roller coasters." He steps forward like he wants to come all the way in her office to chat some more. Samantha quickly fakes a call coming through her Leaf.

"So sorry, but I must take this," she says, holding up a hand and turning away from him. He mutters something apologetic and moves along his way.

Once he's out of sight, she closes her door and takes a seat at her desk. She thinks back to Largo's words and dwells on his final question: 'Who are the leaders and visionaries who will shepherd us across this fragile juncture?' *I am,* she says aloud to no one. There's no time for empathy or regret. Nothing can get in her way lest it be bulldozed completely over. Ten billion smart apes must be satiated if we brave and daring few take the next logical step in evolution. The time has indeed come. Her retinal Leaf pings softly, a reminder of her upcoming schedule that runs well past midnight. She initiates a command, sending an encrypted message to her inner circle. Everything is in place. The unveiling of Loopd>In is imminent, but loose ends remain. The subtle threats still linger, those who could disrupt her plans. The thought tightens her jaw.

Rising from her chair, Samantha strides down the hall to the floor's only window. The city sprawls before her, its lights a constellation of human ambition. Somewhere out there, the next chapter of her plan is waiting. And she will write it, in ink as indelible as the stars.

Only advance, she reminds herself. No retreat. No half measures. No contingency plans. *Only advance.* That wisdom-filled adage propelled and inspired more than any other since she was taught its meaning when she was a little girl.

CHAPTER TWO

THE SON AND THE CRANE

In the heartland of America, where the sky stretches wide and uncluttered, a construction site sprawls across a hundred acres, buzzing with constant activity. Like a well-oiled machine, a myriad of drones, each a cog in this grand design, swarm like a colony of bees assembling the remainder of a massive hive. All diligently following the queen's orders, not one is off schedule or mission. But Dante Largo is not their queen, nor their commander. He is something more akin to a guardian or caretaker—tall and lanky, his six-foot-four frame marked by a long wingspan that once helped make his curveball nearly unhittable. His bright blue eyes, sharp but often distant, rarely betray emotion these days, locked behind five years of practiced stoicism and haunted retreat. A faint scar, above his left eyebrow, tells the story of a line drive that came screaming back at him during a high school game—a reminder of how unpredictable both the sport and life can be. His wavy, Beatle-like hair, a dark mop that once framed the face of a boy who smiled easily, lies beneath his company-issued bright orange safety helmet. His big hands, with long fingers built just right for the delicate grip of a baseball, now spend their days repairing drones instead, his touch more mechanical than instinctual.

A service tech, his role is to ensure this orchestration of technology sings without missing a beat. Like most moments of his working days, everything is functioning as designed and scheduled. He takes a step back from the focus of his work and into the warmth of the late December day. It's sixty degrees, not terribly unusual for this time of the year in the Midwest, just a few short hours south of St. Louis. The low winter sun casts long shadows across the site, turning the exposed beams into sharp lines etched against the sky. Nearby, drones continue to buzz and click as they shuttle building materials between metal and carbon fiber skeletons, each frame towering higher as the day inches on. His last shift before the holiday break, he's restless, and his mind drifts to thoughts of the past, the things he's avoiding.

He takes a moment to appreciate the bustling, congruous movement around him, every drone performing its choreographed routine—welding, sealing, lifting—seamlessly conceived. The technology here is world class. Even though he's worked as a drone tech the past two years, he's still very much in constant awe of the way everything progresses as planned. A precision that borders on poetic. He lets his hand slip into his forest green hoodie and retrieves a thermos of coffee, taking a deep sip as he watches the construction drones swoop and dart between the steel beams like the most agile birds. The site manager, a grizzled old-timer with a bushy mustache, gives him a nod as he walks by, and Dante returns it with a half-smile. The relaxed camaraderie keeps him grounded here—men and machines working together. Dante has been one of less than a dozen on this project since it started. They are in sync, each one trusting the other to get the job done.

He takes a few steps away from the official worksite into the designated break area. Only a few hours remain and he will be off for the rest of the year, getting to recharge his own batteries for close to three weeks. Something catches his boot—a small, jagged rock jutting out of the dirt. He pauses, leaning down to inspect it. Oddly shaped, with rough edges and a pale streak of quartz running through it. On any other day, he might leave it be, but something about it irritates him. He stoops, picks it up and tosses it back into the brush beyond the bush. *Bam!* The act of tossing it, the sensation of letting it go from the release point he thoughtlessly selected, brings him back to another place, another moment.

Suddenly, he's no longer here on the construction site. He's back at Oracle II, on that most wretched day five years ago, a baseball in his hand. He's warming up on the mound, having never felt better in his entire life. His whole body was tuned in, his mind calm, each breath easy, deep, and full. It was his shot, his chance to make the Show.

Dante had developed an almost otherworldly control over his emotions by then, a skill he had sharpened through years of meditation and mindfulness. His father introduced him to Sam Harris's *Waking Up* app before he was ten, and those daily sessions became a touchstone. Especially on game days, Dante practiced the art of shutting out the noise, letting the world blur into the background while he locked in, every part of him—mind, body, and breath—aligned in the calm focus he needed to perform at the highest level. And as always, he was fully unplugged.

Dante's hands, big and capable, gave him a unique grip on the ball. He perfected a curveball that took years to master, the kind of big-league pitch coaches absolutely adored. It didn't matter that he was a right-hander without a zipping fastball. Not anymore. The game shifted back to its roots in recent years due in large part to new AI-assisted strike zones, pitchers were graded on precision and movement as much as speed. This new generation once again strived for getting outs rather than swing-and-misses. They didn't all need to break a hundred miles per hour anymore. It was about strategy, control, and finesse. Just about every team had a Greg Maddux, an artist and maestro on the mound. And Dante was certainly on the path.

But that gameday in late March didn't go as planned.

Dante's arm felt electric. His final warm-up pitch snapped into the catcher's mitt, and he exhaled slowly, rolling his shoulders, settling in. He felt untouchable, weightless. Every cell in his body was tuned to the moment. The crowd buzzed with anticipation. This was it—the day he took his biggest step toward the majors.

Then, in the periphery of his vision, movement. A blur cutting across the bullpen. Someone was sprinting toward him like a bloody madman. Dante barely had time to process before Chew crashed into him, gripping his jersey, fingers digging into his shoulders. His best friend, his rock, the guy who was never rattled—was shaking.

"Deuce—" Chew's breath came in short, ragged bursts. His eyes were wild, bloodshot, and wet. "It's your dad."

The words barely landed, a distant echo in the buzzing stadium. Dante, who was known to many, especially Chew, as Deuce due to that big league curve, blinked at him, confused. "What?"

Chew's grip tightened. His fingers curled around Deuce's jersey, like he was trying to physically hold him together. "There was a shooting," he said, voice cracking. "St. Louis. At his conference . . ." He shook his head, like he couldn't believe the words coming out of his mouth. "Deuce . . ." His lips trembled. His chest heaved. "He's gone." Then Chew crying uncontrollably, a site Dante had never witnessed previously. What on earth was going on?

The ground beneath Deuce ceased to exist. His brain scrambled, trying to grasp the words, to put them into a reality that made sense. But they didn't. They couldn't. His dad was supposed to be flying out after the conference. Celebrate his achievement, this moment, toast to his success. It was all planned. A full weekend in their favorite city to visit.

Gone? A slow, sick feeling curdled in Deuce's stomach. "No," he said, the word barely audible over the stadium noise.

Chew swallowed hard, holding back another onslaught of tears. "I saw the footage, man." His voice cracked, barely keeping it together. "I—I shouldn't have looked. It's—" He clenched his jaw, squeezing his eyes shut, his whole body trembling. "It's the worst thing I've ever seen."

Deuce's heartbeat hammered in his ears. His breath quickened. This wasn't real. This wasn't happening. His fingers clenched tighter around the baseball in his hand, but his grip was weak, unsteady. His body knew before his mind did—knew that the weight in his chest was something permanent, something irreversible.

The ball slipped from his grasp. It hit the dirt with a soft, hollow thud. A noise rose from the stands—a wave of murmurs, an unease spreading like a raging wildfire. He turned, following the stunned stares of the crowd. And then he saw it.

The jumbotron flashed a breaking news banner, the words emblazoned in stark, merciless white.

"MASSACRE IN ST. LOUIS: DOZENS KILLED, INCLUDING TRISTAN HARRIS AND PHILIPP LARGO."

The letters burned into his vision. He stared. Blinked. Waited for the words to change. They didn't. Philipp Largo. Gone. Tristan Harris. Gone.

His father, Philipp. His hero. His last parent.

Now an orphan. Something inside him splintered, cracked like an old foundation giving way to collapse. His chest seized, lungs locking up. He couldn't breathe. Couldn't move. The world tilted on its axis, the stadium warping into something surreal, something *wrong*. The noise—crowd, vendors, announcers—became a dull, incoherent hum, distant and meaningless.

Chew was still talking frantically, still gripping him, but Deuce couldn't hear the words. All he could hear was the silence of everything else. The void. A blur of movement. Coaches rushing over. A trainer saying something urgent. But it was all muffled, distorted. His eyes drifted back to the jumbotron. The words weren't changed.

His father was dead.

The weight of it crushed him, an entire building on his chest. His legs gave out, and he sank to the ground, his knees slamming into the dirt. The impact barely registered.

Chew dropped down with him, his breath ragged, his own grief pouring out of him. "Deuce . . ." His voice broke, shattered. His hand hovered between them, unsure where to land—on Deuce's shoulder, his arm, anywhere that might hold him together. But there was nothing left to hold.

Deuce pressed his palms into the dirt, his vision tunneling. A deep, guttural sound clawed up his throat—rage, grief, agony—but it never made it past his lips.

His father was dead. The man who taught him everything. Who pulled him out of the darkest places. Who showed him how to navigate a world that never quite made sense.

Gone.

A rush of static filled his head. He didn't hear the umpire calling for order. Didn't feel the presence of more teammates surrounding him. The game, his future, his shot at the majors—it all faded into nothing. The only thing left was the hole in his chest, yawning and endless.

Chew's voice cracked again. "I'm so fucking sorry."

And then, through the suffocating silence, through the numbness spreading like ice in his veins—rage. A spark of it. Distant, buried beneath the wreckage. But there. Because this wasn't random. This wasn't just some act of violence in a country still trying to shake off the nightmares of the 2020s.

This was the *MAGA Massacre.* They wouldn't call it that right away. The news would hesitate, dance around the truth. But that's what it was. That's what it would be known as. A massacre. And his father—one of the men leading the charge for a better future—had been at the center of it. For the first time since he saw those words, since the world shattered around him, Deuce sucked in a breath. Shallow. Jagged. And then another.

His vision swam back into focus. The hiss and sway of the crowd. The presence of Chew still gripping his arm like a tether to the world. The dirt beneath his knees, solid and real. The baseball, lying inches away, forgotten in the dust. Somewhere, deep in the marrow of his bones, the beginning of something new stirred.

Not acceptance. Not peace. Something sharper. Something that five years later, would lead him right back to the city that still haunted him.

Dante shakes his head and sighs until he's out of breath, bringing himself back to the present, though the memory persists like a bruise he can't stop pressing. The purr of drones fills the air as they swoop across the site, almost in sync with his pulse, which is starting to slow again. The worksite is hyperefficient, almost flawless, with AI optimizing every part of the process. Soon the high-speed transit system will be complete and interconnected across the country. Having been on the project since it started gives Dante a small tinge of satisfaction, yet for all its technological perfection, it feels strangely hollow. Like everything since his father's murder, it's mostly just a routine devoid of meaning.

A *pop* from his new retinal Leaf pulls him out of his own thoughts and the horror and memories of that fatefully awful day. In his direct view a soft purple glow appears across his retina:

> *Deuce, I went ahead and booked passage for both of us. We launch tomorrow night. It's time. You know what I mean. Can't wait to see you again, my man. It shall be one for the books.*
>
> *—Chew*

A small, tired smile creeps onto Dante's face. Chew, his best friend and former teammate, has been after him for months to make the trip back to San Francisco. Known to all as Chew, David Mastamann has been Dante's best friend for more than half his life. The one Dante stayed in touch with these past five years. And he only ever refers to him as Deuce, the nickname bestowed upon him as a youngster when he first developed that big time curveball. Chew wants Deuce to face the city that haunts him, convinced that going back will offer some form of closure. But it's more than that. Chew wants to rebuild their friendship, to remind Deuce of who he was before abject sorrow tore through him. And though Deuce knows Chew is right, the thought of going back is enough to make his pulse race all over again. After all, he just got triggered and thrown back in time by tossing a damn rock.

Deuce's gaze drifts to the massive crane towering over the construction site's center. The late afternoon sun hangs low, shining a deep orange light that ignites the crane's frame, giving it an ethereal glow. As the light hits the crane's length, it casts a massive shadow across the dirt field, stretching far beyond the site boundaries and over the treetops like a specter reaching into the past. Deuce feels it like a pall, echoing his own unresolved grief—a reminder of what his father helped build and what the world had mostly forgotten.

With the maiden voyage of the HyperLoop dominating the national press, Deuce can't help but think of everything his father did, but few realized it was his hand at play. None more so than the HyperLoop because it came about closely following Elon Musk's reconnection with Sam Harris . . . a reconnection bridged by none other than his father. When the Making Sense podcaster began to make sense for the world's richest man and pull him out of the madness he slipped into during those Terrible Twenties. For Deuce, the ultimate tragedy was that his father's grisly and untimely death drowned his legacy, and over time, the world moved on. And to this day, Deuce wasn't sure of everything his dad had a hand in. It's time to change that, he thinks. Starting in San Francisco.

A second Leaf *pop*. He's only activated the device less than a month and now, getting the hang of it. It's a recent tech breakthrough on the level of fire and wireless as it changes the game of life for every user. Information and communication as simple as a concentrated thought. High tech gadgetry and life sciences amalgamated to reshape, well, everything. The message is again from Chew, as if he's there with Deuce, egging him to shed the past and go forward together into the future in which hope abounds and pain recedes.

"If you can't do it for yourself, do it for him."

The weight of it settles over him like the descending twilight. For five long years, Deuce had stayed hidden, convinced that his father's legacy—overshadowed by the violent spectacle of his death—was out of reach. And that nothing carried any meaning. But today, something indeed feels different. San Francisco no longer seems like a place to avoid. Instead, it's a place he needs to return to, a place where his father's memory deserves rekindling.

As the light slips away, Deuce lets go of the numbness that's held him back since that day five years ago. The crane's silhouette fades into the evening, its shadow absorbed into the darkness, but

Deuce stands a moment longer, watching, resolved. For the first time in years, he feels the faint stirrings of purpose, and he's looking forward to catching up with his closest friend. He responds to Chew that he's ready—and excited—to make the play.

CHAPTER THREE

THE ABYSS

Charisma Sinclair slows to a walk, chest rising and falling in deep, steady breaths. Sweat cools against her skin as she pulls off her sunglasses and surveys the neighborhood she's spent years pretending to belong in. Towering, architecturally ostentatious estates sprawl across manicured lawns, their owners ensconced in wealth so old it no longer recognizes itself as privilege. Every driveway hosts the latest autonomous vehicles, every home a monument to someone's family legacy. She wonders, not for the first time, if they even know what it's like to build something from nothing.

Then there's hers—a modest 3-D printed unit tucked at the edge of the community, an anomaly in this world of opulence. A testament not to lineage but to raw ingenuity, to a life built on intellect and innovation rather than inheritance. She prefers it that way. Or at least she did, until now. One step inside her home and she notices it. An envelope—thick, cream-colored, embossed with an insignia she doesn't immediately recognize—placed dead center on her kitchen island, like a trap laid in waiting. Not slid under the door. Not dropped in the mail. Delivered.

By whom? And how?

A sharp tension grips her ribs, compressing her post-run exhilaration into something cold and tight. She knows, with the kind of premonition that doesn't require opening it, that nothing inside that envelope is good. She stares at it in her hands as if it were a relic from an extinct world. It's thick, almost ceremonial, a weight that doesn't belong in 2049. *Who even sends letters anymore?* Everything important—contracts, legal notices, corporate negotiations—flows through encrypted quantum channels—secured, documented, permanent. Especially with the recent advent of the retinal Leaf. But this . . . this is different. Tactile. Deliberate. A definitive power play.

She runs her fingers along the embossed insignia, her pulse quickening as recognition sets in. A law firm—one of the big ones, the kind that deals in multibillion-dollar lawsuits and existential corporate warfare. A sense of wrongness creeps over her, an icy knot forming in her stomach. She inhales sharply, tries to center herself. *No assumptions, react later*, she tells herself.

Then she sees it. *Cease and desist.* The words *sever all ties with Loopd>In* leap out at her like a physical attack. A rush of adrenaline spikes through her veins, heat rising to her cheeks, her chest tightening as if the air itself is turning against her.

No. No.

Her knees threaten to buckle, but she steadies herself against the cold, polished edge of her kitchen island. The document is dense, packed with legal jargon designed to overwhelm, but the meaning is crystal clear—She has been exiled from her own creation.

The next words make her stomach lurch: *Any attempt to assert intellectual ownership, interfere with ongoing operations, or communicate with active stakeholders will result in immediate legal recourse, including but not limited to financial restitution, punitive damages, and permanent injunctions.*

It reads less like a warning and more like a death sentence. Her vision blurs, nausea creeping up her throat. She blinks rapidly, forces herself to read it again, as if a second pass might soften the brutality of it. But it doesn't. Loopd>In is no longer hers.

She can't breathe. *How? Why?* She forces her mind to move, to untangle the impossibility of it. *This can't be legal.* Her name is on the patents. Her work is written into its very DNA. But there, at the bottom of the page, is the signature that makes her blood run cold.

Samantha Ravensby.

It's a clean, bold stroke and unmistakable in its finality. The betrayal flares like a wound ripped open mid-healing. Charisma moves before she can think. Her legs propel her forward, instinctive, desperate, her body seeking proof—real proof—that this isn't happening. She practically throws herself into her office chair, jabbing the power button on her console. The machine comes to life, screens blinking awake, their cold glow illuminating the panic etched across her face. Her hands slam against the keyboard. Fingers fly, keystrokes sharp and erratic, pounding out the login sequence she's typed a thousand times before. But now, the screen hesitates, lagging, buffering longer than usual. Each passing second stretches unbearably.

Then—ACCESS DENIED.

The phrase blinks at her in bold red letters. She blinks back, uncomprehending. Her hands freeze over the keyboard.

No. She tries again, typing with deliberate, forceful precision. Charisma.Sinclair_Admin. Enter. ACCESS DENIED.

Her breath shudders in her chest. Her cursor hovers over the recovery options. She tries her financial accounts next, hands shaking as she swipes through the verification process.

Account Locked.

She grips the desk. The screen seems to shrink, to loom, to suck the oxygen from the room. A fresh wave of nausea rolls through her. Every piece of her existence is being erased in real time. She swipes to her personal development files. The blue progress wheel spins. And spins. And spins.

Then—FILE NOT FOUND.

Gone. Her mind fractures into static. This isn't real. This can't be real. But it is. The nausea surges. She shoves back from the desk, stumbling to her feet, her breath coming in sharp, uneven bursts. Her body moves on instinct, seeking an anchor, anything to keep her from spiraling. But there's nothing. Just the deafening silence of a life that has been stolen from under her.

Charisma steps away from everything and closes her eyes, standing in the middle of the kitchen, trying her best to summon all those lessons from yesteryear. Mindfulness. Deep recollection. Cadenced and focused breathing. She tries to summon something from her interactions with Samantha over the past months that would lead to this. Unreturned phone calls. Body language in the office and boardroom. Passing comments, tones in correspondence. Nothing overt, but there was subtlety everywhere, wasn't there? She wasn't invited to meet the HyperLoop team following their proposal. She didn't think much of it at the time, but now, it certainly appears to be a bellwether.

She closes her eyes and focuses on the days leading up to this moment. She sees it clearly. This wasn't a fracture—it was a controlled demolition. A calculated move, made by someone who was planning for a long time. Samantha wasn't just taking Loopd>In. She was erasing Charisma from it. A quiet sob escapes her throat before she can stop it. She presses a fist to her mouth, desperate to contain the sound, but the tears come anyway. Hot, silent, *furious* tears.

It wasn't supposed to be like this. Loopd>In was her ticket out. From her mother's shadow. Out of the suffocating circles of influence that dictated who *belonged* and who was merely *tolerated.* She built something *real.* Something visionary. And now, in the span of a single evening, it's taken from her like a child ripped from its mother's arms.

Her gaze moves to the letter still clenched in her shaking hands. The paper crinkles slightly under her tightening grip. It's nothing more than a formality—a taunt, wrapped in legal jargon, a polite way of saying, *Stay down. Don't fight. It's over.*

Samantha knew exactly what she was doing. Charisma had nothing left to fight with. The walls of her home inch closer, the air suddenly thick and oppressive. For a space designed with openness in mind, it now feels cramped. The living room—once her sanctuary of solitude—seems almost predatory. The glass coffee table at its center, normally pristine and uncluttered, now feels sterile, an empty reflection of herself. Two charcoal-gray sofas sit across from each other like silent witnesses to her unraveling, their cool, modern form mocking her. The recessed lighting, always set to a warm, amber glow that match her eyes, now casts long, sharp shadows against the walls, deepening the hollowness in her chest.

She turns toward the sliding glass door, her gaze drifting past the transparent pane to the only thing in her world that still feels untouched—her garden. Beyond the threshold, native irises and California poppies sway in the night breeze, their soft hues muted by the dim moonlight. The manicured hedges stand like silent sentinels, framing chaotic bursts of color. There was harmony here once. A balance between wild growth and cultivated beauty.

This is where she reads. Where she problem-solved in the twilight hours as Loopd>In went from a concept in her mind to becoming reality. Where she sits beneath the open sky, allowing her mind to drift up to the stars. She spends countless nights here, nestled into the worn Adirondack chair, letting the vastness of the cosmos comfort her. She feels closest to her truest self here, untethered, limitless.

It was the *Time & Space* program that shaped her more than anything else—opened her eyes to the incomprehensible scale of the universe. It showed her a perspective beyond the petty battles of power and control, gave her a sense of wonder that no material success could replicate. She recalls the teacher who first introduced her to the world of the cosmos, Mr. Cody. What would he tell her if he were sitting with her tonight? *Look up to the stars and not down at your* feet, his most oft-used maxim. She has mixed feelings and emotions about going any further down this path. Then she recalls what spawned from that national program's wake. The UnPlugger movement that emerged resonated with her deeply, the idea that *disconnecting* from the digital noise meant *reconnecting* with something real. Nature and the tangible world. Together, they were the first steps toward her creation, no, not creation, but the beautiful blend of life and mind sciences that became Loopd>In.

Now, she feels disconnected from everything. She forces herself upright, gripping the counter for balance. The wine rack catches her eye.

Not yet.

Her hands twitch, muscles tightening in protest. She stares at the bottle of Pinot Noir tucked between two others. Her old companion. The one that smooths the edges when they get too sharp. She doesn't even bother with a glass. The bottle is open in seconds, the deep crimson liquid hitting her tongue before she has time to think about it. One gulp. Then another. The warmth spreads through her chest, but it doesn't dull the ache. If anything, it makes it sharper—a cruel reminder that there's no real escape.

Her stomach churns in rebellion. She barely makes it to the bathroom before it all comes back up. Collapsing onto the floor, forehead pressed against the cool tile, she breathes raggedly. Pathetic. Even her body is rejecting her now. With a weak, shaking hand, she reaches for the worn dark green blanket draped over the armrest near the kitchen. She pulls it over her shoulders like armor, curling into herself on the living room couch.

Sleep. Just sleep.

The tears still come, but she's too exhausted to fight them anymore. The weight of everything presses her deeper into the cushions, the quiet rush of the city outside a dull backdrop to her own unraveling.

Tomorrow, she'll still be ruined. Tomorrow, she'll still have nothing. Tomorrow, she won't be able to avoid the truth.

But tonight? Tonight, she lets herself break and fall into the abyss.

CHAPTER FOUR

PERILOUS PACHYDERM

Chew steps into his side-by-side unit, the familiarity of the 3-D printed walls greeting him like an old friend. The look and smell of his compact, efficiently designed living space, identical to Deuce's next door, offers a comforting embrace after weeks on the road. The subtle whir of advanced technology, hidden within the very fabric of his home, showcases modern convenience and a shared life with Deuce, separated only by a wall built from the same innovative process that shaped their twin abodes.

The neural network connection on his new retinal Leaf isn't working properly, so Chew goes old school with the touch screen. After a few taps on a phone nearly as old as he is, he holds up his ID card, and a second later, he purchases two tickets on the HyperLoop. They're for David Mastamann and Dante Largo. Chew chuckles. Seeing his actual name spelled out alongside Deuce's never ceases to amuse. Has anyone called his best friend anything other than Deuce over the past decade? His phone dings, indicating an authorized email. It's his receipt for the trip. He swings his feet from the floor and plops down on his couch. $199 for everything. He cannot believe it sometimes. He remembers when he was a young kid, and a single plane ticket cost over $2,000 to fly to Paris. How could he forget? His mom and dad reminded him of the price every hour of that two-week trip.

But that matters very little this go-around. Neither he nor Deuce has been back to San Francisco since . . . Chew wonders if this isn't a huge mistake. It was only, what, four years? Five? He went through all this in his head before. And he talked plenty with Deuce. He reminds himself why this is the right move, trying to brush away the lingering doubt and fear. Besides, this will be their maiden voyage on the HyperLoop! What better way to initiate this return to their once-favorite city? It's time, damn it.

Chew scrolls through a few pictures of San Francisco. Nights out in North Beach and the Mission. They were epic, but ephemeral. There and gone in the blink of an eye. No other city came close to matching San Francisco. The city was a mosaic of unforgettable experiences for Chew and Deuce, a singular experience—alive in a way no other place could match. The city didn't just exist, it continually pulsed, electric, and boundless, as if the very air carried the energy of all who walked its streets before them. Their memories were filled with the excitement of big-time sporting events. As precocious youngsters they joined in the collective cheer and felt the roar of the crowd. Leisurely strolls through Golden Gate Park offered moments of tranquility and a deep appreciation of the natural world in a major city center, as they wandered beneath the towering cypresses and eucalyptus, where golden shafts of sunlight filtered through the canopy, dappling the winding dirt paths. The scent of damp earth and blooming jasmine clung to the air, while the distant strumming of a busker's guitar mixed with the rustling leaves, turning the park into a sanctuary that felt both wild and welcoming.

They cherished the panoramic views from the city's hills, in which life in the great western metropolis met with natural beauty in stunning harmony that few, if any, throughout the world could match. Biking through the restless arteries of the city, they weaved between vintage streetcars and honking rideshares, past the welcoming glow of taquerias and jazz lounges spilling saxophone notes into the cool night air. The scent of grilled sourdough and sizzling dim sum clashed and mingled, an olfactory signature of a city always in motion, where every turn revealed another burst of life—skaters bombing down hills, muralists lost in their latest masterpiece, lovers wrapped in twilight embraces beneath glimmering marquee lights. Those experiences were the constant backdrop of their time in San Francisco, vibrant and full of life, until an abrupt turn of events cast a wicked shadow over these cherished places, transforming them from scenes of joy to echoes of past demons. Since then, San Francisco has only been a house of horrors for Deuce and Chew. *It's time to change that*, Chew thinks.

He exhales, staring up at the ceiling. Deuce was barely functional after Philipp's murder, and in those early days, Chew was the one to keep him moving. He helped Deuce land the construction gig, giving him something physical to do, something that didn't require being in the public eye, talking to people, or thinking too much. At the time, it felt like the best way to keep him sane. But Chew knows better now. He knows Deuce has been hiding. Knows that, despite his intelligence and the potential Philipp saw in him, Deuce chose a life that lets him disappear into routine. That's what this trip to San Francisco needs to be about—helping Deuce remember who he used to be. Before grief hollowed him out, Deuce was a force—lanky and loose-limbed, yet composed, a quiet confidence simmering beneath the surface. He carried himself with ease. Everything he did looked effortless, whether it was painting the edges of the strike zone with that wicked curveball or holding court in late-night debate, weaving his logic like a craftsman shaping wood. His mind as sharp as his mechanics, a wit as quick as his reflexes, and an intensity that never felt forced, just . . . natural. He didn't simply move through the world. He belonged in it, like he was always on the verge of something greater. And now? Now, he was a faint memory of that promise, a young man treading water in a life too small for him. San Francisco wasn't only about facing ghosts—It was about dragging Deuce back to the surface before he disappeared completely.

Before his mind can slip any further into discomfort and angst, a message comes through from Deuce. Chew halts his nervous pacing as the message's contents seep with positivity. *Ready to make the play.* It sounds like the old Deuce, the one before his life was shattered. Chew feels as though an elephant nearly crushes him and springs up from his chest. The weight of this idea being his, after all. About returning with Deuce to the city they were in when the news broke—It is lifted now with the notion that Deuce genuinely wants to go on this trip. Sure, it sounds good, but the execution will be the trick.

No time to screw around. This momentum needs to keep going. Chew plops down on his living room couch and quickly reviews a catalog of his celebratory pictures. There it is, that's the one: a photo taken of him on New Year's Eve half a decade ago. Wearing nothing but dark sunglasses and a Penguin-style top hat to cover his package. He's bent slightly backward and waving with the other arm as if a news chopper were filming from above. He wishes his abs were still like that. The end-of-the-year holiday has been their favorite since they were very young.

Then he keeps scrolling, pausing on shots of women he's met along the way. A statuesque Brazilian model with Olympian legs and a smile that could melt glaciers. A short, curvy redhead with full sleeves of tattoos and an energy that crackled through the room. A sophisticated older woman from Milan whose perfume still titillates his memory, her knowing smirk making him feel like he was always one step behind in whatever game they were playing. A dancer from New Orleans with the most sensual ebony skin, sinewy grace, and magnetic eyes that contained entire stories. A plain, but beautiful farm girl from Iowa with calloused hands and a tolerance for alcohol matched by legendary sailors. Her inebriated laugh and seductive smile would be etched in his mind forever.

He never had a type. Never wanted one. Confidence, curiosity, and a little mischief—That's what did it for him. Women who made him *feel* something. Women who owned their space. If anything, Deuce used to tease him about having *too* broad a taste. Chew always fired back: "I'm a buffet lover. Keep your single entrée . . ."

Satisfied, he selects a handful of photos—a mix of adventure, indulgence, and nostalgia. He adds one of the San Francisco skyline at night, taken at Sausalito's peak, and arranges them all into a collage before sending it to Deuce. It's still so easy with the old phone, he's not sure if he will even take the time to get the network connection fixed before they head west. He settles deeper into the couch and locks onto the phone's screen. In the next instant, it all goes dark. It's been so long he forgot it had to be charged like they did decades ago. Before it completely shuts, the last thing he sees are his daily numbers of optimal sleep, total movement, and biorhythms. He thinks about rooting around the place and looking for an adapter, and a cord, and what else? He opts against it since it would be too much of a hassle. He fiddled on this phone far too long.

It is relieving though to know that Deuce is looking forward to this upcoming year-ender in San Francisco. His sentiment was genuine, Chew is sure of it. But it also makes him nervous. He can't push too hard or Deuce will shut down. Too much at once, and

Deuce might back out entirely. Chew needs to get this right, thread the needle carefully.

As the quiet of the evening settles around him, Chew feels a sense of calm determination. He and Deuce will return to San Francisco, not just to reminisce about the past, but to create new memories, to reclaim the city that once held so much joy for them. It's time to face the ghosts of their past and lay them to rest, once and for all. They've both kicked the can down the road for far too long, in their own ways. For Chew, it feels damned good to know that elephant is long gone and Deuce is on board. Now, he has to make sure his best friend stays that way.

CHAPTER FIVE

SEASONS

In the quiet of the evening, Deuce sits alone in his car, a shared little red sedan that costs him only twenty bucks a month, yet the interior is something to behold. The expansive digital dashboard in front of him displays a range of vehicle diagnostics and entertainment options, all encased in an intuitive design. The seats, brilliantly crafted from recycled polyester and bamboo, adjust perfectly to his posture, providing a level of comfort that belies the car's modest expense. Soft ambient lighting bathes the interior, its hues shifting subtly with the onset of the night. With voice-activated controls, touch-sensitive surfaces replacing traditional buttons, and Jonah, his personal AI system since his early teenage years, managing every component of the automobile, it epitomizes the prefect integration of technology and daily life.

Outside, the sun has long dipped below the horizon, the night wrapping itself around the world. The towering crane, a colossal sentinel marking the construction site, is at rest. Another week is in the books. Another year, too. Deuce won't return to work for another three weeks. The air around him is thick with the scent of accomplishment and the satisfying promise of short-term freedom. But freedom can be a funny thing—Deuce had plenty of it in the past five years, and it hadn't done much for him.

He's tried everything to quiet his mind and ease his pain. Booze made him reckless. Pills numbed him into stagnation. He dabbled in stimulants for a while, chasing a rush that never lasted. But psilocybin was different. It didn't erase anything. It reframed it. It let him step outside himself, observe his grief without drowning in it. It was less an escape and more a reconciliation—one he was unable to achieve through any other means.

He retrieves his backpack from the back seat and opens the front compartment. His treat awaits—a hermetically sealed brownie, infused with CBD extracts, protein, ATP, and two micrograms of psilocybin. A true culinary marvel. It's small, less than a few grams in total. Deuce savors it in a single bite, letting the flavors and ingredients meld on his tongue. The warmth of it spreads subtly, a slow unraveling of tension from his chest.

"Jonah," he says softly, "play *Tame Impala*'s *Seasons*."

The car responds with a smooth chime, and the first notes begin to wash over him. Kevin Parker's voice, ethereal and layered, floods the cabin. The speakers, hidden within the frame of the vehicle, create an immersive soundscape, wrapping him in music as if he's floating inside it. The fusion of alt and progressive rock, blended with electronic elements and Parker's mesmerizing falsetto, immediately soothes him.

The Marvel on Mars changed everything, popular music included. When astronauts from twelve different countries touched down on the Red Planet together in unison, something shifted back on Earth. The moment had been bigger than any one nation, bigger than even science itself. At long last, humanity left its fingerprints on another world. And as the world looked up, the music changed with it. *Space rock*—both the genre and the aesthetic—surged into prominence, a response to the collective awe of a species reaching beyond itself.

And Tame Impala? They became more than just a band. They became *the* band. The last of the great holdouts. No AI-generated lyrics and sounds. No synthesized compositions churned out by predictive algorithms. Real music, made by real people, in an era where the distinction had all but disappeared. Kevin Parker refused to let technology dictate creativity, and because of that—and the explosion of space rock—his work only grew in reverence.

Deuce lets the music carry him away, his post-work treat kicking in fast, amplifying his emotions. His feet tingle, his legs sweat, and his heart races as the music swirls around him. He glances at his reflection in the rearview mirror, proud of what he sees—particularly the fact that he's still here, still moving forward. His floppy hair dangles above his eyes, and he thinks he might need a trim before the trip. He stares into his own bright blue, almond-shaped eyes. The sadness is almost gone, replaced by a profound sense of luck. And a newfound appreciation for life. He garners at least some of this sentiment each time he uses psilocybin.

His dad used to play him Tame Impala when he was a boy, back when they'd take long road trips to visit family and friends. Those journeys were filled with music, and Deuce grew to love this band especially. To him, they weren't just another act. They were a symbol of sheer brilliance, of authenticity in an era that had long since lost touch with those concepts. His father always said that great music—real music—had the power to shape history, like great ideas did. And his dad, Philipp Largo, had always been a man of ideas.

"Jonah, let's get out of here," Deuce says. "Authorize the journey back home. Let's go see Chew." The dashboard comes to life with a gentle wave of color, an aurora of soft blue and silver. Jonah, the AI operating system that's been his constant companion for years, responds with a familiar warmth.

"Assuredly so, Deuce," Jonah says, its voice measured and articulate, a perfect blend of vintage charm and modern precision. The AI was programmed to sound like a mixture of a classic airline pilot and an old-school radio host, its tone exuding both authority and casual confidence. "Estimated drive time will be forty-five minutes. Would you like a scenic route tonight?"

Deuce smirks. "Nah. Just get me home, buddy. I'm looking forward to seeing an old friend."

"As you wish, Deuce. But do keep your seatbelt fastened. I'm rather fond of your continued survival."

The banter isn't new. Jonah has been a part of his life for the better part of the last decade, the only consistent voice in a world otherwise unraveled. It wasn't real companionship, not in the way Chew was, but it was something.

The electric car softly motors along the highway, the AI synchronizing with the flow of the autonomous traffic system. Deuce gazes out the window. Every car around him is gliding forward, moving at precise intervals, never colliding, never stalling. Not a single human hand is on the wheel.

His father would've loved this. The goal should always be: Zero collisions, zero congestion, zero emissions, he used to say.

Philipp Largo had always believed that people should be freed from the tedium of menial tasks, that the future belonged to a world where humans could focus on ideas, creativity, exploration, travel. Plus, he knew driving was the most dangerous things most humans did every day, especially during the years of rampant smart phone and social media use where distractions abounded every second. He had worked toward a reality where automation and AI weren't just tools of convenience but the next step in human progress. And now, here it was—his vision manifesting in perfect, silent harmony.

Deuce swallows. *Is it possible to live a full life—an examined life—without constantly being reminded of what was lost?* He exhales. The weight of the question hovers in his mind, unanswered. But then, out of nowhere, a surge of something else—something lighter, something electric—takes hold of him. Excitement. Excitement to see his old friend again, to step out of this stasis he built around himself. He hasn't seen Chew in months, and the thought of reuniting stirs something unexpected inside him. Maybe this trip to San Francisco won't only be about confronting demons of the past. Maybe it will be about something else entirely. Maybe it will be about proving to himself he's more than just the son of Philipp Largo. Maybe it's about finally stepping out from the shadow of grief and reclaiming the life he put on hold five years ago. Or maybe—just maybe—it's about setting things right. About taking the first real step toward something that matters again. Emotions and synapses stirred by the effects from psilocybin course through him.

As the highway lights streak past in fluid motion, Jonah accelerates effortlessly into the night, and for the first time in years, Deuce doesn't feel like running away from something. He feels like heading toward it.

CHAPTER SIX

MOTHER'S MERCY

The last remnants of her once-promising venture with Loopd>In weave through Charisma's mind, not merely as broken aspirations but as fragments of a future unjustly confiscated. Her thoughts pirouette between strategies of legal recourse—demanding restitution and vindication—to whims of fantastical retribution where she imagines orchestrating Samantha's downfall with the precision of a chess grand master. But she knows all of this is mindless fluff unless there's any real action behind it. She quiets her mind, and uses her retinal Leaf to scour through her contacts. When she lands on one who might be able to help, she places a call.

"Gabriella, please! You have to help me. I can't get to anything. I can't retrieve anything. I archived all of my stuff using Loopd>In's network. All my backups were on Loopd>In gadgetry. I never gave it a second thought because Loopd>In is *mine*! But now I don't have a single thing in my arsenal. All I'm asking for is something with my personal files. That's not a crime. It's nothing. Will you please help me? Please!"

"Charisma, calm down. You're talking a million miles a minute. Take a deep breath. You're gonna give yourself a heart attack."

"Sorry, it's just that hardly anyone has responded to me. No one has reached out. It's like as soon as Samantha's cease and desist letter arrived I turned into a ghost. Or worse! Like she found a way for everyone who I ever worked with to forget that I even existed."

"Charisma, listen to me. I want to help you, but I have to be careful. If those files only exist within the Loopd>In network or are stored on anything owned by the company, well then, I'm really sorry. There's nothing I'm gonna be able to do. There's no way I'm crossing that woman. Not even for you. Samantha made it clear you were persona non grata."

"Wait! What does that mean? What else did she say? C'mon! Please . . ."

Charisma has had conversations like this recently. The brave few former coworkers, many of whom she hired directly, who took her call or returned her messages. Most wouldn't even do that. But for the ones who did, it mattered little. They all ended the same: Charisma pained at the end with the notion that no one on the inside could or would help her. As soon as her call with Gabriella ends, a maroon sports car pulls into her driveway. It's her mother, coming over unannounced and uninvited.

In the morning light filtering through her kitchen window, Charisma Sinclair's appearance reveals the strain of recent events. Her chestnut hair, usually glossy and meticulously styled, hangs in unkempt waves, framing her oval face and accentuating her high cheekbones and full lips, which now seldom curve into a smile. Her olive skin, normally radiant, appears sallow and drawn, the dark circles under her deep-set, amber eyes betraying sleepless nights. Charisma's striking features, reminiscent of Mediterranean beauty, bear the weight of her current despair.

Her mother, Carmen, enters without knocking, strolls into the kitchen and stands face-to-face with her daughter, sharing the same striking features that hint at a vibrant past, but also showcasing the twenty-eight years she has on her daughter. Carmen's face, though lined with age and worry, retains the strong jaw and expressive eyes that mark the shared lineage. Their resemblance is striking, a mirror of time reflecting the potential of youth against the backdrop of experience and resilience.

"Mom, why are you here?" Charisma's voice is hoarse, her throat tight. She scrubs a hand over her face, trying to shake off the weight pressing on her chest. "I hate you seeing me like this. It's—"

"It's a-okay, is what it is, Charisma," Carmen cuts her off. "C'mon, darling. This isn't you. You're one of the strongest, smartest young women on this planet. Please, talk to me. What can I do?"

She doesn't respond but instead mopes back into her bedroom and falls into her sheets. Carmen follows right behind, noticeably distraught with her daughter's temperament and despair. Charisma turns over, wipes her face, and takes a few deep, concentrated breaths. Her room, originally a model of modern minimalist design, is littered with the remnants of Charisma's attempts to fight Samantha's treachery. Legal documents are strewn across the floor and her black futon, mingling with discarded tissues soaked with frustration-fueled tears. Charisma sits up and points to the letter she received from her former company.

Carmen studies the legal letter from Loopd>In's corporate headquarters. With each moment, the wrinkles on her face seem more pronounced, reflecting the disappointment and concern that this situation has brought upon her daughter. Charisma's mother has a reassuring tone as she says, "Well, reading between the lines here, they're simply changing the name of the company you built. We can push back, honey. I'm certain of it. Remember: Be water, and you'll find the path."

Charisma, exhausted and defeated, can't summon the energy to respond. She turns away from her mother and once more buries her head beneath the tangled sheets, her thoughts racing. This must be what Eduardo Saverin felt like when Zuckerberg jammed him out of Facebook. Her room, once a haven of innovation and creativity, now serves as a tattered battlefield where her dreams shattered. Outside, the world moves on, oblivious to her anguish. The morning sun yields faint shadows on the white walls, creating a stark contrast between the promise of a new day and Charisma's looming despair. As though the room itself mourns her loss.

While the physical world goes about its business, Charisma's mind is a centrifuge, spinning fragments of betrayal, exhaustion, and helpless fury so fast she can't separate one from the other. Her eyes sting, her head throbs, and her heart feels heavy. Even with her mother's best intentions and influential contacts, there's no turning back time or undoing the perfidy that has cost her a multibillion-dollar business. It's a wound too deep to heal. And oodles of time that cannot be given back. *Time.* By far and away our most valuable asset.

Carmen gently places a hand on Charisma's shoulder and says, "You've been in bed since I arrived, and you darn well know I don't like wasting time on my Leaf or jumping into any kind of VR. Get your butt up and meet me in the kitchen. We'll prep our own meal today. It will be fun. We can talk through all of this. Please, honey, stay strong. Don't allow this to wreck you."

In response, Charisma sits up again and lets out a huff, her messy hair falling around her like a chaotic crown. Her mother's presence steadies her, an anchor against the weight threatening to pull her under. She knows she can't remain in this state of paralysis. She must find a way to move forward, even in the face of overwhelming odds. Charisma rises from her bed, her eyes reflecting a mix of exhaustion, despair, and a small dash of hope. Her mother's cinnamon-scented presence offers a glimmer of solace in a world turned upside down. She leads Charisma into the kitchen, but quickly changes her mind once her feet hit the cold, hard linoleum tile.

"You know what?" she says with a wide smile turning back to her daughter. "Why don't we let Andre take us up to Santa Rosa? I think that's precisely what you need right now. Let's get out of here for the day."

Charisma nods hesitantly. She doesn't know what to say to her mom so she remains silent and obedient. The idea of escaping her current reality is appealing, even if only temporarily. Carmen's new car, driven by an automated software named Andre, waits in the driveway, an embodiment of the world's ever-advancing technology, ready to transport them to a different space, perhaps offering a temporary respite from Charisma's troubles.

They step inside, and the car comes to life, its sensors and systems engaging in unison. The journey ahead, while uncertain, promises a chance for Charisma to breathe, to think, and hopefully, to find some clarity amid the chaos. As the car glides smoothly onto the street, the familiar streets of her neighborhood fade into the background, replaced by the open road leading to Santa Rosa. The drive is quiet, each lost in their thoughts. As Charisma stares out the window, the landscape becomes a blur, each passing mile deepening her introspection. All things Samantha Ravensby. All things Loopd>In.

The scenery outside shifts unnoticed as Charisma's mental state is awash with scenarios of confrontation and triumph. Each imagined victory over Samantha injects a surge of adrenaline, a hint of the old fire that once fueled her ambition and innovation. The betrayal that not too long ago seemed like an insurmountable blockade now morphs into a series of challenges she feels compelled to navigate and overcome. The next moves on the chessboard percolate in her mind.

CHAPTER SEVEN

HEARTS & MINDS

The porch light turns on above them at its immediate scheduled time, its dull yellow glow barely cutting through the deepening twilight. A gust of wind kicks up loose gravel in the yard, rattling against the porch railing as Chew pulls Deuce in for a firm, lingering embrace.

"Great to see you again, old friend," Chew says, gripping Deuce's shoulder.

Deuce exhales. The scent of cedar and saffron drifts from inside Chew's place, familiar yet distant, like something from a past life.

"No one is old here," Deuce replies, managing a tired grin. "But you're looking sharper than ever, my man."

Deuce leads the way into the place and flops down on Chew's living room sofa, oddly in good shape for having been in his possession for close to a decade. Built during the 3-D printing boom of the 2030s, the inside is mostly minimalist: the single burgundy couch that Deuce occupies, two reclining chairs, and a kitchenette.

It looks and smells as if someone just began the moving-in process, but this has been Chew's home base for years. The exception, as always, is his book collection. Two towering wooden bookcases flank a formidable, glass-paneled credenza, their shelves packed with works that shaped him. In an era where hard copy books surged back into prominence—no longer just artifacts of a pre-digital world but emblems of depth and discernment—Chew's collection stands as both a personal archive and a testament to his insatiable curiosity.

Sagan, Dawkins, and Sam Harris dominate one shelf, their musing on the cosmos, consciousness, and evolution marked with countless underlines and margin notes. Yuval Harari's sweeping analyses of history and humanity rest beside Cixin Liu's hard-edged, sci-fi magnum opus, exhilarating and terrifying in equal measure. And tucked between them, Coleman Hughes—his essays sharp as a scalpel, dissecting modern discourse with clarity and reason, a voice of principled dissent in a world too often ruled by emotion. He's always been one of Chew's absolute favorites. His own personal North Star.

These books aren't decoration. They're battle-tested companions, pages softened by years of reading and rereading, ideas woven into the fabric of who he's become.

"So, Deuce, lots to unpack. I—"

"Unpack?" Deuce asks, cutting Chew off before he can complete his thought. "I thought we needed to *pack* pack. I got your message: We launch tomorrow night."

"Yes, I meant . . . nothing. We have a full week out west for all that." Chew seems like he's walking on eggshells whereas any misstep could send Deuce spiraling, pushing him to bail on their trip altogether. Like he often does over the past half decade, Deuce stares blankly into space, gazing down the darkened hallway, which leads to Chew's bedroom. In an instant it's as if his mind transported to an entirely different place.

"You gotta be excited to ride the HyperLoop, huh?" Chew asks with a charge in his voice as he paces his living room floor. "All these years in the making. This is a big damn deal."

"I can't remember the last time I was excited about anything." Deuce sighs.

"No, no, no you don't. Not this time. I'm not letting you go down that path. It's nothing but a dead end. You know this. Your path leads back to San Francisco. *Our* path. From there . . . we'll see."

Although they still communicate almost daily, the two best friends haven't been in the same room together for many months. Their work has them on the road more often than not. For very different reasons.

"I know what you're trying to do, Chew, and I appreciate it. I really do. But I'm becoming increasingly aware that my path leads nowhere. At least for now. I'm content getting by on the jobsite. Out of sight, out of mind."

"And what about the pact with your dad all those years ago? Doesn't that matter more now than ever?"

Deuce doesn't answer right away. His eyes twitch and dart around the room, unfocused, not on anything in particular but on an evening long past.

They had sat on the back porch, the night thick with summer air, cicadas humming in the dark. Philipp was quiet for a long time, staring at the horizon, a tumbler of whiskey cradled between his hands.

Ten-year-old Dante—he hadn't received his widely-adopted nickname—pulled his knees to his chest, the one to break the silence.

"What are we supposed to do now, Dad?"

Philipp didn't answer immediately. He exhaled slowly, his breath curling like smoke in the warm night air. Then, he turned to his son, his blue eyes reflecting something deep, something profound.

"We go harder, son. We go as hard as we can to make up for the physical loss of Mom, but like she's still watching us all the time. We push forward, every single day, like she'd have wanted us to. No half-measures, no sleepwalking through life at any point. Overdrive, always. For her."

Dante swallowed hard, nodding. He didn't fully understand the weight of what his father was saying, not then. But he had sworn, right there and then, to honor it.

Now, years later, Chew's words cut through the memory like a blade. For years, Deuce abided by that pact. It drove him, pushed him to excel in the classroom, to refine his stuff on the mound until it was major league ready. But now, five years after his father's murder, the promise feels like a relic from another life.

His mother's death had been different. A tragic accident, a freakish twist of fate. Sandra Largo was an avid cyclist, taking on RAGBRAI—a grueling but joyous ride across the state of Iowa that she conquered for years. Then, one July morning, she was gone, struck by a drunk driver outside Cedar Falls. A life full of motion, ended in an instant.

When it was just Deuce and Philipp left, his father found meaning in the loss. He demanded that his young son try and do the same. And for a while, Deuce did. But then Philipp was stolen from him too, and meaning no longer seemed to matter.

"That pact died the day my father died. You know this better than anyone, Chew."

"Your father died, but that pact shouldn't. You owe it to him and yourself."

"So, I'm supposed to live the life of three people, not just two, with one being the incomparable, but forgotten Philipp Largo?

Not bloody likely, Chew, I'm afraid."

Chew leans against the bookcase closest to the hallway. He anticipated a moment like this for months. Ever since the HyperLoop schedule announced the completed general construction. He knows this can go one of two ways, with one direction being Deuce backing out of their trip. But he's also grown weary of watching Deuce shrink into someone unrecognizable, his fire dimmed, his purpose eroding seemingly every time he sees him face-to-face.

"What would your father want for you now?" he asks. "It's been a half decade."

"You should know," Deuce responds sharply, bouncing up from his temporary seat on the couch. "You spent nearly as much time with him as I did."

"And thank the gods for that," Chew exclaims with fervor. "I'd be nowhere without him. Well, certainly not where I am today."

"You give him too much credit, my friend. You'd have found your path just fine without him."

"I'm really disappointed to hear you say that, Deuce. If anyone on this planet didn't get his fair share of credit, it's most assuredly your father."

Deuce gives Chew a familiar look of exhaustion and frustration, breaking eye contact and shuffling his feet. He stares back down the hallway with a shrug while the look on his face goes solemn and blank.

"Look man," Chew says, determined not to allow their conversation to sway into other matters as he has been wont to do these past five years. "We're at the point where I'm genuinely worried about you. Staying invisible on the road is no way to live your life. Not for you. I feel like if you don't make a move soon it could end up being too late."

"Then why did you help me get this job in the first place?" Deuce snaps back.

"Because that was then," Chew responds before Deuce can continue. "That's what was best for you at the time. But it's high time your era of hiding and mourning comes to an end."

"Good of you to make that call for me."

"Look, for now all I want is to go back to our once-favorite city. Ride the HyperLoop. Enjoy time away like we used to. Ring in this new decade in style, ya know?"

"Yes! Absolutely," Deuce exclaims with verve and excitement in his voice. "That's why I signed up to go in the first place. So why all this consternation?"

"It's not that, Deuce. It'll never be that between us. We're brothers forever. It's not the same without you around, especially the old you."

"Don't give me that, Chew. You're doing better than ever, you're everywhere. Changing the world just like you wanted since we were young rascals."

For the past four years, Chew served as the tip of the spear for the McWhorter Foundation. Its mission: establish and successfully operate tech and specialized labor training centers throughout urban America. Chew was handpicked by the founder, John McWhorter, after he went outrageously viral following a heated exchange with a reporter covering their District Championship junior year of high school. Chew was the only black player on the team. Rather than ask about his two-hit, multi-RBI game or how he called the game behind the plate for Deuce who went the distance on the mound, the reporter focused on the race card. Chew took umbrage and, while calm and focused in his retort, he didn't hold back:

Reporter: *Do you think this win means something different to you since you're the only minority on the team?*

Chew: *You should be ashamed to call yourself a journalist. It's 2040, dude. Aren't we over this nonsense? Guess not as there are still fools like you who like to play these idiotic games. Well, I have a sound bite for you: For the overwhelming majority of us sane, thoughtful humans the amount of melanin in my skin matters as much as the color of my hair. You should consider listening to folks like Coleman Hughes rather than Coates and Kendi. I can promise you that my fellow brothers and sisters who have over these last few decades are far better off because of it. Now, does anyone want to ask me about popping that slider into the gap in the eighth inning?*

Chew leaned back in his seat and gave the room an ocular pat down, assessing who dug his response and who might have been put off. He smiled wide, beaming confidence and pleasure since the reporter didn't fire back, instead sitting befuddled, nearly shell-shocked. The clip went viral faster than the Hawk Tuah girl did the year before he was born. Chew had hit nail on the proverbial head, due in large part from his tutelage at the feet of Philipp Largo. From there Chew's career took off. He didn't bother with college as he was precisely the young upstart McWhorter was looking for when launching his initiative. And although it was McWhorter's connection to Largo, which helped seal the deal for Chew, he always credited Deuce's father much more for strongly encouraging him to read the likes of Hughes, McWhorter and Glenn Loury during his formative years, most of those books still adorning his shelves. In fact, Chew attributes just about all his success to the guiding hand of Philipp Largo. After all, he played such a significant role for all of Chew and Deuce's generation. This is the very meat and potatoes Chew wants to get into with Deuce now.

"And after you won your Cy Youngs and World Series, you were going to do some world-changing too," Chew says, now pacing slowly in his living room.

"The world changed for the better," Deuce says, looking directly at his friend as if he were addressing a large crowd on a serious matter. "Like it's done on the aggregate for the past century. The only difference being we all recognize and appreciate it now. The shit of the matter is that mine did not. It went in the opposite direction. You want to know where I go from here, huh? You want me to step into my father's shoes, or something of the kind?"

"I don't want you to be your dad. Hell, even with the benefit of a half decade's worth of hindsight we don't know everything he was involved in. Everything he influenced. I just want you to get back on track of being you again. Your zest for life and the natural world. Your never-ending curiosity. That can't die off with your father. It feels like . . . I don't know . . . that in a lot of ways death actually won. He's all but forgotten and you're a shell of the guy who almost took the mound that fateful day in San Francisco five summers ago."

"So that's what we're attempting to do then? Go back to the place where it all changed? Well, what do we have like twelve, thirteen hours before departure? How early does one need to arrive at the HyperLoop?" Deuce laughs for the first time since he arrived. He walks over to the kitchenette and peers through what scant offerings Chew has in his fridge. "Whaddya say we head out for a bit tonight? Kind of like we used to when we'd sneak out the night before a big trip. Nothing big. Maybe a few beverages and laughs to sharpen that edge before we head west?"

"What do you have in mind?" Chew asks, happy as a clam that his friend appears to be upbeat and somewhat eager to make this excursion happen.

"You're here far more than I am," says Deuce. "Let's go to the most happening spot around. No, scratch that. Let's go someplace that plays good music."

"I'm with ya there," Chew says with his infectious grin. "I know just the place."

CHAPTER EIGHT

WELCOME TO JUAREZ

The restaurant's floor-to-ceiling windows frame the bay, where the tide rolls in slow, steady waves, brushing against the dock with the patience of a timeworn ritual. Across the water, the San Francisco skyline beams like a constellation set adrift. Inside, lantern-style pendant light cast pools of warm gold onto polished teakwood tables, their glow reflecting in the rippling glassware. Sparse tonight, the space still buzzes with distant conversation and the occasional chime of silverware meeting porcelain. Charisma and Carmen sit by the window, their table positioned at the restaurant edge, where the quiet is thick enough to suffocate. The scent of seared tuna and miso lingers, mingling with the faint brine in from the shore. Between them, the weight of an unspoken history presses against the space like the tide beyond the glass—inevitable, creeping, impossible to ignore.

Carmen leans in, her fingers tightening around the stem of her untouched wine glass. She studies Charisma's face, searching for cracks in the silence, her brows drawn in tight concern. When she finally speaks, her voice is measured, gentle, but unable to mask the urgency beneath.

"Charisma, talk to me. What's going through your mind?" She pauses, her fingers tapping lightly against the table, a restless habit from years of political maneuvering. "I've never seen you this quiet for this long. You hardly spoke the entire way here."

Charisma looks up, her eyes meeting her mother's. There's a vulnerability in her gaze, a rare glimpse into her inner turmoil. "It's just . . . seeing you, being here with you . . . it brings back Juarez. How different everything was before."

Carmen goes solemn, lowering her head, and sighing deeply. There was a rupture in Charisma's relationship with her mother, a definitive before and after. In her youth, Carmen Sinclair was the epicenter of their world, a locally elected official who enjoyed hosting grand and important gatherings almost every week, drawing dozens, sometimes hundreds of people into her orbit. Local dignitaries, international power players, influencers of all kinds, all seeking advice from her—advice, connections, money. Carmen was a magnetic force, orchestrating deals and moving the dial of influence. But then something changed. At first, it was merely another issue her mom needed to tackle. It didn't seem like anything significant shifted. But it never got better, only worse. What appeared as a singular challenge became all-consuming. Carmen Sinclair, the woman was a powerful and charismatic figure, morphed into someone who could barely get out of bed. Her vigor, confidence, and influence melted away, much like a chocolate bar left in the blazing summer sun.

Doctors came and went. For a while, she saw a world-renowned 'specialist.' When she returned home, she was worse than before she left. Almost completely despondent. Broken, like a little feline who suffered a year's worth of physical abuse and was cripplingly frightened of every move and living thing that made a sound.

It would be several years later before Charisma would learn the full story. An immigrant family who her mom had been extremely close to had been rounded up and deported while Carmen was out of town. The mother of the family, Anita, was their housekeeper and primary gardener for the past year. Carmen considered her to be part of the family. Charisma trusted and loved her like she was mom number two when she was very little.

Upon her return to the city, Carmen went scorched-earth to right the wrong. She pulled every string, called everyone she knew who could do something. Threats and coercion were employed at every turn. But it was too late. They were already sent back to their former home in Ciudad Juarez. So, she boarded the first flight she could get and made her way to the treacherous Mexican border city. At the airport, mere minutes before she set to depart, she was finally able to connect with Anita. She promised her friend that she would rectify everything and have them returned to the Bay Area within the week. It turned out to be a false promise. The family, all four members, were slaughtered in a home invasion before Carmen crossed over into Ciudad Juarez by way of El Paso. The local press suggested they were wrongly targeted as a family who had been cooperative with local authorities working to stem cartel warfare.

From this, Carmen Sinclair never recovered. PTSD was the most frequently used term to describe her condition. In the years following, she would eventually be able to get out of bed, perform rudimentary tasks, and hold a job at the Public Library. But she was a brittle shell of her former self.

As Charisma processes the entirety of this tragic memory while trying to enjoy a plate of sushi with her mom, fear creeps over her like a hangman's mask. She sees herself going down a similar path now that Samantha Ravensby ran roughshod over her. She recoils and immediately loses her appetite. How could she not see all of this sooner?

"And now, you're worried you'll turn into me?" Carmen asks, both lost in the tragedy of all those yesterdays. "Our histories don't have to repeat. You're brilliant, Charisma. Always have been. Learn from my folly. Keep the wonderful, worldly perspective you've had since you were a toddler. Don't think that you'll get through this. *Know it.* And know that you will be far stronger and more accomplished on the other side of this struggle."

Charisma looks directly into her mother's eyes and tries not to blink. She sees the path as clear as she sees the Bay in the background. First, there is the hint of massive success. Wealth, notoriety, achievement. But it is nothing more than a giant ruse as crushing defeat and suffocating depression soon follow. A most cruel jape. The reflection she sees back at her is horrifying. *No!* Charisma's story does not have to emulate her mother's, just like she said. She doesn't have to follow in these fallen footsteps. She can walk a different path and fight back. For the first time since she received the letter from Samantha Ravensby's attorney, Charisma feels a genuine sense of resolve. She can step out of the way of the hangman's noose before it's fastened to her neck. She is capable of a walloping counterpunch. But she knows she will need help. Big time. She sits a little straighter, her hands no longer fidgeting, no longer curling into nervous fists beneath the table. A slow breath in, then out. The weight of helplessness that settled over her since the letter arrived doesn't lift entirely—but it shifts. Lightens. It doesn't own her anymore. Now, more than anything else, it's a dear old friend who's top of mind. *Where on earth is Mulva Warfarin now that she really needs her*?

"I think I'm good, Mom. I appreciate you coming all the way out here. You've definitely helped me work some things out between the ears . . . Like you taught me all those years ago. Let's get out of here. What would you like to do next?"

Her mom does not respond right away. She offers a slight smile and returns to forking through her Greek salad. Sadness and depression abate for Charisma temporarily. The fire that's burned inside her since her youth feels aflame once more. Charisma knows her next move. A deep dive to uncover the whereabouts of a special someone she has not seen in years. Someone who can tip the scales back in her favor. As she tacitly plans her next steps, the aroma of cinnamon wafting from the other side of the table teases her senses. Charisma can't help but feel a mixture of gratitude and determination. She won't let Samantha Ravensby become her personal Juarez. She owes it to her mom, if nothing else.

They are only one of two tables seated in the entire restaurant. The place became silent, almost unnervingly so. Charisma grips the stem of her wine glass, her thumb circling the rim in slow, deliberate strokes. Across from her, Carmen pushes a cherry tomato around her plate with a fork. Not eating, just moving. A muted chime rings as the kitchen doors swing open, and Charisma exhales sharply, annoyed at her own tension. She sits straight up in her seat, rolling back her shoulders, feigning nonchalance, but the stiffness in her posture betrays her. The air feels thick, expectant, as if waiting for something to break.

Charisma can't help but feel shame in how she's viewed her mom. She's not that ruthless, for if she was, she would have seen Samantha Ravensby coming from a light-year away. Samantha Ravensby might have stolen her company, but she would no longer steal an ounce of her future. Pity and empathy for her mother evaporates from her mind, and she recalls Mulva. A loyal, trusted, and ferocious ally that she will unleash upon her foe. How could she not have thought of this sooner?

"I just want to spend some more time with you, honey. Help you through this however I'm able. Is there anything specific you'd like to do while the sun stays with us for a while?"

"I'm going to find an old friend, Mom. Someone who can help me fight back. Success is not final. Failure is not fatal. It's the ability to persevere that matters most when it comes to the human condition. You taught me that a long time ago. Let's let Andre take us on a little cruise through Wine Country. Starting tonight, I'm getting back to work."

"I knew it wouldn't take long for you to bounce back. Let's go have some fun, drink some great wine. It's been too long. Back in my days of despair I felt entirely alone, especially after your father left me. I felt like I had no one to fight alongside me. But you do. Find her. And don't stop fighting." Carmen squeezes her daughter's hand, the pressure firm, reassuring. "I love you so much, honey."

As they step out of the restaurant, the calm surroundings of Sausalito's waterfront are the perfect backdrop for a prolonged and tight hug between mother and daughter. They haven't been this intimate and vulnerable with each other in a long, long time.

"I love you too, Mom. You've always been my favorite human. By far. And not even because you're my mother, but because . . . well, you're who you are."

They make their way back toward Andre. With every step she takes alongside her mother, a newfound resolve strengthens her stride. The air, crisp and filled with the scent of the sea, seems to clear her mind, focusing on the path ahead.

The story of her mother's downfall, once a memory filled with pain and anguish, now ignites a fierce, determined Charisma. Carmen's story is no longer just a tale of loss and despair; it becomes the fuel to Charisma's burning resolve. It's a clear reminder of the consequences of defeat and the price of allowing one's adversaries to triumph. In this moment, Charisma refuses to follow in the footsteps of her mother's tragedy. Instead, she sees her mother's story as a catalyst, compelling her to fight back with renewed vigor.

"I won't let her defeat me," Charisma whispers softly, her thoughts fixated on Samantha Ravensby, the architect of her current despair. The drive to not just recover what she lost, but to avenge her mother's unspoken sorrows, solidifies within her. Charisma knows that defeating Samantha won't only be a personal victory; it will be a tribute to her mother, a way to reverse the legacy of loss and to rewrite their family's narrative with a story of snatching victory from the jaws of defeat. And she will do this with one of her closest, dearest friends from her childhood. The one and only Mulva Warfarin. Finding her is certainly the next move on the chessboard.

CHAPTER NINE

BEYOND ANDROMEDA

It's been said that in space no one can hear you scream. At the Cosmic Chalice space bar, no one can take or make a call. It's 100,000 square feet of celestial attractions, far-out light displays, and a thumping sound system fit for the gods celebrating victory or creation. The cosmos isn't just a theme at this place—it's an experience. Overhead, a digital sky mimics the swirling expanse of a nebula, its gaseous tendrils shifting deep violets and electric blues, punctuated by simulated supernovae that pulse with each beat of the music. Holographic asteroids drift lazily above the dance floor, their surfaces textured with the pockmarked scars of cosmic collisions. Along the perimeter, a seamless 360-degree display projects the slow rotation of planetary giants—Saturn's rings ripple with artificial light, while Jupiter's swirling storms appear to churn in real time. In the farthest corners of the bar, patrons lounge beneath the soft glow of artificial auroras that cascade down like liquid ribbons of light, shifting through every imaginable shade of green and gold.

At the center of it all is a massive, levitating sphere—a

three-dimensional star map constantly shuffling between different galaxies, charting known celestial bodies alongside speculative exoplanets. Every so often, the bar's AI system zooms in on a random locale within the universe, bringing an undiscovered world into stunning clarity, complete with fictionalized atmospheric details and hypothetical alien landscapes. The entire space buzzes with an energy that makes patrons feel less like they're in a nightclub and more like they've stepped aboard some intergalactic star cruiser, barreling toward the farthest reaches of the known universe.

The Cosmic Chalice boasts that it's completely unplugged. While the attendant doesn't collect an entrance fee at the door, he does require the guys to either turn over or power off any digital devices. Chew laughs and acknowledges the request, powering off his Leaf with a concentrated thought. Deuce has heard of similar spots springing up near places where his work took him over the past year. It's certainly his kind of scene.

"This what you have in mind?" Chew asks as they enter the bar's main hub. Deuce hears Chew, but doesn't respond right away. He feels like he has been drugged, but in a most excellent way as the walls move in a trance-like fashion syncing to the constantly shifting light patterns and lava flows that molt and gyrate over the walls and ceiling.

"I've heard of places like this, but it's something else in-person. Feels like we've taken a trip to Andromeda."

"Let's belly up," Chew suggests leading the way to the main bar. The venue breathes with a steady pace of movement and sound—not packed to suffocation, but alive with the effortless flow of bodies drawn in by the cosmic ambiance. Small groups cluster near the glowing bar, sipping iridescent cocktails that reflect the array of lights, while others drift through the floating orbs of projected galaxies, their conversations dissolving into the music's gravitational pull. The dance floor sways in slow, hypnotic waves, bathed in undulating blues and purples, each step tracing the contours of the ever-changing landscape. Deuce and Chew plop down in their seats as the only two posted up at the bar.

"Good to see humans still working the service game," Deuce says softly to Chew. "Guess you can't ask people to unplug if robots are the ones slinging the drinks and keeping the rules."

Chew turns and studies him for a beat, eyes sharpening with something like relief. Deuce can feel the change in his friend's expression, the subtle lift at the corners of his mouth, the way his shoulders ease. It's like Chew is watching a piece of him come back to life—maybe a piece he thought was gone for good. Deuce knows he's been quiet for too long, hiding while on the road, maybe even scaring the people who care about him most. But just saying something insightful, something obvious and real? He can tell it landed.

"You know, man," Chew says. "For all the benefit of having our own personal assistants the past two decades, I'm really starting to doubt whether robotics will ever match the capability and nuance of *these* hands." He wiggles his fingers in Deuce's face. Deuce's first impulse is to ferociously debate his friend over such a grand statement, but he knows Chew is right.

"What are we drinking?" he asks instead. "I'll follow your lead."

"Let's have a stiff one right here, mosey around this place, and see what's what."

Chew locks eyes with the lone bartender, a short male in his mid-20s, probably right around their age plus or minus a grade or two.

"Two Jamesons on the rocks, my man," Chew says as the song fades away and there's a temporary respite from the blasting music before the next song springs to life.

"Ugh," says Deuce after his first sip. "I haven't had anything this potent in years."

The bartender nods approvingly that he can activate

the transaction.

"Good thing," Chew responds, using a quick scan with his retinal Leaf and pays for the tab. "Other than opiates, there is no worse poison to use to hide. I assume you still rock the psilocybin?"

"Nothing better," says Deuce, still feeling some mild lingering effects of the treat he took after leaving work. "Use as needed, which is only a few times a month." He's taken aback watching Chew down half the contents of his drink with one pull. "Your work driving you to drink these days?"

Chew huffs and bobs his head. It's a typical Chew-move Deuce has seen hundreds of times before, knowing his friend is looking for the precise words in his response. "Truth be told, I'm worried beyond the pale. All this progress and problem-solving . . . An entire generation of us truly enlightened . . . It could all be for naught, and quite soon."

"Wait, you just said that we're still not even close to replicating the magic of human hands. I can vouch for that. On every construction site I've been on—"

"It's not that," Chew interrupts, looking downward to what's remaining in his glass.

The first song from the second side of *Stadium Arcadium* blares from every direction. Deuce can't recall the song's name, but with his subsequent sips of Jameson he's found himself in a most relaxed state with some of his all-time favorite music serving as the perfect backdrop. He's also glad that Chew isn't dwelling on him for the time being.

"It's something your dad told me before he died."

Chew believes that the mere mention of his father will trigger him, but Deuce has never informed his friend that's not really the case. Instead, it's like gazing into a void. As soon as the name of Philipp Largo is said, Deuce simply zones out of veracity. It's a trick, a mechanism he learned a few years ago in the wake of his agonizing grief.

"We don't have to talk about this," Chew continues, his voice a light scream trying to rise above the thumping music. He stretches out his back and then tightly crosses his fingers, using them to stretch out both arms. Deuce gets the sense that he's really starting to scan the room, take notice of any ladies who might be taking notice of him.

"Go on," Deuce says without making eye contact. "What did he have to say on the matter?"

"That all the signs would be there if our eyes were open. That around the corner lurked something nefarious he called *Homo Deus*."

"I know all about *Homo Deus*," Deuce says, sipping his drink little by little. He wonders why he didn't bring more psilocybin. Drinking is for savages, he thinks.

"If you know all about it, then I must ask: How concerned are you?"

"Concerned? What, that a small group of rich and powerful fucks are going to pull the levers to not only evolve past us simple *Homo sapiens*, but also achieve death's end? Doesn't seem so bad to me. Give us peasants something to shoot for, right?"

"I'm surprised you're that cavalier. I don't think it's that funny, my man. And I don't think it would work like you say. If it were that simple there would be anarchy. No, first they'd need control via subversion and distraction."

"Right around the time we were born every expert, everyone in the know was sick to death over AGI supplanting us on the evolutionary food chain. Or that it would turn us all into paperclips. And look what happened! Turns out that everyone having their own personal C-3PO by their side growing up was a good thing."

"That's only because of how it was coupled and complemented by the *Time & Space* program."

"That's debatable at best," Deuce fires back, swiveling quickly in his seat and making direct eye contact with Chew for the first time since their banter began.

"It's difficult for me to square that it's so hard for you to give your father the credit he deserves," Chew says, motioning to the bartender that he'd like another round. "What gives with that?"

Hindsight is 20/20. Has there ever been a more prescient maxim? Deuce heard his father say it growing up referencing that first year of the 2020s. And now, thirty years later, with the benefit of all that subsequent hindsight, Deuce isn't sure what to make of it and how his father really fit in. He knew around the time he was born the old US of A was mired in division, polarization, and constant loathing. He knew the '20s were indeed terrible in that regard. Countless theses, thought pieces, and award-winning documentaries dissected the times. Echo chambers due to exorbitant social media use. Millions locked into their screens and attuned more to their digital avatars than the real world. But more than anything else, Deuce knew so much of this strife and unnecessary struggle stemmed from the fact that at that time less than one in four Americans read books on anywhere near a consistent basis. When the first round of AI unleashed an epistemological bankruptcy with respect to anything of value or substance on the internet, it didn't take long for people to return to an old, favorite pastime. Something that could be trusted and treasured: reading hard copy books. Yes, this coupled with the *Time & Space* program and thusly every little boy and girl in the country having the legitimate opportunity to be instilled with a Carl Sagan-esque wonder about existence and the cosmos . . . yes, thinks Deuce, that too assuredly helped in the great healing America so badly needed.

But how much his father was actually involved, Deuce wasn't sure to this day. Maybe it was because he was so often chasing dreams of grandeur on the ballfield. Or maybe it was because after five years he still wasn't ready to confront the finality of his father's life. That in Deuce's mind, he was only at the cusp of achieving true greatness and recognition . . . and that in all the world there hadn't been a greater tragedy.

"I don't know how to respond to that," Deuce says, turning back and facing the bar. The volume of the music has ebbed, the crowd at the Cosmic Chalice has grown by a dozen or more, but Deuce and Chew remain the only ones posted up bar side. "It's probably because I—we— got such an early education directly from him. By the time they started teaching all that in schools it was second hand for us."

"Well, I know one thing," Chew says right before he polishes off the remainder of his drink. "There's no way we'd be riding to San Francisco on the HyperLoop without your dad's involvement."

"I think that's debatable too."

"C'mon, man! You can't be serious!" Chew slams his drink down, lets out a great huff, and beams a look at Deuce like he's fed up.

"What, just because he was allegedly the one who bridged the gulf between Musk and Sam Harris?"

"There's no 'allegedly' about it and you know that to a near certainty. Look at what Musk became in the twenties—a lunatic! And one glance at what he's accomplished since . . . One doesn't have to be Sherlock Holmes to piece that together."

Deuce is keenly aware of the list, as is just about every other sentient being on planet Earth. The Marvel on Mars, the retinal Leaf, and now the HyperLoop. All accomplished with the venerable Sam Harris by his side for years, whispering sage counsel in his ear following their estrangement for most of the twenties.

"You know, he never told me how he did it. Never even alluded to it. Did he to you?"

"No, not really," Chew says, now seemingly distracted, scouring the room. "Philipp Largo never concerned himself with getting credit."

"Yeah, probably the salient reason why no one remembers him today."

"That's not true, Deuce," Chew says, pausing his ocular survey of the place. "I damn well do and so do you. Plenty of others and tens of millions more just don't know it."

"That's the real reason we're going to San Francisco, isn't it? You think somehow I'll get inspired, get reignited to be involved, jump headfirst into the fray."

"Not at all," Chew responds without hesitation. "I just want to go to our once-favorite city, have a ton of fun, and make some new memories with my best friend." He smiles wide and mischievous, his classic look since he was a boy. "Enough of all this for now. Let's commence the action tonight. I'm feeling good, right where I want to be."

Deuce looks up and notices two women across the room, their eyes locked on Chew. One, tall and lithe with a drape of dark curls, sways effortlessly to the rhythm, her pale skin catching the glow of the shifting lights. Her gaze is sharp, assessing, but playful—like she already knows exactly how this night will unfold. The other, shorter but striking in her own right, wears her platinum-blonde hair in a sexy, chin-length bob, her eyes look piercing even from a half room away. She leans in close to her friend, whispering something that makes them both giggle before turning their full attention back toward the guys.

Chew gets up from his seat, runs a hand through his dark hair and grins wide, his posture shifting as if he's just stepped into a familiar game. Deuce doesn't hesitate. He rises from his seat and follows his old friend across the room, ready to make a proper introduction.

CHAPTER TEN

MULVA WARFARIN PART I

The night sky ignites with brilliance, each lightning bolt a jagged tear in the fabric of darkness, followed by guttural roars of thunder that seem to rattle the very bones of the earth. The rain doesn't fall so much as it slams against the glass, a relentless cascade of water that distorts the world beyond the window into a smearing, shifting mirage of streetlights and tree branches bowing under the howling wind. The Pacific Northwest storm rages, its eighty-mile-hour gusts roaring like some vengeful spirit tearing through the landscape. Roof shingles peel away and tumble like discarded playing cards, power lines dance and snap in the distance, and the thick scent of damp earth and ozone seeps into every crack and crevice.

Inside her dimly lit room, Mulva Warfarin does not stir. She remains stoic, unmoved by the chaos outside, her gaze fixed on the barricaded window as if she were studying an opponent rather than sheltering from a force of nature. This beast of a storm is touted as the year's most potent one, predicted to hammer southern

Oregon for the next forty-eight hours—a relentless bombardment of chaos. Yet for Mulva, floods, mudslides, wildfires—a cyclic spectacle of nature's fury—means nothing to her now.

As she plugs in her neglected phone, the screen jumps to life, banishing the gloom of her dimly lit room with its sudden glow. She hasn't charged the device in over a week, being mostly disinterested in the digital ties that bind the rest of the world. And while she's heard amazing things about the new retinal Leaf, she has yet to try one out herself. To Mulva, the tangible weight of a phone, the tactile press of buttons, connects her to a reality she can control when she so desires. She flexes her fingers, pressing them into her palm, then splaying them again, a quiet ritual. The storm rages on, but she remains still.

The device buzzes as it powers back on, and a few notifications flood the screen, but one message stands out—an old school text that seems almost anachronistic among the alerts. It's from Charisma Sinclair, a name that conjures a spectrum of memories, vivid and intense. Her chest tightens. She was at once her best friend, the love of her life, and in so many ways her idol. Charisma could do or accomplish anything within the realm of advanced engineering from the age when they first met as preteens. Charisma, for all her wonder about existence and the cosmos and all the big stuff, was also a brilliant tactician and problem-solver who could get down to the most minute detail to uncover how anything worked and subsequently work backward to figure out a fix, a new design, an improved functionality. Even as a kid, Charisma could look at a broken device and understand it before anyone else even saw the problem. Mulva remembers clear as day the summer Charisma built a fully functioning drone out of spare laptop parts and a dismantled VR headset, just for the fun of it. "*Wanna see something cool?*" she had said, eyes alight with the thrill of creation. Minutes later, the drone was zipping around the backyard, responding to Charisma's voice commands like an eager pet.

Mulva wouldn't have been surprised no matter how high her friend could've climbed. But now, for her to reach out to Mulva in such a way sends a shiver and a thrill throughout her body. Her breath hitches. The message is succinct: "*I need you now more than ever. Get a hold of me ASAP . . . PLEASE.*" The words are punctuated with an urgency that pierces Mulva's habitual reserve, igniting a spark of concern that flares into determination.

She sits motionless for a few moments, letting the import of the message sink in. Her fingers hover over the keypad, hesitant yet compelled. In the storm's intermittent illumination, her face is a tableau of conflict and resolve. The past rushes back like a flood—memories, feelings, unresolved questions. She grips the phone tighter. With a decisive movement, she taps out a response, her commitment galvanized by the knowledge that Charisma, her once inseparable companion, needs her.

Time, a nebulous concept, loses its grip on Mulva's consciousness. Five years? Six? It matters not. What endures is Mulva's unwavering affection for Charisma. The bond forged in their teenage years transcends time's passage. The message, clearly a digital SOS, carries an unspoken plea—a friend in dire need. Charisma, in a moment of vulnerability, summoned Mulva. Was she truly forgotten all this time? The specifics remain elusive, wrapped in the urgency of the message, a modern-day distress call.

Mulva's room is an exercise in impermanence, as if she never intended to stay long. The mattress, bare except for a rumpled gray blanket, sits directly on the floor, the frame long since discarded. A single wooden crate serves as both a nightstand and bookshelf, stacked unevenly with well-worn paperbacks—Vonnegut, Didion, Wolitzer, and a tattered physics book she's been meaning to return to. A folding chair leans against the far wall, unused, its metal frame rusting at the hinges. The desk, littered with old receipts, scattered sketches, and a few empty pill bottles, is a graveyard of half-formed ideas. A faded duffel bag, always half-packed, rests by the door like a silent reminder that she's never fully settled anywhere.

Meanwhile, the storm has not let up an ounce, only increasing in intensity. Wind rattles the window frame. The distant wail of a snapped power line underscores the storm's fury. She continues to scan every inch of the room and at the same time formulates her plan. In one corner, the medicine cabinet stands slightly ajar, its contents a tempting array of prescribed sedatives, stimulants, and Mulva's favorite—psychedelics. With a practiced hand, she pockets a few goodies—a temporary escape from the confinement of her own mind.

Her name, Mulva Warfarin, a personally chosen moniker, a defiant act against a foolish father who found humor in the trivial, particularly a 90s sitcom episode he would recount with glee. Mulva, a name hissed with a sneer, was her rebellion against the man who saw her as an extension of his amusement.

The storm outside mirrors the turmoil within Mulva's heart. Once more, she finds herself at a crossroads, a precipice where the path behind is littered with fragments of a fractured past, and the road ahead shrouded in uncertainty. Amid this internal and external chaos, a singular thought prevails—Charisma Sinclair was once her light in the dark, and now she will do whatever she can to see her friend through this storm.

Mulva, sensing the gravity of the situation, closes her eyes for a moment, tuning into the primal rhythm of the rapture outside. Her love for Charisma propels her into action. She slips into her weathered coat, its fabric as familiar as a second skin, and steps into the maelstrom outside. Cold rain slashes against her face. Thunder cracks continually overhead. The relentless downpour serves as a baptism, washing away the inertia of confinement. She sets forth, determined to brave the elements and challenges that undoubtedly lie ahead. The storm, with its thundering and breathtaking theatrics, becomes her cloak, masking her movements. Time to retrace the bonds of a friendship weathered by time, yet enduring, like a lighthouse guiding Mulva through nature's wrath toward her most cherished friend.

CHAPTER ELEVEN

DOUBLE DOWN

In the cozy confines back at Chew's place, the soft glow of recessed lighting casts a warm, golden hue over the walls and his minimalist décor. The faint scent of burnt incense lingers in the air, mingling with traces of whiskey and whatever exotic candle Chew lit. The bass-heavy tunes from the Cosmic Chalice still reverberate in Deuce's bones as he sinks into the familiar embrace of Chew's well-worn couch. He glances toward the bookcases, surmising that he shares at least half of Chew's collections of the works visible on the shelf.

Sitting next to him, sprawled in languid confidence, is the woman who's been flirting with him since they left the space bar. Blonde with streaks of rebellious red, her black dress clings to her frame, the strap slipping teasingly down her shoulder. She watches him with half-lidded eyes, a slow smile curling her lips. She inches closer, her fingers tracing absent-minded circles on his knee.

"I'm sorry," Deuce says with a scratchy voice. "I don't want to lead you on."

Her fingers pause, then resume, slower this time, as if testing him. "What, are you coming out of a bad breakup or something?"

The sarcasm is sharp, but there is some curiosity behind it. Deuce doesn't answer right away, instead looks back toward the bookcases. Sagan, Harris, Dawkins, Cixin. Existential philosophy stacked against sci-fi classics. Books like these have served as both he and Chew's armor, a monument to the knowledge they've collected like artifacts over the years.

"How about a drink?" Deuce asks, trying to shuffle away from the present awkwardness. "I'm sure my friend has ample stock of—"

"I don't want a drink . . ." She stares intently, dark red lipstick now smeared across her face. When she fully realizes he isn't interested, she looks at Deuce like he's a person with leprosy, or a bum, or both. He recoils and his stomach sinks knowing it won't be an easy chore to get her out of here especially considering her friend is enjoying time in the bedroom with Chew.

She pouts like a toddler for a few moments before she springs to her feet, rushing past Chew's bookcase and down the narrow hallway toward the bedroom door. The candles cast dancing shadows on the walls, adding to the sensuality of the scene. He briefly considers pleading with her to stop, but opts against it. The pounding on the door is frantic. Emily answers, a blanket wrapped around her naked body, dark hair tousled, cheekbones catching the low light. She's breathtaking. Even disheveled, there's something regal about her, a presence that makes the mania around her seem insignificant.

"Hey, hey! Take it easy," Chew says, wearing only his infamous skintight leopard speedo, as he dashes into the scene, all smiles and giggles. "Ladies, please," he chuckles, arms raised in mock surrender. The blonde slurs something incoherent before grabbing Emily's hand, pulling her out of the apartment in a frenzied rush. The front door slams behind them, leaving the apartment in stunned silence. It's all over in less than two minutes.

"Lemme get a hit of that," Chew says, sighing and settling down next to Deuce on the sofa. Rather than having another alcoholic beverage, Deuce has lit the remnants of a joint that from the looks of it was last smoked days, maybe weeks ago.

"Dude, she was repulsive," Deuce says to his defense. He feels guilty Chew didn't get to close out the night he planned. "I was fine chatting with her, but she made a move. I shot her down. Then she went ballistic the moment she heard you going to pound town. Sorry, man. I just couldn't. I didn't like anything about her."

"Yeah, but her friend was hot. Whew!" Chew smiles wide.

"Yes, she was. Her name is Emily, by the way," exhaling a waft of stale smoke.

"Emily! That's right. Man, I was really struggling coming up with that. Yes, for sure—Emily is an uber-babe!"

"And quite cool. I had a nice chat with her at the Chalice."

"Why didn't you make a move then?"

"I was going to. I went for a round of drinks. By the time I got back you had reemerged from the shadows and swooped in. You had her on the dance floor seconds later."

"So, you're saying you liked my gal?"

"Emily."

"Yes, Emily. I won't forget her name again. You liked Emily? You should've said something, man."

The joint burns down, and Chew stares back at him in astonishment.

"C'mon, Chew," Deuce continues. "It's been this way since grade school. You know it to be true."

Chew props himself up on one elbow, studying Deuce like he's said something completely absurd. "Aw, man, you c'mon," he says, shaking his head. "That's not—" He pauses, eyes narrowing slightly, as if replaying a dozen old memories at once. He opens his mouth again, but nothing comes out. Instead, he lets out a soft chuckle and flops back down. "Hmm, never really thought about it like that." He exhales, staring at his ceiling. "But you know you could've always called dibs and I would've backed off."

Deuce smirks. "Like that would have changed a thing," he says, shaking his head. "But I'm in no mood to argue about it tonight. Let's listen to some groovy tunes. How does old school Tame Impala sound?"

The collection of the western Aussie band's early work howls from Chew's surround sound setup. *The Bold Arrow of Time* is first up. Deuce is high and relieved. He senses Chew processing this information. All of it was true. Tonight is a perfect example. But the pair do not get into it any further. They opt to let Kevin Parker and the band he made legendary take the air for the rest of the evening. Chew lights a fresh joint, rolls off the couch, and sprawls out on his living room's carpeted floor. His dark, athletic frame stretching out in a showcase of exasperation. No more words are said between the two best friends. Just the comfort of each other's presence and the excitement for tomorrow's journey.

Deuce thinks about Emily some more. Then he thinks about all the other stunning gals who dug Chew more than him. Was it because he didn't have mom growing up? Was he really that clueless when it came to women? His heart races like a sprinter making the final turn. His emotions turn sad and hollow.

Growing up without mom was like putting an asterisk on every single record ever achieved. It hit hardest during the quiet moments—the ones that should've been celebrations but felt hollow instead. Like his first complete game on the mound in middle school, when he instinctively scanned the crowd, expecting to see her face beaming, only to remember in the next instant she wasn't there and never would be again. Or the time he and his dad built a telescope from scratch, and he wished he could show her the rings of Saturn, the way they shimmered in the eyepiece like something out of a dream. Those moments stuck like splinters. And maybe, deep down, that's why he let so much slip past him—why Chew always ended up with the girl, why he never fought too hard for anything outside the ballfield. Because chasing something meant risking disappointment. And he was damned tired of heartbreak and disappointment. All those moments and memories, especially the good ones, didn't matter nearly as much because she wasn't there. Nothing but dust and a memory. It was awful. But Deuce made that all-in deal with his dad: Overdrive. Every day. For Mom.

It was difficult, especially early on. But his father was the greatest teacher and turned him on to so much during his formative years. Always kept his mind occupied and the fire of curiosity burning bright, especially by teaching him a deep appreciation for time and space, and a fluent knowledge of our backstory—familial, national, and as a species. Even through the grief of losing mom, Deuce knew that he had still hit the cosmic lottery having been born healthy, in this country, and during this era.

His spirit brightens somewhat upon this reflection. Deuce can feel the haunting vibes of San Francisco subside. He's genuinely looking forward to getting there—via the HyperLoop—with his best friend and end the decade with some real joy and aplomb. Maybe he'll meet someone like Emily.

CHAPTER TWELVE

MULVA WARFARIN PART II

The rain streaks the McDonald's window in erratic, silvery trails, tracing the faded glow of the parking lot like veins of liquid light. Charisma watches the storm's final gasps, the heavy clouds retreating, leaving behind the kind of damp, lonely quiet that follows upheaval. Inside the booth, her fingers circle the rim of her coffee cup, its warmth doing little to thaw the cold weight in her chest. She finally speaks, her voice barely more than a whisper.

"You never knew how I truly felt . . ."

Mulva doesn't answer right away. She stares out at the darkened lot, letting the words settle between them. Charisma studies her, the way her buzzed hair frames her angular face, the way her fingers clench and unclench against the table. There's no trace of the firecracker she once was—the girl who used to crack the world open with her laughter and razor wit. What's left is someone aged beyond her years, worn down by whatever battles she's been fighting on her own.

Finally, Mulva let out a slow, measured breath. "You're right, Charisma. Absolutely right. I always assumed. It was such a difficult time, filled with confusion and heartbreaking disappointments."

The words hit Charisma with an ache she wasn't prepared for. A lifetime of regrets compressed into a single sentence. For the past hour, they've talked without pause, their conversation an unbroken thread of words looping back through the years, tightening old bonds that had frayed but never fully snapped. Charisma clings to the ease of it, the way their voices still fit together despite everything. The rain drums a steady rhythm against the glass, a metronome ticking away the moments they've already lost.

Mulva shifts in her seat, restless energy coiled beneath her skin. It's the same way she used to fidget before making a decision that would change everything. When she speaks up again, her voice is distant. "I fled when the storm was at its worst last night. They weren't going to allow me to leave unsupervised, so I didn't give them a choice in the matter."

Charisma straightens slightly, suddenly more alert. Mulva mentioned leaving the facility, but she skimmed over the details—too fast, too light, like skipping a stone across the water. Now, Charisma clearly sees the weight in her eyes, the exhaustion that clings to her like an overworn coat.

"Mulva . . . what happened?" she asks.

Mulva exhales, staring down at the chipped laminate of the table. She turns her cup slowly between her palms before answering. "It wasn't a hospital, Charisma. Not really. More like a holding cell with better wallpaper." Her voice drops lower, almost lost beneath the hum of the fast-food joint. "They keep you comfortable enough that you stop questioning why you're really there."

Charisma feels a prickle at the base of her neck. "Jesus. Did you have to—"

"I didn't hurt anyone," Mulva cuts in, shaking her head. "Didn't need to. The storm did half the work for me. The power went down around midnight. No cameras. No locks on the emergency exits that still worked. I walked right out into the rain like it was meant to happen." She huffs a dry laugh. "The only challenge was getting off the property without tripping one of their bullshit perimeter sensors. But they weren't built for a night like last night. Ferocious winds like you see once a generation. Downed trees everywhere. It was terrifying and thrilling in the same breath. I hitched a ride out of town with some local heading south before they even knew I was gone."

Charisma lets the weight of Mulva's words settle in. She's picturing it now—Mulva slipping out of a faceless, sterile building, her shoes sinking into wet earth as the storm raged all around her, her heartbeat competing with the thunder. The image sends a charge of something electric through Charisma's nerves, something close to admiration. She walked out of there with nothing but her own stubborn will and the storm at her back. *All to come help me.*

Mulva shakes her head, running a hand over her buzzed scalp. "I should be afraid they'll find me, drag me back. But I don't think they care. I wasn't a problem for them most days. They probably wanted me out of the way."

Charisma's fingers tighten around her coffee cup. "You're not going back," she says. "You're coming with me."

Mulva finally meets her gaze, and for the first time all night, Charisma sees a crack in the tough exterior—a blip of uncertainty, of something unspoken hanging between them. Her lips twitch, signaling something like amusement or disbelief ghosting across her face before vanishing. She looks down, tracing the rim of her cup with one finger. "You always had a way of making things sound so simple." Her voice is softer now, lacking the edge that usually slices through her words. "But nothing about me is simple. And nothing about this world is fair."

Charisma exhales slowly, absorbing the weight in her friend's voice. *Neither am I. Neither is this fight.* She doesn't say it, but she wants to. Instead, she leans in, resting her elbows on the table. The McDonald's around them purrs with a quiet sterility, a relic of a corporate empire that continues to thrive with the shifting tides of the times. The walls are lined with screens displaying AI-generated employees hawking burgers and nostalgia, looping prerecorded smiles that never falter. Outside, the rain has dwindled to a soft mist, but the sky remains heavy with unspent thunder.

A soft mechanical rustle cuts through the silence as their server rolls up to the table. It's a near-perfect replica of R2-D2, save for the McDonald's golden arches stamped onto its cylindrical body. The droid chirps once, a synthesized facsimile of hospitality, before extending two trays with the mechanical precision of a factory assembly line.

"Jesus," Mulva mutters, eyeing the little machine. "This place used to hire minimum-wage teenagers."

"That was before Disney bought them out," Charisma says dryly, grabbing her tray. "No more disgruntled kids forgetting your fries—just seamless efficiency and corporate-approved charm."

Mulva snorts but takes her tray anyway, poking at the synthetic burger like it might come to life and bite her back. "Yeah, well, I'll still take a sullen teenager over a soulless automaton any day."

"And yet, here we are," Charisma says, staring at the table, the weight of their conversation pressing down on her again. She looks up, meeting Mulva's eyes. "Listen, I don't care how complicated this is. I need you, Mulva. I've never needed anyone more in my entire goddamn life."

The confession lands like a stone between them, sending ripples through the silence. Mulva stiffens, eyes locking with Charisma's, wary and searching. The first real, unguarded thing Charisma said all night, and it rattles both of them.

"You always did know how to twist my arm," Mulva says, the hint of a smirk pulling at her mouth. "Fine. Tell me. What am I getting myself into?"

Relief rushes through Charisma so quickly it almost leaves her lightheaded. She grips Mulva's hand across the table, holding on tight.

"Samantha Ravensby stole my company. My life's work. I'm either going to take it back or take her out."

Mulva tilts her head, her gaze sharpening, the fog of old emotions momentarily lifting. "And you think I can help?"

"I know you can." Charisma's voice is steel now, unwavering. "Because if there's one person I know in this world who can burn down the walls of a fortress, it's you."

Mulva exhales through her nose, shaking her head as she glances toward the window, rainwater streaking down the glass in erratic lines. "You always did know how to sell a revolution."

Charisma smirks, squeezing Mulva's hand again before letting go. "Then let's start one."

Mulva grips the edge of her tray, knuckles whitening. Charisma watches the change roll through her—something stirring beneath the surface, something Mulva hasn't shown since they've been back together. The way her gaze sharpens, how her posture shifts ever so slightly forward. Like she's coming back to life, piece by piece. Charisma knows that look well. It's the one Mulva used to wear when the world needed shaking. The one that meant she was all in.

With a deep breath, she shoves her half-eaten burger aside and locks eyes with Charisma. "Alright. But I have a condition."

Charisma lifts a brow. "Name it."

"We do it my way. No legal battles, no playing nice. You're not going to outmaneuver someone like Samantha Ravensby with boardroom politics and well-placed press leaks. Or any other crap like that. We're gonna hit her where it hurts. And we won't stop until she's got nothing left."

The steel in Mulva's voice sends a shiver down Charisma's spine, but she doesn't flinch. "I'm listening."

Mulva leans back, fingers tapping rhythmically on the table as her mind starts spinning, assembling the first pieces of a war plan she hadn't known she'd been waiting for. The old instincts are still there, lurking beneath years of detachment. There's something thrilling—dangerous—about feeling them click back into place.

"We start with intel," she says. "If Samantha stole Loopd>In from you, she didn't do it alone. I guarantee you, there's a weak link somewhere—an assistant, a lawyer, some poor bastard she's screwing over even harder than you. We find that person, and we exploit them."

Charisma exhales slowly, nodding. "*And then?*"

Mulva shrugs, a slow, sharp grin spreading across her face. "Then we make her wish she never fucked with you."

The constant beat of rain against the windows fills the pause between them. Charisma studies her friend, the energy of something dark and familiar burning in Mulva's expression. The same look she used to wear when they were kids, plotting their latest rebellion against whatever system wronged them that week. Mulva Warfarin, her oldest friend, her fiercest ally, the person she trusted with everything. This is the moment Charisma Sinclair knows, without a shadow of a doubt, that she's going to win. She slides her tray away and wipes her hands on a napkin, the decision settling in her bones. "Then let's stop wasting any more time."

They rise together, stepping out of the booth in sync, their movements fluid, electric with purpose. As they stride toward the exit, the R2-D2-like server chirps a farewell in perfect, cheerful monotony. Mulva throws it a two-fingered salute as they push through the door into the cool night air.

The rain tapered off to misty droplets, clinging to their skin as they walk toward Charisma's car. Mulva stands by as Charisma unlocks her self-driving vehicle with a flick of her wrist.

"So, what's the name of your car's AI?" Mulva asks, glancing at the smooth, dark body.

"Andre," Charisma replies. "And he's taking us straight to the heart of San Francisco."

Mulva smirks, sliding into the passenger seat as the doors hiss shut behind them. "Alright, Andre," she mutters, stretching out as the electric motor comes to life. "Let's go raise some hell."

The city lights beckon in the distance, gleaming like an invitation. As they accelerate onto the highway, Charisma leans her head back against the seat, the weight of despair loosening, making room for something far more potent.

Resolve. Revenge. Redemption. And beside her, Mulva Warfarin, the storm Samantha never saw coming, ready to set the world on fire.

CHAPTER THIRTEEN

GORGEOUS GHOSTS

The Spirit of St. Louis HyperLoop complex stands as a monument to ambition, a gleaming titan of metal, fiber, and light, wrapped in the velvet veil of the December night. Its architecture is both alien and organic—an immense, branching structure that seems less *built* and more *grown*, its arms stretching skyward like some futuristic megatree drinking in the cosmos and even making the St. Louis Arch seem a relic. The entire structure radiates energy, a living nerve center of human ingenuity, its veins coursing with the light of millions of microprocessors working in seamless synchrony.

As Deuce's car glides between two identical models—one a deep, forest green, the other a polished, radiant red—the glossy exterior reflects the city's artificial glow like a vision from another world. The human energy of thousands of fellow travelers, the faint hum of electromagnetic currents, the distant whirl of HyperLoop pods gliding into their docks—It all blends into this mechanical emblem of progress. This would be yet another crowning achievement in the legacy of Elon Musk, but both guys knew it had Deuce's dad's fingerprints stamped all over the edges.

Deuce and Chew retrieve their lightweight, carbon fiber luggage from the car's back seat, their movements deliberate, unspoken excitement and trepidation shift between them like a static charge. Before stepping forward, Deuce checks the trunk one last time, though he knows nothing was left behind—a habitual caution, a ritual born of years of drifting place to place.

Before them, Musk's masterpiece unfurls in its full, titanic glory. The octopus-like sprawl of the HyperLoop stretches into the night, the sheen of its metallic limbs twisting and rotating in a delicate, synchronized dance of design and engineering. Beyond even the loftiest skyscrapers, it does not merely scrape the sky—it claims it.

Deuce exhales low and slow, shaking his head. "Unreal, man. It's . . . unreal." The weight of history presses against his chest. He looks over to Chew who nods approvingly while licking his teeth back and forth as he stares at the complex's façade.

This wasn't just a transit hub—it was a declaration. A manifestation of human will, a direct rebuttal to every cynic who ever said civilization was in decline. And at the heart of it all—hidden in connections, bridging divides, and forgotten conversations—was Philipp Largo.

As they close in on the main hub, the Spirit of St. Louis continues to rise before them like something out of a dream. Deuce slows his stride, taking it in—The enormity, the vagary of where structure meets sky, the way it seems less like a station and more like a living entity, expanding and twisting into the night. It's one thing to read about it, to watch the launch videos, to follow the progress updates over the past decade. But standing here, where it bellows with the pulse of a city within a city, Deuce feels the sheer weight of its reality.

"We can't be late," Deuce says, adjusting his bag strap over his shoulder. His voice is casual, but every other sense is titillated at the prospect of riding on this thing.

"Man, I never thought I'd see the day we could just hop on something like this and zip across the country in minutes," Chew says. "While never leaving the ground."

Deuce exhales, taking one last long look at the structure. "It's almost . . . too much." He drags a hand through his wavy hair, his gaze shifting between the looming HyperLoop and the sprawl of city lights beyond. "Like standing at the edge of something, knowing you're about to leave a whole part of yourself behind. Traveling was always a big part of our lives, Chew. After this, it will never be the same." He shakes his head, trailing off.

Chew follows his gaze. The Spirit of St. Louis sprawls across the core of the city, a feat of engineering that makes even the world's most advanced airports look outdated. The enormity is dizzying—a fusion of a stadium, a launch terminal, and something beyond imagination.

And it's all accessible. To *everyone.*

That part sticks with Deuce the most. For years, travel—real travel—was the privilege of the few. Even after AI and quantum computing eliminated inefficiencies and helped drive down costs, barriers remained for so many. This structure doesn't just move people—it moves *possibility.* It's a promise that mobility isn't a privilege anymore.

The closer they get to the entrance, the stronger the faint electric charge in the air becomes—something subtle but omnipresent, like standing near a silent thunderstorm that never breaks. The low buzz of electromagnetic currents beneath their feet is almost imperceptible, but Deuce feels it in his bones. *Damn. We really made it here.*

As they get closer to the main entrance, Deuce feels like a man stepping onto another planet. His movements are stiff, careful—like he's waiting for something to snap him out of this. Chew doesn't press, not yet. Instead, he lets the moment linger as they step through the entrance.

Inside, the immaculate interior gleams, illuminated by hanging orbs of soft white that mimic constellations. Walkways float on near-invisible suspensions, carrying travelers smoothly through different levels. The very air feels hypersterilized, but not cold, filled with a faint scent of ozone and polished steel.

Deuce slows beside Chew and for a second, something glimmers in his own reflection on the polished floor—an expression he hasn't seen in himself in years. Not fear. Not excitement. Something much heavier. He catches Chew glancing sideways at him, watching him closely. Always watching, as if waiting for the right moment to push.

"Hell of a sight," Chew says, his tone easy but deliberate. "Your dad would've loved this."

Deuce doesn't answer right away. He grips the strap of his bag and continues his walk toward the gate. The words land like a stone dropped in a deep well, echoing down into something Deuce has tried to seal off. He knows what Chew is trying to do—nudge the memory forward, open the vault. And he's not wrong. Philipp Largo would have loved this place. Not just for the design or the innovation, but for what it represented. A statement, an unmistakable leap forward.

"Yeah," Deuce says finally. "He certainly would have."

The thought burns through Deuce's mind. Philipp Largo, one of the true architects of this new era: Buried. Forgotten. Just another name, another face in the crowd lost to history. Deuce slows his pace again, glancing at the passengers moving through the terminal—tourists, business travelers, families. All of them about to experience something remarkable that was built on the foundation Philipp Largo helped to lay. But his name isn't anywhere. And Deuce, more than anyone, feels the weight of that. His jaw tightens as he scans the massive digital displays listing the HyperLoop's main contributors—names of investors, engineers, and public figures who helped champion the project. But not his father. Not the man who was instrumental in bringing Musk back from the brink when the first blueprints were still napkin sketches.

Chew keeps walking, but Deuce pauses in his tracks. A familiar frustration curls in his gut. This wasn't just about the past. The world moved forward on the back of his father's mind, and no one seemed to care. Maybe that was how progress worked—build, forget, repeat.

Or maybe that was all bullshit and Deuce was fed up with hiding his head in the sand anymore. For the first time in years, something more than grief stirs in him when he thinks of his father. A need, a hunger, to reclaim what was lost. To make sure Philipp Largo wasn't some obscure ghost haunting the periphery of history. He doesn't know how yet, but one thing is for certain in this instant: This will not stand. He adjusts his bag again and catches up to Chew at the gates of entry. His pulse is steady, but his mind is electric with new thoughts.

Chew sighs, shaking his head. "I try to remember everything your dad told me. Told us."

A quiver of something shifts in Deuce. He feels alive.

"My favorite," Chew continues, grinning, "was when he said, 'We're nothing more than slightly evolved chimpanzees, and it's rough out there—so give yourself a break.'"

Deuce finally lets out a laugh. A real one.

Chew doesn't say anything.

Deuce wipes a tear from his eye and does his best to hold back any more laughter so he can respond. "He had some good ones.

Hadn't heard that one in ages. You always did know when to drop a good one-liner, my friend."

Chew shrugs. "Originality is the art of concealing your sources. And being around your dad all them years surely helped my cause."

For a second, things feel lighter. Like the demons surrounding them might stay in the past, at least for the night. Deuce halts once again. Chew stops beside him, searching his face. "You alright?"

Deuce's fingers drum absently against his thigh, his gaze moving toward one of the massive screens displaying the HyperLoop's upcoming routes. The destinations glow in brilliant white text:

- Western route: Denver – Las Vegas - San Francisco | 17 minutes
- Eastern route: Indianapolis – Pittsburgh - New York | 33 minutes
- Southern route: Oklahoma City – Dallas – San Antonio – Monterrey – Mexico City | 48 minutes

Deuce lets out a sigh. Then he mutters, almost to himself: "Do you ever think . . . I don't know. If time actually heals anything?"

Chew doesn't answer right away. Instead, he follows Deuce's stare to the list of destinations. To the flashing arrival times. To the reality of where they're heading.

San Francisco. The place where everything changed. Finally, Chew claps a hand on Deuce's shoulder. "Let's find out," he says, guiding them forward.

Deuce doesn't hesitate. As they move into line, he perks up when he recalls something he recently read. "You know what they're calling the fusion reactor that's powering this entire place?"

Chew shakes his head. "I don't think I even know my own name right now. I've never been equally thrilled and terrified to go on a ride."

"Hypatia II," Deuce says, a proud smile breaking across his face. "The very first one was built on the ruins of Alexandria. This one's right off Lake Superior."

Chew lets out a low whistle.

The legend of Hypatia—the brilliant and beautiful thinker viciously destroyed by hatred and ignorance—was one of countless lessons from Philipp Largo. Seeing her name etched into the future, two millennia later, feels to Deuce like although she lost the battle, her spirit still won the war . . . her brilliance honored and celebrated by a world that damned near burned itself back to the Stone Ages.

They inch forward. Ahead, the travel pods appear from seemingly nowhere, gliding into position. Opaque, super smooth, a hundred feet of smooth, reflective material that reminds Deuce of Chicago's Bean sculpture—except these aren't just for show.

Chew leans in. "What are these made from again?"

Deuce exhales, tilting his head. "Anything and everything Musk's team could get to work."

"Musk is *the* man," Chew says, watching the multitude of pods shift into docking positions. "Hard to believe he was such a maniac and troll a few decades ago."

Deuce turns to face him. "Vision without execution is merely hallucination."

The warm station light catches the edge of Chew's features—a glimpse of someone who once knew exactly where he was headed. Chew blinks. "Huh?"

Deuce nods back. "That was my personal favorite maxim from my dad. You mentioned yours. I really thought about mine for a few moments. When you mentioned Musk's past hijinks and bullshit, it hit me. Dad often used to mention it in the same breath as he did with Elon, especially once he got reconnected with Sam."

Chew lets the words settle before he drapes an arm over Deuce's shoulder. There's no rush in the line. No frantic sprint to gates, no last-minute dashes. The station moves like clockwork, built on precision and ease.

"I sure wish he was here with us," Chew finally says. "I'd cut my arm off for just *one* more weekend with the guy."

A surge rushes all through Deuce's body at the thought of another weekend with his dad. Or even just one more hour. But he's grown tired of allowing emotions like this to sadden him. He closes his eyes and quiets his mind. Like he was taught so many years ago. Like he used to before taking the mound. Laser focus. Deep mindfulness. Trying to thread the needle between warrior-like competitor and Jedi-like mind control. He's determined to not go down a dark path. No longer. He can feel his father's presence around him the deeper inward he goes. Like he's Luke and Philipp is Obi-Wan. He opens his eyes and beams the kind of smile at Chew that shows off all his teeth.

"AI and nuclear fusion," Deuce says, looking up and all around him in the final moments before boarding time. "Working in unison to make this all happen. It's incredible, Chew. While we're ruminating on all quips and lessons from the guy, I thought of one more." He pauses for effect and looks Chew right in the eye. "He said that although the twenties were indeed terrible, being around to see the rise of commercial AI *and* Caitlin Clark at the height of her powers when she played at Iowa was as astonishing as anything he witnessed in his life. The juxtaposition and the irony of both happening basically at the same time. And we all know how they only got better with age. Let's go catch our ride to San Francisco, my friend."

They step forward. Retinal scans blink in approval for their boarding. A final and curious CID-A authorization requests permission to trial a new customer experience called Loopd>In.

Chew nods at Deuce a final time before boarding. A silent acknowledgement. The pods seal shut. The HyperLoop radiates with the most positive energy and promise of boundless opportunities. As the pair launches westward, ghosts are left behind them in streaks of neon light.

CHAPTER FOURTEEN

THERE THERE

And the gods made love. Alone in her office tucked into the Golden Gate Nexus, Samantha agonizes over how many times she should repeat this line. She's completely torn. Part of her instinct strongly suggests she should do so at each and every milestone. But she loathes redundancy. And while this might not be the most important speech she ever made, it could very well go down as her most memorable. Every line, every utterance needs to be perfect. No waxing philosophical, no going on tangents or off script. She decides three times will be enough. At the beginning, middle, and end. She reviews her list: sentience—fire—agriculture—the written word— electricity—flight—nuclear power—the internet—AI—and now this . . . what she and her beautiful band of barbarian scientists and engineers are about to unleash upon the world.

I've done it, she whispers to herself. This is the next, long-awaited step. Tomorrow, Loopd>In will be available on selected pods throughout the brand new HyperLoop system. A tech breakthrough of this magnitude is often unnoticed by the masses until it becomes ubiquitous. Not this time. Much like the advent of commercial AI being available for every Tom, Dick, and Harry right around the time she turned forty, Samantha knows this will slap people right across the face the first time they use it. And for those who don't want to be doers, well then, they'll finally have their ticket to paradise without having to put in the work. With Uncle Sam's help most likely coming with the next Congressional session, they can remain there for as long as they like. *Not quite all the way there.* We still need to figure out how to safely emulate the speed of the HyperLoop pods in a fixed position, so the experience equals that of which each user will go through while traveling in Elon's latest spectacular game changer. *But we'll get there soon enough.*

She turns on her screen using her retinal Leaf. Everything is connected. The show will start in a few moments. She looks around for her handheld mirror and once she finds it, she gives herself a look-over, still astonished at the results of her latest CRISPR therapy. She laughs at the thought of impersonating Buffalo Bill in *Silence of the Lambs*, still her all-time favorite film.

I'd fuck me . . . Still such a silly girl sometimes. *But I mean, c'mon!* Who wouldn't? She looked better now than the day she turned forty. The screen comes alive right on time with her core teams in attendance spread out over five countries and five different time zones.

"Good day to you all, whatever time in the day it may be for you," Samantha says, opening her address to the top employees of Loopd>In. "But it is *tomorrow* that I want to talk to you all about right now . . ."

Samantha remains the only one in her office. She carefully curated and crafted her global team with an infusion of best-in-class software engineers, life science specialists, and VR programming renegades who drooled of building Loopd>In once she seized complete control of the company and eradicated any and all internal threats. All of these experts, of course, were guided by their AI counterparts, all set out on a singular mission, which would be realized in a few short hours. Samantha considered making this speech from the confines of Loopd>In's headquarters, perched heavenly atop the Jovian high-rise in downtown San Francisco, but thought better of it in the eleventh hour. *No, what I'm about to say must be delivered here.*

"Each and every one of you are a crucial part of the next monumental step forward in the story of our species, *Homo sapiens,*" she says with unbridled enthusiasm, lighting up as if showered with praise, not bestowing it. She takes a deep breath and reminds herself not to come off as too smug or condescending at any part of what she's about to convey. "I'm no poet, so I harken back to my favorite songwriter and musician to help me describe these leaps of paramount importance for our band of slightly evolved chimpanzees who dominated life on this pale blue bot for over a millennia." She pauses again and looks up at her office's ceiling. The meeting's video feed is dually synced with the camera from the monitor and her retinal Leaf. Above her, an artist friend of hers rendered a brilliant sexual dance of the Milky Way and Andromeda personified as Adam and Eve. She allows the image to display in silence for nine, ten seconds, all the while fondly reflecting on the man who coined that term. No, not Sagan with his eloquent verse and prose whenever painting pictures with words of the cosmos and existence. No, her thoughts are on the man who in death she kept to herself because she could. *Oh Philipp, if only you could be here with me today . . .*

"Whenever our distant ancestors first discovered the ability to harness fire, well, the only way to describe it from my eye comes from the immortal words and lyrics from the late, great Jimi

Hendrix, *and the gods made love . . .*"

She waits to see if her phrase of the day elicits any kind of response from the other side of the screen. A few smiles, but mostly a cadre of tech warriors hanging on to her every word, at least from her eye.

"So too was it when we evolved from hunter-gatherers into farmers. The advent of the written word brought us closer together in mind and soul as a species, and electricity transformed daily life from toil and suffering into a venerable and productive middle class. The rest of our gargantuan leaps of progress mixed in their results. As a country, and let's be honest, as a species we handled the internet and social media like utter fools, like savages. We all know we could've done so much better with those tools, and we did, with AI. But now this . . . this next great leap, what we are about to unleash. It cannot be fouled up. And we've all made sure of that, haven't we?" She pauses and deactivates her Leaf, killing the dual screen feed momentarily. "Loopd>In, along with its first partner, the HyperLoop, will equal the playing field for all. We've already achieved so much with universal power springing forth from the wonders of harnessing nuclear fusion . . . With dreadfully high costs of living being reduced to fractions of what they were a generation ago. But it's *our* product, *our* gift to the world that will essentially be the coup de grâce when it comes to class. When it comes to the haves and have nots. And we're accomplishing all of this without a lick of government intervention or involvement."

Part of her wants to pause for an extended period and ask for questions. Hear the adoration emanate through the screens. *No. Not today.* She must deliver this unencumbered and with crisp efficiency. It shall serve as her public statement relative to what is now going to be available for HyperLoop passengers and, soon enough, the rest of the world.

"The gods made love when it came to AI and finally we handled something so powerful, so impactful, with grace and wisdom and because of that we're where we are today. Its predecessors might've whacked us out and made us distrustful—and hateful—of each other for years, but I believe the lessons from those follies paved the way for such excellency when it came to the adaptation and regulation of implementing AI, or more apropos, AGI, within our daily lives. From the brilliance of our younger generations to the planet healing, the work and execution we achieve with these lifeless partners by our side is nothing short of the most remarkable accomplishment of all."

She stops right there, not allowing herself to go any further down that rabbit hole. She doesn't want her most significant message lost in the mists of describing how nature returned to harmony.

"But out of all these feats . . . from fire to fusion . . . nothing dents the fairness question in life. That for millennia only the rich and powerful could explore their greatest fantasies and dreams. To go wherever they desired so their senses could feast upon all the splendor. That is until now, because of us . . ."

She accomplished what she set out to do. The rest is a cursory overview of tomorrow's debut launch, some specific laudatory musts, and a heartfelt thank you to her teams. The stage is set. There will be no one to stop her this time.

CHAPTER FIFTEEN

HEADS, SPIKES, WALLS

The sun drapes San Francisco in gold, its warmth soaking Charisma's skin after weeks of damp chill. The breeze off the bay still carries a crisp bite, but under the sun's glow, her muscles relax, tension unwinding with every step. She pulls her phone out of her pocket and reactivates it for the first time today. Its glow illuminates as she books passage for herself and Mulva into the heart of the city. The Bay Area Transport—BART—is experiencing issues with retinal and facial scanning, prompting them to rely on the old-school mobile device procedure. After the archaic process, they are notified of a ten-minute wait until the next train arrives, followed by a ten-minute ride.

Charisma taps her temple, and the Leaf stirs to life—a whisper of light flickering beneath her vision. It's seamless, as always. No buzzing, no lag. Just data blooming across her sight line like mist on glass: transit alerts, environmental readings, a ping from Mulva's location. The technology is so embedded now, it's easy to forget it's there—part prosthesis, part intuition.

She remembers when it first launched, when skeptics called it invasive or unnatural. But to her, it was always inevitable. A stepping stone. The Leaf didn't replace the real world—it layered on top of it, like a lucid dream you could navigate at will. In many ways, it mirrored what she once hoped Loopd>In would become: not an escape, but an evolution.

Despite annoyance at having to turn her phone back on, Charisma takes pleasure in the congruence and symmetry of the moment. Although she carries it everywhere she goes out of habit, she hardly ever uses it anymore, proud of resisting the digital tether that entrapped her parents' generation. Mulva, standing behind her, is zoned out, lost in music playing through nearly invisible earbuds. Charisma admires Mulva's rhythmic movements, a dance hidden beneath a jet-black hoodie that bears no brand. The music is hers alone, but the way she moves—fluid, deliberate, completely unbothered—makes Charisma feel like she's witnessing something intimate, a performance only Mulva knows she's giving. Charisma wonders if her life's string of random events is going to end where it began. *Congruence.* Beauty is symmetry. All around us. But a quick and violent end would not be beautiful. Charisma knows this. Avoiding that is still within her control. So, what is the next move then? What play on the chessboard makes the most sense? At her disposal is a powerful weapon. *No, c'mon!* Mulva is so much more than a weapon. She is an asset and an ally. She is a friend willing to do anything. And she proved herself time and again.

As Mulva continues to flow and weave to her music unencumbered, Charisma thinks back to the night when their mutual stories hit their first crescendo. The night when Mulva almost decapitated Lance. Of course, she was not Mulva Warfarin then. That was back when she was still Krissy Picard. Cute, cold, and cunning Krissy. She got hauled away once her plan—whatever the end game truly was—got foiled. All because Lance was able to get his little SOS message out, unbeknownst to his captor.

Christ, it took her less than a week to pull that off. Charisma shudders at the notion of what her friend would have done to him. It also excites her, given her current predicament. Lance was an asshole, sure, but nothing compared to Samantha Ravensby. He had forced himself on her, drunkenly, at a high school party earlier in the year. It was gross and totally unacceptable, but Charisma did not want to retaliate. She didn't think the juice was worth the squeeze. That did not matter to Krissy, however. As soon as she heard the news, she concocted a plan and executed it five days later. Charisma was always equally thrilled with and terrified by her friend's cunning and ferocity.

She followed Lance Ludwig, that smug, elitist son-of-a-bitch, home from soccer practice. She lured him into her good graces with the promise of T-3000, back when that crazy designer drug first hit the streets. He should have known better, since his antics at the party were now well known throughout school, and Krissy and Charisma were close friends. But he could not resist the temptation, having heard stories from some of his friends in college about going on the wildest and most sensual trip of their lives shortly after ingesting the latest designer drug.

Less than a minute after stepping into Krissy's garage—or what he thought was her garage—he was knocked unconscious. When he came to, he was strapped very tightly to a bolted down wooden board with what looked to be a crude medieval guillotine that loomed in his periphery. His phone sat on a table out of his reach, but not too far away for voice command. He sent his distress message right before Krissy re-entered the room.

"Any last words," she smiled. "I want to make this quick. Your face disgusts me." Krissy was decisive and loud with her declaration. Her message was getting across in spades. "Fortunately, no one will see it any longer."

"Wait, wait, please! No!" The fear took total hold of him in that instant and he lost all control of his bodily functions. Krissy delighted at his terror and didn't even mind the smell, but she did not notice that he had activated his phone and sent a call for help. Maybe she erred because she didn't really want to go through with it. Maybe in some bizarre way she wanted to get caught. But her rage was real and she sure as hell was sick of pretty boys like Lance Ludwig getting away with anything they did or said. Removing his head from his neck would send quite the message. Krissy reveled in the notion of being a true American anti-hero. They would tell her tale for generations to come. Kill the head and the body dies. Fuck the patriarchy.

"Little Lancie poo-poo in his panties? Awe, poor boy. Well, at least you shouldn't have any remaining following your heart's final beat," said Krissy. "Let's get this over with, shall we? I've read that people, after being decapitated, can actually see their headless, lifeless body for a few seconds. Something like the brain is still functioning for a few brief moments following the act. Will you blink a few times for me, so I know for sure? That'd be fabulous. I would really appreciate it."

She allowed him to scream and sob for too long if she was serious about going through with it. The door got knocked down and with it, Krissy was promptly arrested. The story made national news. Lance tried to play the part of the aggrieved victim, but tales of his assholery soon became common knowledge and he was eventually kicked off his beloved soccer team.

Charisma pleaded with her mother to do something, anything, for Krissy, as this was all done on her behalf. That is when she knew her mom was truly gone. She didn't even have it in her to pick up the phone and try. Before the nightmare in Juarez, Carmen Sinclair would've done anything her daughter asked that she deemed noble and worthy. Certainly, no longer. In the end,

Krissy received five years in a mental asylum. Charisma visited her every week during the first year. Whenever Charisma asked if she had really planned to go through with it, Krissy always gave the same response, a classic line from their beloved *Game of Thrones*: heads, spikes, walls.

Krissy Picard never came out of that asylum. She died in there sometime around the beginning of year two. And Mulva Warfarin was born.

As they depart the train, Charisma and Mulva step into the spirited and eclectic heart of San Francisco, each stride carrying with it determination and uncertainty. The city's pulsating energy seems to mirror Charisma's internal conflict. She envisioned this moment countless times—the triumphant return, a decisive confrontation with Samantha Ravensby. Standing amid the city's towering structures, a sense of doubt creeps in, clouding her once clear purpose. As she traverses the streets of San Francisco, stride for stride in reflective silence with her beloved friend, Charisma can't help notice and appreciate the city's transformation. The once prevalent issue of homelessness has diminished significantly, replaced by psychedelic wellness centers and affordable neighborhoods, many of which were built using the same 3-D tech that constructed her own home. Places of healing, mentally and spiritually, for those in society who need it most, were as prevalent as gas stations and vape shops had been in the first memories of her youth. The urban core, vibrant and thriving, booms with the energy of a city reborn from the ashes of its troubled past in the 2020s. The revitalized neighborhoods, bustling with life and activity, stand as a shining example of a world-class metropolis that not only recovered but flourished, embracing a future where the well-being of all its citizens is a priority.

This renaissance of the cityscape serves as a parallel to Charisma's internal journey, as she navigates the complex web of her emotions and intentions. The contrast between the city's hard-fought revival and her own turbulent quest underscores the notion that redemption and change are indeed possible, but they require confronting and overcoming the deep-seated challenges within. This realization dawns on Charisma as she moves through the streets, now hand in hand with Mulva, each step taking them closer to a confrontation that could very well redefine them, much like the city that reshaped itself.

CHAPTER SIXTEEN

A WORLD OF ICE & FIRE

Chew steps into the luxurious cocoon of his HyperLoop pod, and a world of crafted comfort wraps around him. An embrace of softness—cushions, pillows, and easement—surrounds him. The Loopd>In touchscreen software he signed up for grants him control, a prelaunch combination of groundbreaking technology and personal imagination, about to hurtle him out west at a staggering seven hundred miles per hour. Before him lies a small, elegantly designed capsule, the CID-A, glowing with a soft internal light. He swallows it, feeling a slight effervescence as it descends, marking the initiation of his virtual journey.

Simultaneously, Chew activates the retinal Leaf provided prior to boarding. The latest in neural technology, this model is different from his own, customized and branded by the same software that controls his pod. Immediately and seamlessly, it integrates with his visual and cognitive faculties. The Leaf syncs instantly with the capsule's biochemical signals now coursing through his bloodstream. As the CID-A dissolves, it releases nanobots that construct a neural scaffold, linking Chew's nervous system directly to the Loopd>In interface.

Contemplating his favorite band's new album—*Seasons*—for the journey's soundtrack, Chew pivots, with a single concentrated thought, toward a medieval battle cry, immersing himself in a world previously confined to screens. George R.R. Martin's legendary creation materializes vividly. Leading a band of cutthroats through the Riverlands, Chew's mission crystallizes: Rescue a highborn lady from impending doom.

The transition is instantaneous, as if reality itself were rewritten. A gust of wind whips past Chew's face, carrying the crisp scent of damp earth and distant woodsmoke. His boots sink slightly into the Riverlands mud, the weight of his armor pressing against his shoulders, solid and unyielding. The misty veil obscures the weak sunlight, grounding every sensation as he treads forward, each step cushioned by the soft, damp terrain. Somewhere in the distance, a horse snorts, its breath misting in the frosty morning air. The scent of burning wood fills his nostrils, mingling with the sharper tang of metal and sweat. He flexes his fingers, the chilled steel of his gauntlets tightens around his knuckles, the cool bite of the wind threading through the gaps in his armor. This isn't just a game. It's a revelation.

Chew has spent years inside virtual spaces—first as an escape, then as a hobby, and eventually, as an extension of himself. But this? This isn't an escape. It's a world that feels more vivid than the one he left behind. The air, the cold steel of his gauntlets, the dampness in his boots—it's not a simulation anymore. It's reality, or something damn close to it.

A deep, unsettling thrill coils in his chest. He's always been aware of the risks—how entire generations before him were swallowed by screens, how people lost themselves in curated feeds and fabricated identities. He's read the studies, the warnings, the think pieces from people who don't understand what it's like to step into a dream and have it respond to you. But he doesn't need a study to tell him what's dangerous. He lived it.

Chew grew up watching his father disappear behind screens—news feeds, investment portfolios, endless simulations of the future, all of them more important than his own son. When he was little, he'd sit in the next room, hoping, waiting, but the door stayed closed. And by the time he was old enough to understand why, he had already inherited the habit. Virtual worlds didn't reject you. They didn't forget you existed. They took what you gave and gave something back. For the first time, he wonders if he'd even notice if he stayed. This experience is unlike anything before. And it's not even close.

As Chew's virtual saga concludes, the victory in the world of Westeros yields a bittersweet triumph. His heart, still hammering with the reverberations of battle, now syncs to a different rhythm—the unrelenting velocity of the HyperLoop. The change is jarring, like waking mid-fall from a dream. For a split second, his body struggles to recalibrate, muscles tensing against the strange weightlessness pressing against him. The pod moves with such flawless precision that he barely feels the motion in the traditional sense—no turbulence, no jostling, just a constant smoothness, as if gliding through a vacuum. The only indication of their speed is the soft vibration coursing through the seat and into his spine, the occasional smear of landscape stretching past the transparent overlays on the pod's curved walls. He catches fragmented glimpses of America at impossible speeds—desert highways twisted into golden blurs, cityscapes melting like oil on water, mountain peaks dissolving before they can fully form in his mind. His equilibrium tilts; there's no force pulling him forward or back, only the unrelenting surge of momentum swallowing time itself.

The transition from the VR realm to the tangible world leaves him momentarily disoriented, his senses having great difficulty grappling with the shift. Emerging from the cocoon of the HyperLoop pod, Chew steps into the vibrant beat of San Francisco's Golden Gate Nexus—the west coast's answer to the Spirit of St. Louis. The night air is cool against his skin, sprinkled lightly with the salty kiss of the bay. The city lights shimmer, a mosaic of life in constant motion, reflecting the dynamism of a place reborn again from the ashes of its past trials.

Chew's mind races, threading together the experience of his virtual adventure with the tangible presence of the city he once knew. The complex purrs with the cadence of progress and the reminder of tales of old ghosts, including the specter of that darkest day when he and Deuce faced the unthinkable. The city, like Chew, bears the scars of its history, yet stands resilient, its shine and grit still mixed together after all these years and defining what makes San Francisco so unique.

The city center unfolds before him, its skyline both unchanged and unrecognizable. The HyperLoop's journey was so fast, so seamless, it feels like he teleported into a place that exists in two timelines at once—the city of his past and the one he steps into now. Five years. Five years since he had last sprinted through these streets, lungs burning, his voice hoarse from shouting Deuce's name. He fought his way through crowds, his mind stuck in a loop of disbelief, desperate to be the one to deliver the news before Deuce saw it on a screen or was informed by someone else. Philipp Largo had died.

And now, he's back, here at the Golden Gate Nexus like he's emerged from the other side of a wormhole. He's no different. Not really. No matter how much time passed, no matter what tech advanced, no matter how fast the world moves, nothing moves fast enough to outrun the past.

His breath comes unevenly. His hands shake. The HyperLoop should have prepared him for this moment, but nothing could. Time and space are all Chew can think about as he looks for Deuce to emerge from his pod and into the Nexus. Time moves without hesitation, carving through moments like a blade through water and stone alike. It bends for no one, yields to nothing, yet leaves no soul untouched. It neither waits nor wavers, but in its wake, it reshapes everything.

CHAPTER SEVENTEEN

KILL THE GIRL

From the air, the city seems to be on lockdown, as if anticipating an imminent attack. Swarms of drones buzz and stream through the night sky, not in defense but in construction. The cutting-edge tech promises to elevate San Francisco to even greater heights, captivating Charisma and Mulva as they marvel at the automated harmony.

"We should grab a drink before we go to the hotel," Mulva suggests, her voice barely audible over the mechanical whir. Even her usual caustic outlook softens in the face of the technological spectacle unfolding above. It's past six o'clock, the city transitioning from a vanilla sky to a canvas of seasonal colors and lights. Choosing Jack's Century, a hole-in-the-wall pub, they settle into a back-corner booth beneath a hazy red glow.

"Two double Makers'—up," Mulva orders swiftly as they take their seats. The bar exudes a haunting ambiance, adorned with pictures from the post-WWII era when San Francisco became the Mecca of the counter-culture movement.

"I'm not sure getting spun out on the sauce is a great idea tonight," Charisma hesitates, voicing a concern that was swirling in her mind.

"Enough half measures," Mulva interjects, her tone cutting through. "Samantha Ravensby and others like her will never know justice in this fucking system. So I'm gonna give it to her. That's why you summoned me out of the nuthouse, right? I'm your blunt instrument. Now all you have to do is get out of the way and let me do my thing."

The weight of the decision hangs in the air for Charisma. Unleash, contain, or something in between? The allure of revenge clashes with the looming repercussions. Doubt creeps in, but she can't let Samantha get away with it. It's a wicked fork in the road indeed.

"All our life we were told we'd be the agents of change," Mulva says as the waitress sets down two short glasses full of the Kentucky bourbon. Charisma looks at them as if they contain lethal poison rather than alcohol, trying to recall the last time she drank anything other than red wine. She cannot. "We were told we were 'oh so close,' 'right on the cusp.' All we had to do was lean in and push a little bit further, together, and soon we would have our day. That equality—and then some—would be ours. We both know that was complete and utter bullshit. Cunts like Samantha Ravensby—turncoat traitors—That's who won out. The game was rigged against us since that Jewish fairy tale about Eve eating the forbidden fruit. To me, Samantha Ravensby stands for everything that went wrong when women had a real chance. And I mean to cut the head off that symbol, that is, if you'll allow me."

In a ferocious and maniacal fashion, she sucks down the glass of liquor with three powerful gulps, slams the empty glass on the table and looks up to the ceiling. She exhales sharply, nostrils flaring. Her throat tightens, shoulders going rigid, like a coiled spring wound too tight. A deep, guttural sound escapes as she tilts her head back, her entire body vibrating with barely contained aggression. Charisma is taken aback, but her sensations tingle at the prospect of witnessing Mulva 'do her thing.' She takes a sip from her drink and eases back into her seat.

"You're right, my dear. I've known the entire time that you're right. I used to rail about personal responsibility on my blog and podcast. About all that enlightenment bullshit we were fed as kids. Truth is, unless you're uber wealthy—or vastly fortunate in other ways—this whole American experiment is a sick joke. Samantha Ravensby knew it. She knew it and played the game."

A tremor runs through Charisma's hands as she lifts the glass. She tilts back, willing herself to down it in one go, but the bourbon scorches her throat. She coughs, sputtering half the liquid onto the table. The burn spreads anyway, seeping into her limbs like fire licking dry wood. She wipes her mouth with the back of her hand, breath quickening, jaw tightening. The heat of it—of the drink, and of her fury—rushes through her, pulsing in her chest, her fingertips, her skull. The dim red glow of the bar makes everything feel heavier, the weight of the past pressing in from all sides. Outside, everything seems to move in restless waves, bright reflections of a half dozen colors beam through the window beside them, but inside this booth, inside this moment, Charisma is on the edge of something irreversible.

"As much as they want to celebrate all this new progress, nothing has changed. It's all a veneer meant to keep us in line. What happened all those years ago broke my mother. All my adult life I tried to learn from her missteps and mistakes. I tried so hard to do right by her. I tried to play the part of the strong, forward-thinking, thick-skinned, charismatic . . . All.The.Things-kind-of female leader and entrepreneur. I tried like hell, and I lost." She looks down at what remains in her glass. Maybe half a shot's worth. She shoots it in a single gulp and wipes her mouth. "Now whaddya say we go and gut this bitch together—go out with a bang, ay? Sound good, my dear?" Charisma drops her voice, letting the husky drawl of Kathleen Turner slip through her words. She doesn't do impressions often, but when she does, Mulva's reaction is always the same—eyes lighting up, a grin spreading before she even finishes the line. Charisma knows it's a rare glimpse of something different, something unexpected from her. Maybe that's why Mulva eats it up every time.

"Now you're speaking my language," Mulva says, a full smile twinkling as if she is a young kid on Christmas Day. "Sucks it has to end like this. Maybe in a parallel universe it's the other way around. Like the shoe is on the other foot, or something. Hell, maybe we'll find out once this is all over."

"I really wish that was the case. I don't believe in any god, but I sure do miss Her. Unfortunately, we're born, we live, then we die. All we have is our legacy. And mine—ours—will be one for the ages: decisive vengeance against those who wronged us. Those who lied, cheated, and stole what wasn't theirs. We'll return those misdeeds against them with the power of ten-thousand suns."

"Talk to me, baby! I'm ready to mount the charge right now!"

"Isn't it New Year's Eve tomorrow? Why don't we go out with a bang, for real? Pencil out the details of our plan tonight, party tomorrow, and when the calendar flips over . . . strike. That's the play, my dear. She'll never see it coming on a holiday. Probably will be hungover to boot." Charisma slumps back in her seat and lets out a prolonged and deep sigh. "It's been so long since I really let my hair down. Probably since that weekend you visited me in college when you got that weekend reprieve. What a waste of a life, but I did enjoy it, you know? I just never allowed myself to indulge because of—"

"It's not a waste of a life at all," Mulva says. "Not by a million miles. You're simply killing the girl tonight. Killing the girl and letting the woman be born. And like you said, it's all about legacy. Well baby, they'll be talking and writing about us for years. Now that's a legacy."

They clink glasses and order another round. A weight lifted for both of them, and the early onset of the booze's temporary warmth comfortably blankets them both inside and out.

CHAPTER EIGHTEEN

REALITY BYTES

Amid the bustling crowd of departing and arriving passengers, Deuce and Chew lock eyes the moment they step into the majestic California city. The weather calls for jackets, typical for this place—rarely too cold, rarely too warm. Deuce grabs Chew under his elbow, guiding him away from the crowd, seeking solace from the comings and goings.

"Did that just happen?" Deuce's voice is unsteady, his breath hitching. "Did we . . . move at the speed of sound, and I can still feel it?"

Chew rubs his palms together, flexing his fingers to reassure himself they belong to him. "It was—" He exhales sharply, shaking his head. "Man, I don't even have the words. That wasn't travel. That was—"

"Time folding in on itself," Deuce finishes. "Like we skipped over reality instead of moving through it."

They glance back at the massive HyperLoop hub behind them—an architectural marvel of shimmering glass, solar spires, and interwoven transit lines radiating energy. Pods glide effortlessly into place, swallowing passengers whole before vanishing into unseen tunnels at impossible speeds.

"I'm still catching up," Chew admits, pressing a hand against his chest. "Like my brain needs a second to recalibrate. Like—"

"Like the world we just left was more real than this one," Deuce mutters.

For a moment, they stand there, silent, absorbing the weight of what they've experienced, trying to comprehend it.

"What did you do?" Deuce asks. "There were so many enticing options to choose from."

A loud bellow from a tower at the HyperLoop's main hub signals the departure of another set of pods. San Francisco's new complex—known as the Golden Gate Nexus—outshines even the Spirit of St. Louis: Five hundred acres of sprawling loop systems coupled with a high-speed rail connecting San Francisco to Portland, Vancouver, and Los Angeles down the Pacific coast like a perfectly constructed spine holding together North America on its western edge. Light art displays guide travelers while offering mesmerizing patterns and cinematic visuals at every turn. Gigantic white spires arch up every hundred feet, the skin adorned with thousands of solar panels intertwined with fiber optic glass.

"I went full medieval," Chew says, his voice lower now and more contemplative than usual. "I was in some battle—horses, steel, the whole deal. I could feel the weight of the armor on me, the kickback when I swung my sword. And the sounds . . . man, it wasn't just hearing it. It was like my brain was there, sorting through a violent skirmish, tracking footfalls in the mud. I can still feel it in my bones."

Deuce clenches his jaw. He hadn't thrown a pitch in years, but the second the simulation took hold, he was right back on the mound, under the blistering lights, the dirt packed firm beneath his cleats. His fingers curled instinctively around the ball, feeling the raised seams, the tacky surface warmed by his grip. He took a breath, long and slow, inhaling the scent of infield grass and stadium popcorn. The roar of the crowd swelled in his ears—Not a dull, artificial noise, but a living, breathing beast that rose and fell with every movement.

He checked the catcher's signals. Fastball, inside corner. He nodded. Wound up. Released. The ball exploded out of his hand, a controlled bullet slicing through the air, barreling toward home plate. The batter swung—a fraction too slow. The ball cracked into the catcher's mitt, a perfect strike. The rush hit like an electric current through his bloodstream. He went again. And again. Slider. Curveball. Changeup. Every pitch came easy, like he'd never left. Like he was that kid on the verge of making it—before everything fell apart. The game moved forward in a blur, but he was there, fully present, his body tuned like an instrument, his mind locked in. This was what he was made for. This was his reality.

And then—it was gone. Like a dream yanked from deep sleep, he was suddenly back in the HyperLoop pod, his breath heavy, hands clenched into fists. He could still feel the seams of the ball against his fingertips. His arm ached in that old, familiar way—the good kind of ache, the kind that came after a game-winning shutout. His brain fought to separate memory from illusion.

And it wasn't just nostalgia. It wasn't just a cool simulation. It was real. More real than this. He stepped onto the streets of San Francisco, the crisp air hitting his skin, the city stretching before him like a place he lived in another lifetime. The last time he was here, he was chasing a future that died before it could start. Now, standing in the shadow of the Golden Gate Nexus, he couldn't help but wonder:

What if this trip is another simulation? What if nothing is real?

"We're not in *Super Mario World* anymore," Chew says, though there's no humor in it.

"No kidding." Deuce forces a breath, shifting his weight, gazing all around him at the spectacle of Golden Gate Nexus. "For all our technological leaps, story-wise, we're still running with the same kind of tales and tomes from our parents' and grandparents' generations."

The banter is familiar, but something about it feels hollow. It lacks the usual bite, the playful edge. Deuce senses it in the way Chew's voice tightens, the way his eyes stray toward the skyline instead of meeting his. There's a heavy weight between them, something unspoken but thick in the air. They're both a little scared—fear, doubt, and astonishment at what they experienced sure, but they're back.

Back to San Francisco.

They hadn't been here since *that* weekend. Since the news that shattered everything. Deuce exhales, slow and steady, forcing himself to take in the city. The biting Northern California air, tinged with salt from the bay. The quiet glide of electric cars along the streets leading in and out of the Nexus that were once choked with gas-powered engines. The distant rush of air traffic threading between the city's towering high-rises. For years, this place had been a specter in his mind, a mirage of everything that could've been. Now they were here again. And once more the world was shifting under their feet.

Chew crosses his arms, eyes lingering on the Nexus behind them. "We've been hearing about UBI for months now, ya know?" he says, his voice measured. "It's coming. Early next year."

Deuce nods. The federal government toyed with the idea for decades, but it was no longer an abstract debate. It was imminent.

"I know," he says. "And after what we experienced, it makes way too much sense. The timing of it. Everything."

Chew raises an eyebrow. "I'm tracking with ya, man . . ."

Deuce kicks at a loose pebble, watching it roll across the pavement. "What we went through—*this*—is the real product. The real deal. The next frontier. The HyperLoop's just the delivery system. For now. Once you put this in people's homes, allow them to plug into any fantasy, any setting, and suddenly, there's no reason to wake up. With Universal Basic Income, there will be no reason to work. No reason to leave the house. No reason to exist outside of whatever world they decide to jack into."

Chew exhales, shaking his head. "Hell, I felt it. That wasn't some game with extraordinary effects, Deuce. My mind is still sorting through it like it was something that actually happened."

Deuce looks up to the skyline. The steel and glass rise above them, their surfaces reflecting the city's artificial glow. Everything looks polished to perfection, efficient, a utopia on the surface. But beneath it, he can feel something else—something potentially eroding.

His father had seen it coming: *If a man doesn't have a legitimate reason to awake soberly every day, then a heap of trouble he will make . . .*

Deuce swallows, the memory of his father's voice cutting through the city's movement like a blade. That was the problem, wasn't it? We spent the last two decades fixing the world and landing on a new one. The Marvel on Mars, infrastructure and automation connecting continents, nuclear fusion powering just about everything, benevolent AI assistants for all, and the *Time & Space* program enlightening an entire generation of Americans. Dubbed the Great Correction by many, it was a multitiered endeavor to set the species on the right path following the tumult and turmoil of the Terrible Twenties. A project whose mission it was to end scarcity, remove the need for struggle, and to remind people to look up to the stars and not down at their feet—or more apropos, their phones. But what if struggle was the only thing keeping people upright?

Chew exhales, running a hand over his jaw. "What would your dad think about all this?"

Deuce lets out a dry laugh. "Thinking about that old raconteur again, huh?"

"Hard not to," Chew says, nodding toward the skyline.

Deuce glances back to the Nexus once more, the steady splendor of light threading through its structure. The future is here. And it's virtual. He'd felt it in his bones, the same way he'd felt the weight of that ball in his grip, the same way Chew swung that sword in his simulation. But this wasn't just some new, mind-bending technology. It was sedation.

"It's like he always said," Deuce says. "The road to hell is paved with good intentions."

Chew smirks, shaking his head. "A bit cliché for Philipp Largo, wouldn't you say?"

Deuce stares at his friend and pictures his father's face in his most animated moments. "Yeah. Probably." He exhales, pushing his hands in his jacket pockets. "He often lamented that for all our technological and engineering wonders, we're still just slightly evolved chimpanzees . . . and could easily blast ourselves back to the Bronze Age should the wrong two or three dominoes get knocked over."

Chew smiles wide, joy rising up in his eyes. "Now that's more like him."

Their laughter fades. The city stretches before them, hundreds, maybe thousands of autonomous electric vehicles moving in and out of the station. All Deuce does is issue the command via his retinal Leaf to get picked up. But he can't seem to shake the feeling that they saw the future. And he's not sure if that's a good thing.

CHAPTER NINETEEN

THE STONED APE THEORY

Their hotel is a one-star dive, a locally owned dump with a dark purple exterior nestled in the outer reaches of the Outer Mission. The room emits an annoying and heavy stank, the beds rival concrete slabs, and the temperature dances a dozen degrees every time they fiddle with the gauge. It's a relic from the twentieth century, quite similar to an off-the-highway motel with no voice activation system. They had to secure the room with a credit card, but none of this bothers Mulva. She's asleep within seconds of her head hitting the pillow.

Frustrated, Charisma abandons the pursuit of sleep and stares up at the ceiling, its surface riddled with hairline cracks that stretch like brittle veins across the aging plaster. A stain near the corner—water damage, maybe, or something worse—blooms in an uneven ring, its darkened edges resembling a spreading inkblot. A single flickering bulb in the hallway outside sends irregular rays of light creeping through the gap beneath the door, breaking the room's stagnant dimness. She exhales sharply, rolling onto her side, but the images behind her eyes are no better. The past is waiting for her. Always waiting. In these restless moments, memories of her very first encounter with Samantha Ravensby flood her mind.

It all began in Santa Rosa four years ago, an entire olympiad ago, a span equivalent to high school or college. To Charisma, those four years feel like a lifetime. Samantha, taking a seat in the plain, cookie-cutter coffee shop, greeted Charisma with an unexpected compliment.

"Wow. You're far more attractive than your LinkedIn profile," Samantha remarked. The shop, not a chain like Starbucks, lacked the local Bay area charm of several of its contemporaries, appearing rather ordinary.

Charisma, initially taken aback, replied with a reserved, "Thanks, I guess." Samantha reached out the previous week via the business social networking site. After witnessing Charisma's presentation at an innovation expo in Oakland, she expressed interest in Charisma's concept. Despite the ostensible connection, Samantha's face remained unfamiliar.

Samantha clarified, "I didn't mean for that to come off the wrong way. But you really are striking."

Accepting Samantha's invitation, Charisma entered the café with the mindset of a seasoned entrepreneur. Her software, on that absolute razor's edge of innovation, was not just a tool but a potential revolution in the making. Its capability to seamlessly integrate artificial intelligence with human cognitive processes promised to redefine the tech landscape. Loopd>In was more than a mere product; it embodied a latent seismic shift in technology, capable of influencing markets and altering the very fabric of virtual interaction.

Charisma's ambition, however, transcended the lure of financial success. Her vision for Loopd>In was infused with a deeper purpose: to leverage this groundbreaking technology for societal betterment, to rectify injustices, and to offer a semblance of redemption for the pain and suffering endured by her mother. To Charisma, the concept's expansive potential was not only in its market value, but its capacity to effect genuine, lasting change, offering a tangible pathway to rectify the fractures and ethical foundations of the tech world.

"I appreciate the compliment and right back at you," Charisma responded, looking at Samantha thoroughly and with deep inquiry. Despite appearing a decade or two older, Samantha's supreme attractiveness was distracting. Charisma, recognizing the precious value of time, however, set a boundary: "I have thirty minutes. I'm all ears."

Samantha acknowledged the challenges Charisma faced, drawing from her own past experiences. She spoke of doors shut in her face despite her talent and vision, of rooms where she was the smartest person present but never taken seriously, of men who praised her ideas in meetings only to steal them behind closed doors. She built her first startup from nothing, fought tooth and nail for funding, only to have the project stripped from her hands by executives who saw her as a liability the moment she became a threat.

"I know what it's like," Samantha said, her voice low but cutting. "To be underestimated. To build something extraordinary, revolutionary and watch people with power try to wrest it away before it's ready. I spent years learning how to beat them at their own game. And I'm confident I can show you how."

Charisma hesitated, but the words struck a nerve. She had fought to be taken seriously her entire life. She worked harder, longer, smarter, just to get a fraction of the opportunities handed to others.

As the waiter interrupted, Samantha dismissed him with the wave of a hand, continuing to share her unique proposition.

"Charisma, I've been looking for a software solution like yours for the past few years. Something that can link the user's neural connectivity to desired advertisements as organically as a passing thought. You're so far ahead of the curve, you don't even know."

Charisma, opening up and letting her guard down, explained her perspective. Everything she was building was a stepping-stone, a portal into a different world with the potential to bring about significant change. To achieve this, she needed more capital, limiting her interest to prospective investors or those with connections to investors.

Samantha, unable to offer immediate financial support, presented an alternative that piqued Charisma's interest—a platform to link Charisma's software with a built-in customer base potentially in the *billions*.

Charisma, intrigued by this third category, listened intently as Samantha delved into her knowledge of the HyperLoop—a revolutionary mode of travel set to surpass the impact of autonomous automobile fleets from a decade ago. Samantha posed a thought-provoking question, asking Charisma if she considered monetizing idle passenger time with her software, envisioning the perfect fit for the coming HyperLoop pods.

Charisma reflected on her eureka moment a year earlier and the infinite possibilities it spawned. She felt confident that she was out front in the dawning age of digitization synchronizing with the frontiers of the latest in life sciences. The vision, initially focused on augmented reality and the retinal Leaf, now expanded to a new level with Samantha's revelation. The potential seemed stratospheric, and Charisma couldn't shake her mother's adage: *If something seems too good to be true, then it probably is.*

Unlike so many of the leering VCs and condescending industry veterans she dealt with, Samantha wasn't talking down to her. She spoke with the confidence of someone who already won, but the intensity of someone with something to prove. There was no hard sell, no exaggerated promises—just exuding certainty, as if her success were inevitable and Charisma's, if she made the right moves. And so it was in that coffee shop, Charisma decided to trust Samantha, marking the beginning of a journey that would lead to the synthesis of Loopd>In with various devices into the wonders of CID-A. As Charisma grappled with whether this innovation was really Samantha's or hers, she questioned the true nature of Samantha's motives in introducing her to the Muskian world of the HyperLoop.

Their discussion shifted to the powers that be hindering humanity's progress decades ago, categorizing psychedelics alongside narcotics and thusly stifling research for more than a generation. Charisma shuddered at the lost years of exploration, attributing it to older white men calling all the shots, always being in charge. Psychedelics, once demonized, found redemption in legitimate labs and universities, addressing the mental health crisis, and giving rise to the Stoned Ape Theory. She recalls Samantha's poignant words that day. "Psychedelics will soon serve as the bridge between our primitive past and a more enlightened future."

A team of anthropologists discovering 'shroom-based' components in the remains of apes fueled what was once dismissed as a silly theory—The true missing link between chimpanzee and man, spawning sentience and consciousness six million years ago. The wide acceptance of the theory coincided with the emergence of legitimate psychedelic centers, tackling the mental health crises across the country.

The breakthrough came when a Santa Barbara lab isolated compounds from psychotropic drugs, merging them into advanced communication technologies that could be fused into neural networks. CID-A, the by-product, represented a leap forward for mankind on par with agriculture and electricity. And in doing so became the final technological breakthrough Loopd>In would need in order to put it all together and create a revolutionary final product.

Back in the present, Charisma has a difficult time trying to square Samantha's role in all of this. The puzzle is difficult to put together, her memories fuzzy. She gazes at Mulva, sleeping peacefully—a variable and x factor that Samantha never anticipated. She exhales slowly, a breath she didn't realize she was holding. The tightening in her chest loosens, like a rope slackening after years of slow, suffocating tension. The muscles in her shoulders uncoil, the weight pressing against her ribcage finally lifting. Charisma is reassured. It has always been Mulva. In the quiet of the late night, Charisma resolves to confront her past, to face the decisions she made, and to chart a new course for her future, no matter how uncertain it may seem. With the first light of dawn creeping through the curtains, she finally drifts into a fitful sleep, her mind teeming with the exchanges of that pivotal conversation and the weight of what looms ahead.

CHAPTER TWENTY

BOON FOR THE CAUSE

Chew leans out of the back seat window, fully extended like a frenzied canine, feeling the crisp San Francisco air rush past his face. The city is alive, an intricate weave of light and motion as interactive ads beam across glass-paneled facades, responding to the movements of pedestrians below. Overhead, the Golden Gate Nexus dominates the skyline from their vantage point, its bioluminescent solar panels casting an ominous glow over downtown. To the south, the building known as the Spire rises through the low-hanging fog, its towering frame of reinforced timber and carbon-negative glass reflecting bursts of color from passing hover traffic. Air taxis thread through the vertical corridors of the city, their navigation lights tracing silent pathways between the high-rises.

"Let's get out of here!" Chew squeals. He triggers the halt option via his retinal Leaf, and their driverless Tesla Splendor smoothly pulls over to the curb. Fleets of automated cars cruise by at a steady thirty miles per hour, their exteriors shimmering with dynamic advertisements that hop between languages and visuals depending on who walks by. Storefronts light up with holographic signage, projecting three-dimensional sales pitches into the air. Overhead, kinetic billboards scroll breaking news and stock updates along the sides of skyscrapers, their light reflecting off the damp pavement like scattered constellations. Bicyclists and roller skaters zoom through and dance throughout the traffic, safe in the knowledge that an errant driver checking his phone won't kill or maim them. Even at night, San Francisco moves with a restless energy, its artificial luminescence and lively action in the streets challenging the darkness.

"What's the plan?" Deuce asks, his curiosity piqued by Chew's sudden impulsiveness. "I thought we were heading to our place first."

"Yeah, but we're passing it, so I wanted to stop and check it out since we're right here," Chew explains.

"Check what out?"

"Loopd>In. Their headquarters is in that badass scraper called the Jovian right there!"

They gaze up at the forty-something story wood-framed structure, adorned with sparkling solar glass blocks like resplendent crown jewels on a giant king's garb. Recent advances in synthetic timber have made wood the primary construction material for modern skyscrapers, and this is the tallest of its kind they've ever seen.

"It says they're on the top floor," Deuce notes. "No way we're getting all the way up there, especially at this hour."

"C'mon! Where's your exploratory spirit, my man? Let's give it a run and see what we can shake loose."

Chew bolts through the front door, not waiting for Deuce. Two security robots, with circular flashlights for eyes, roll into action, giving them an odd, personified character. Chew explains they're here to see his cousin who works on the top floor. Deuce, reluctantly following, whispers, "What in the hell are you doing?"

"Just stay calm and let me handle this. I'm as good with the robots as I am with the ladies."

Deuce gives him a look, suggesting Chew has lost his mind. Chew, feigning the search for identification, informs the robots he left everything at home, including a functioning retinal device. The larger robot informs him that no one on the top floor is in the office. Chew quickly scans through his Leaf as he turns his back on the ersatz security team, confirming that a woman named Samantha Ravensby is the CEO. He decides not to claim her as his cousin and, with a jab from Deuce, signals they're leaving.

"Relax, one sec," he whispers to Deuce. "I got what I need."

They make haste departing the building's lobby and go back out into the night. In the core of the city, San Francisco is as illuminated in the evening as it is by the sun in the middle of the day. The city, with its fusion of history and modernity, reflects their own journey—an intricate combination of nostalgia and a keen eye toward the future.

"What in the hell was that all about?" Deuce asks. "You want to get us arrested before our trip even starts? Messing around with security robots—only you, Chew. Only you."

"I had to go in there, man. Loopd>In's Cloud didn't have any pictures of staff, not even their board or executive team."

"So?"

"So, I figured there might be one in the lobby. And I was right. Look at this beauty!"

He shows Deuce the picture of Samantha Ravensby he just snapped. Deuce doesn't seem impressed.

"That's Samantha Ravensby. The Loopd>In CEO. Quite the fox, isn't she?"

"I can't believe I'm even surprised," says Deuce, throwing his arms up. "We bounced in there and risked this entire trip to see if you could confirm if their CEO is a babe or not?"

"Yeah, well, most big tech companies have pictures of their chief hanging somewhere prominently in a public space. My hunch paid off. So not only is she in charge of a company ready to take off with groundbreaking tech, but she's a ten to boot!"

Deuce rolls his eyes. "Now what?" But suddenly, something seizes him at his core, telling him he has seen this woman before. He just can't place the context.

"Now? Nothing to do but find her and make our move. I'm meeting that woman while we're here, I can tell you that, my friend. What her company developed is going to change the world. I'm not sure it's going to change it for the better, but there'll be no going back once it's unleashed on the masses. It'll be bigger and more life altering than smartphones, Leafs, social media, AI . . . you name it."

"How do you propose we find her?" Deuce asks, turning back to Chew.

Chew doesn't answer right away. He swipes back to Samantha's image on his screen, staring at it for a beat longer than necessary. "I don't know. But I'll figure it out."

Deuce studies him for a second. "You're really this determined over some CEO you just learned existed?"

Chew exhales sharply, still looking at the screen, then finally pockets his device. "I looked her up because of what happened on the HyperLoop. I mean, what the hell was that, Deuce? We just lived inside a different reality roaring across the country at 700 mph, and it all felt as real as standing right here. Someone designed that. Someone perfected it. And that someone looks to be her."

Deuce nods, but his skepticism lingers. "And you just happen to think it's a bonus that she's gorgeous?"

Chew grins, flashing that easy charisma. "I mean, I'm not blind. But this isn't just about that." He shakes his head, the excitement in his voice now mingled with something else. "I need to meet her because—who the hell even *is* this woman? Where did she come from? A company on the verge of launching something that could put 99.99 percent of humanity on the sidelines, and she's an unknown? That doesn't sit right with me."

Deuce's gaze drifts from his wildly spirited best friend to the slowly passing cityscape, his window view and then back.

Chew is onto something. His instincts scream at him to dig deeper.

"Alright, fine," Deuce concedes. "But what happens when we do find her?"

Chew flashes a wolfish grin. "Now that's the fun part, my man. We see if she wants to play. We see if she'll divulge her end game anyway. Chances are I'll get on her good side."

"That I believe, Chew. Your record is unmatched in that arena, to be sure. Especially when you're incentivized like this."

"I know there's other stuff we want to do, too. But a little treasure hunt spliced into this trip will make it all-time. One for the books, like we used to say." Chew takes Deuce by the arm and looks him directly in the eye. "But this really is all about you. About us . . . and the past. I feel like a fun distraction interspersed with that is a boon for the cause. Now let's make our move."

"I still don't know what the move is!" yells Deuce.

"Neither do I," says Chew, laughing as he orders up another driverless chauffeur. The car pulls up in seconds, and they get in. "Just drive," Chew exclaims with delight. "TBD for now until I direct otherwise. Drive, baby, drive."

Under the swath of San Francisco's night sky, Deuce and Chew pause at an intersection, the city continuing to thrum all around them. It's been five years since they walked these streets—their most cherished cityscape, introduced by Philipp Largo during their adventurous youth. Now, surrounded by a torrent of lights and the splendor of advanced tech, the city feels both familiar and utterly transformed.

Chew's excitement is palpable; his energy charges the air between them. He views the quest to spot Samantha Ravensby as the spark that might rekindle the spirit of discovery in both of them. To Chew, San Francisco's blend of historical charm and cutting-edge buzz provides the perfect setting for their new journey—one marked by potential healing and the rush of new experiences.

Chew peeks over at Deuce from the corner of his eye as the city unfolds all around them, its electric shimmer reflected in the windshield, the streets filled with holiday revelers and night life enthusiasts. But Deuce is quiet, somewhat unsettling Chew as he knows this version of his best friend: heavy with introspection, tightly wound. He's worried the past is once again trying to surface like a ghost refusing to stay buried. San Francisco was their go-to travel playground, a city gifted to them in their youth by Deuce's father. But it was also the backdrop to everything that broke. Chew doesn't know the full story, not really. How could he? Deuce kept it buried deep down for so long. But he knows enough to understand that coming back here isn't just some trip down memory lane. Going into this journey there would be pain points, bumps in the road. It had to happen though. He knows that much. And he feels a reckoning brewing.

CHAPTER TWENTY-ONE

MOUNTAINS & BEACHES

They walk the city streets for an hour, Mulva doing most of the talking, her voice a constant melody of plans and schemes. The night air of San Francisco is brisk, the kind that brushes against your cheeks with a cool reminder of the ocean's proximity. Only a few hours left in the decade. Soon the second half of the twenty-first century will commence. Anticipation is palpable in the air, but for Charisma, it's so much more than just the turn of a year. A clock ticks in her head as loudly as a siren calling for a coming storm. She knows it's still not too late to do anything, make any move, charge in any direction. The weight of this pending decision presses down on her with each step..

"By the time that bitch takes her final breath, you'll be safely laid out on a beach. Warm, half-naked, victorious with a belly full of wine. Use your imagination for any other spoils of war," Mulva says, the tone of her voice underscoring both the assurance and the daring.

Charisma smiles weakly, trying to match her pace with Mulva's darting strides. The city around them is alive with kinetic energy, cyclists and joggers weaving through the night, scooters buzzing past, and the occasional laughter and chatter of groups enjoying the seasonal spirit. The holidays fill the air and the sites, lighting and décor along the fencing carve out their path. Trees wrapped in festivity. The joyous atmosphere, however, feels distant to Charisma, like a dream she's observing but not a part of.

"You don't like my plan, do you?" Mulva asks, her intuition picking up on Charisma's silence.

Charisma gently takes her by the arm, slowing her to an eventual standstill. "Your plan is fine, Mulva. It's me. I'm a mess."

"You're not. The rubber is about to hit the road and you're getting some butterflies. No worries, I get it." She sighs deeply, looking into her friend's eyes like she needs to be convinced. "All you have to do is let me handle this. Trust me."

"So, not only am I asking someone to fight my battles for me—which I can't stand—I'm also going to lose you all over again. This time forever," Charisma confesses, her voice breaking slightly.

Mulva's response carries with it bravado and resignation. "I didn't come here for a long time, but a good time," she says, but Charisma isn't amused. "It's simple then," Mulva goes on. "You come with. You can stand over her right as her light goes out rather than me play a recording."

"Yes, but in neither option do you escape," Charisma says, her voice scratchy and conflicted.

"So it goes."

They resume their walk, now heading toward the city's latest attraction, the recently completed Phantasm Fountains City Park. The park's entrance is an explosion of colors, LED lights dancing in intricate patterns, casting otherworldly shadows on the ground.

It's a mesmerizing sight, a symbol of the city's rebirth and resilience, yet it does little to lift Charisma's spirits.

Mulva lights a smoke, the tip flaring orange against the electric blues and purples cast by the park's LED-lit murals. She stalks between the archway entrance like a panther guarding her lair, her boots scuffing the pavement in restless loops. Charisma watches her pace, the glow of moving colors speckled over Mulva's face, deepening the tension in her sharp features.

"You know, we besmirch the patriarchy all the time—and for good reason," Mulva mutters, exhaling a stream of smoke that vanishes into the cold air. "But things *are* different nowadays."

She keeps moving, hands buried in the pocket of her hoodie, head down like she's talking more to herself than to Charisma. Around them, the city's newest attraction is alive with energy—patterns of light dance along the walkways, street performers strum digital guitars and sitars, and distant laughter drifts from a group of teenagers huddled near a neon-lit fountain.

"Most of that bullshit from our parents' time was put to rest, thank god," Mulva continues, still pacing. "Cancel culture, uber-sensitivity. What did they call it? Wokeness? All that fades when you're an unplugged spacewoman, baby." She looks up to the night sky and a look of ease and peace stretch across her face. She looks back at Charisma, her expression changing into an unreadable stare in the swirl of colored light. "But this Samantha chick? It's been top of mind since you told me the story."

Charisma watches as Mulva flicks her cigarette onto the ground and crushes it beneath her boot, her frustration manifesting in the sharp motion. "How's that?" Charisma asks.

"It seems like something new, and possibly even more sinister, is rising these days."

A gust of wind rushes through the park, sending stray pieces of confetti from a nearby celebration scattering across the pavement.

Charisma's gaze follows the fluttering scraps of color as Mulva's words settle like a stone in her chest.

"Yes, for sure," Charisma finally says. "The uber-elite seem to get away with anything and everything they desire. It was a concerning trend until a real-world example knocked me out of the ring and upended my life completely."

Mulva stops walking. Just stops. She presses her tongue against the inside of her cheek, eyes locked on the pulsing multicolored artwork projected onto a concrete wall. "So, it's not just an elitist, bourgeois class, but a protected class as well? Like they all have some kind of impenetrable shield covering them from harm or repercussion?"

Charisma exhales, crossing her arms as if bracing herself against something unseen. "Well, it's always been that way with the top of the upper caste, hasn't it, Mulva?"

"Don't make me guess, darling," Mulva says, finally ceasing to pace and taking a seat on a park bench nestled along the trail. She lights another smoke. Charisma realizes she hasn't seen anyone else smoke tobacco since they've been in the city. Mulva was always in a class by herself.

"AGI. Quantum computing. CRISPR. New breakthroughs in life sciences every week. The super rich and well-connected aren't striving to just become trillionaires anymore. Nor are they looking to extend their lives by decades. They want—"

"Immortality," Mulva says cutting her friend off and eyeing down a family of four slowly walking out of the park and briefly interrupting their flow.

"Not just immortality, Mulva. They're aiming for something far more profound. They want to transcend the limitations of *Homo sapiens*. They aspire to achieve what futurists term *Homo Deus*—a new form of human, enhanced way beyond our natural capacities."

Mulva's eyes narrow as she processes this information. "And your pal Samantha is the kind of chick who would be shooting for something like that."

"Exactly," Charisma confirms, taking her friend's hand as they resume walking. "These visionaries aren't just looking to live longer. They seek to elevate their existence to what might be considered godlike. Through the integration of advanced genetic engineering, AI, and cybernetics, they envision a future where such humans possess divine control over their biology, intelligence, and lifespans." Mulva doesn't respond, but shakes her head in disgust. Charisma, more upbeat than she was since they arrived in the city continues: "Let's keep walking and check this park out. Nothing is decided. We have ample time to make the right move. Our chessboard still has plenty of options."

Mulva grinds her teeth but falls in step beside Charisma, the tension in her jaw betraying her frustration. Charisma can feel it—the unspoken fight still burning in her friend, the relentless urge to push forward no matter the cost. If Mulva had her way, she'd move mountains for Charisma. She'd tear them down, rebuild them, reshape the entire landscape if only Charisma would let her.

But Charisma isn't ready—not yet. She knows the decision she makes tonight will define her, for better or worse. The park, with its lights and laughter, feels like a crossroads, a place between the past and an uncertain future. They walk on, two figures against the backdrop of a city that's seen more than its share of darkness and light.

CHAPTER TWENTY-TWO

LET IT HAPPEN

In San Francisco's incomparable heart, under a canopy of stars and city lights, Charisma finds herself lost in thought, her mind a maelstrom of conflicting emotions. The bustling streets, alive with the spirit of the impending New Year, are pure incongruity to her inner turmoil. She can't escape it, the pit in her stomach growing wider and more acidic by the moment. Eyes closed, she immerses herself in the digital sanctuary of her retinal Leaf, summoning a cherished passage penned by her favorite public thinker. In the midst of the frenzy going through her mind, she seeks refuge in these words, drawing from the wisdom that guided her through moments of despair:

"If one has even a rudimentary grasp of time and space, as well as the immutable laws of physics and nature, how could you NOT be an eternal optimist? After all, there is SOMETHING rather than NOTHING, even though the odds would say otherwise given everything we know."

This reflection isn't just a comfort. It's been a cornerstone of her worldview for several years. Charisma's adoration for Sam Harris is akin to someone worshipping the pivotal figures of pop culture—Harris was her Beatles, her Michael Jordan. His thoughts on living an examined life, straddling the divide between rationality and spirituality without succumbing to religious dogma, profoundly shaped her from the time she was fifteen. She never got to meet him in person, but once, as an eager teenager at a packed lecture, she had the nerve to stand up and ask him a question. His answer not only acknowledged her curiosity but encouraged it, making that moment as exhilarating as watching Jordan nail a jumper to clinch a championship game.

For Charisma, it was the icing on the cake after being the first class to go through the *Time & Space* program. That, more than anything, expanded her understanding of the universe and reinforced her drive toward optimistic rationalism. The principles she learned throughout the multiyear program resonated deeply with Harris's teaching, uniting scientific curiosity with a genuinely hopeful outlook on humanity's potential.

Now, as the year end's euphoria swirls around her, these memories converge with the twisted realities of her current predicament. She questions the cost of revenge against Samantha Ravensby. Is it worth sacrificing her freedom? Or Mulva's? The city's energy, pulsating with life and possibility, reminds her of the boundless potential of humanity, yet here she stands, still contemplating a path that could end in darkness.

Samantha Ravensby, through deception and lies, reduced Charisma to ashes. A victim of circumstance, Charisma ponders the morality of the revenge plot. Her mother faced challenges, too, but she never resorted to violent schemes. The overwhelming desire for retribution tugs at Charisma, questioning the price of her freedom against the pursuit of justice.

The city roars with life—cheering strangers, the distant drum of music, hypnotic lights streaking across glass facades—yet Charisma feels utterly alone in her own storm. She paces in short, agitated strides, arms crossed so tightly against her chest it feels like she's holding herself together by sheer force. Her mind loops through the possibilities, each one clawing at her with a different kind of pain. If she lets Mulva do this, will she feel relief? Satisfaction? Or just another kind of loss? Samantha deserves to be ruined, but does she deserve this? *What other justice exists?* The legal system would bring failure and financial ruin. The media would laugh at her. There would be no consequences, no reckoning.

Charisma presses her fingers to her temples. If she simply walks away, is she a coward? If she follows through, does she become the very thing she's fought against her whole life? The question burns through her: Does revenge heal, or does it hollow?

A sudden gust of wind brings change in the air, carrying with it the faint strains of a familiar tune. As it weaves its way into Charisma's consciousness, she recognizes it immediately. "Time to Pretend" by *MGMT*, wafts through the air, transporting her to a time when life brimmed with hope. The music resurrects memories of her mother's presence, her childhood home's surround sound system filling their mornings with majestic melodies. Music was air in her home growing up. It was life. Charisma's affinity for such music persists into her adulthood, grounding her in a world that often seems devoid of solace.

As the song's enchanting melody envelops her, Charisma clutches Mulva's hand, and they sprint toward the source along with hundreds, maybe thousands of others. It's as though a live concert with one of her favorite bands started a few blocks away with no previous promotion or advertisement. However, swiftly as the music arrived, it dissipates into silence, leaving them bewildered. The ephemeral euphoria of the moment vanishes, leaving Charisma breathless, her options seemingly exhausted.

"I can see the strain on your face, Charisma," Mulva says as they stop in front of a retail shop. "I can sense it in every breath you take. The weight of this decision is crushing you . . ."

And in the next instant, another sound emerges, a familiar opening chord that resounds deep within Charisma's soul. Tame Impala's "Let it Happen" unfolds, igniting a torrent of emotions.

"Can you hear it?" Charisma's voice cuts through the night, confident and clear as she tries to shed the baggage of torment and indecision. "It's like the universe is reminding us—reminding me—of who I am, of the optimism and curiosity that brought me here and made me who I am. Look at all these people!"

The city continuously pulsates with lights and drones, arrays of colors and inexplicable laser and artificial tech paint the night sky. As the masses, which must number in the thousands, converge on this ethereal concert from out of nowhere, Charisma and Mulva join the pilgrimage, racing toward the sonic sanctuary.

The song becomes a guiding force, leading them through the city that twists and unfolds like a puzzle with no clear exit. Streets spill into alleys, alleys into underpasses, each turn revealing something new—a wave of bodies pressing forward, street vendors shouting over the music, which grows louder by the second, flashing holo-billboards casting shifting illusions onto sidewalks.

Charisma and Mulva push through the chaos, darting past revelers who seem caught in their own maze of distractions—some laughing, some dancing, some frozen in place, mesmerized by the dizzying lights above. Every path forward feels uncertain, the roads stretching and winding, bending reality like the music itself. And then, through the gaps in the crowd, Charisma catches sight of Mission Dolores Park, its sloping expanse dotted with figures standing atop the hills, silhouetted against the city's glow. The crowd moves as if magnetized, funneling toward the park, where the music roars from an unseen source beyond the tree line. For a split second, Charisma recalls lazy afternoons from her youth, sprawling across the park's sun-drenched grass, the scent of weed and laughter mixing in the air. No time for nostalgia now.

The crowd surges. The music grows louder. Charisma grips Mulva's wrist and follows the throng toward the park's entrance, a shared electric anticipation coursing through all. Tears flow freely down Charisma's face as the power of the song washes over her, an elixir that finds a way to remedy the wreckage of her reality, transporting her to a time before her mother's fall, and way before Samantha Ravensby's intrusion. The impact of majestic music, her healer and time-traveling companion, reverberates through her. The streets teem with people, all drawn to the celestial sounds of Tame Impala, creating a shared moment of awe and wonder.

Amid this emotional climax, Charisma faces her internal conflict head-on. The desire for revenge against Samantha Ravensby battles with her innate optimism and belief in a better future. The music, serving as a lifeline, reminds her of her mother's love and guidance, of her own aspirations, and the path she once sought so strongly to forge. *Be water,* she reminds herself.

Mulva, usually quick with a retort, remains silent, the tune's thrall lacing through her mind, body, and spirit. Finally, she nods, a tacit acknowledgement of the transcendence happening all around them. The city, with all its beauty and despair, momentarily dissolves into the sounds of psychedelic and harmonious sounds. And as Charisma and Mulva turn the final corner, they, like the captivated masses, gaze upward, astonished and blown away by what is unfolding in front of them.

CHAPTER TWENTY-THREE

SEND A RAVEN

The Mission District surges with nightlife revelers as Deuce and Chew roll through in the back of their Tesla Splendor, the windows down, the city reaching in with open arms. The air carries the briny tang of the bay, mingling with the rich spices of street food sizzling on open grills—charred steak, fried onions, something sweet and smoky laced with chili oil. A block away, a bass-heavy groove drifts through the night, weaving between bursts of laughter, the clangs of metal on metal, and the hiss of a crowd moving together as one.

Deuce lets it all wash over him. *San Francisco.* The city had been a playground of wonder when he was young, a place where anything felt possible. Now, it feels different—familiar, but altered. A reflection warped by time.

As their ride slows for a turn, something new creeps into the city's layered noise—a rhythm, faint but persistent, threading through the night. It's almost lost beneath the myriad other sounds, but something about it sticks in Deuce's ear. A slow build. Echoing vocals. A warbled, drifting synth.

Then, Chew jerks upright, eyes darting toward the source. He insists that their AI chauffer hit the breaks. "Stop the ride!" Chew's voice cuts through the air, and his head swivels as if he spotted a supermodel in a skimpy swimsuit. "Did you hear that?!" His excitement is infectious, and despite Deuce's initial reluctance, he can't help but be drawn into the moment. They disembark and are immediately engulfed in the celebratory fever of the city.

The source of Chew's excitement quickly becomes clear. "It's Tame Impala! I can't believe it!" Chew exclaims as they hit the street on foot. "Are you kidding me?! Playing down here tonight? How could this not have been announced? Only in San Francisco!"

"No way," Deuce says, trying to keep up. "It can't be them. We would've heard . . ."

The music grows clearer as they turn the corner, spilling out from an open plaza ahead. A mesmerizing glow washes over the crowd, the towering face of a high-rise glimmering with rolling images. Then, suddenly, the music cuts. A new light floods the street—sharp and commanding. Deuce looks up just in time to see Elon Musk's face taking shape across the skyscraper's surface. His expression is unreadable, his presence unmistakable. The noise around them fades as all eyes lock onto the projection. Here's the man who brought them to San Francisco via the HyperLoop, led the way on electric and autonomous transportation, and took humanity to Mars.

Deuce's memories of the Marvel on Mars were vivid, wrapped in the warmth and wild celebration that engulfed their home that day. It was more than just a gathering. It was an event that had the whole neighborhood buzzing with excitement, spilling into every corner of the house. The living room, where Deuce sat cross-legged on the plush carpet next to his buddy, Chew, was alive with a kind of energy and enthusiasm that could light up the entire block.

Philipp, always the gracious host, moved through the crowd with a tray of drinks, his face lit up with a broad, satisfied grin. Every few minutes, he would pause to clap a friend on the back or offer a new guest a warm welcome, but his eyes frequently darted back to Deuce and Chew, making sure they were soaking in every moment of the historic event. The room erupted every so often into cheers and applause when communication transmissions came through. Hope and triumph filled the room as images of astronauts from twelve nations took that monumental step on Martian soil broadcasted across the screen.

Grown-ups toasted with raised glasses, their conversations steeped in awe and wonder, punctuated by laughter and occasional tears of joy. A scene of utter jubilation, where every handshake seemed firmer and every hug held longer, as if everyone tried not to let go of the moment's gravity.

Amid this bustling celebration, Deuce remembered looking over at Chew, who sat next to him with eyes as wide as the ocean. They exchanged looks of pure astonishment, sharing a silent, profound connection over the significance of what they witnessed. This wasn't just a scientific achievement. It was a moment of unity, the epitome of human potential that Philipp had always preached about. Now, years later, as Deuce is once again back in San Francisco under Musk's expanding legacy, he can't help but wonder about Musk's presence and intentions on this night, right before the dawn of a new decade.

Only Musk's face looms on the façade, solitary and commanding. Moments of silence pass. An unmistakable strum of a familiar and haunting guitar chord sequence envelops Deuce's ears and soul. A new tune fills the air while Musk's image vanishes. The song is from a band even older than the legendary group from Perth. Donovan's "Atlantis" plays as images of Martin Luther King

Jr., the Kennedys, John Lennon, Gandhi, and Tristan Harris, highlight the skyscraper. It's like a hallucinatory fever dream. *This can't be real. Any of it.* Deuce's face is covered with tears as the crescendo of the song explodes from the hidden speakers.

The images are unrelenting. From famous faces gunned down by insanity and violence, it moves to children fleeing schoolyards. Deuce remembers it all growing up and so too the fear that comes during alerts and drills when in those formative years. That fear manifested itself as a part of him in some way, like a new bulge along the breast eventually forming into a killer cancer. It's coming, and there's nothing to stop it. Or worse, it takes the one thing in life he loved more than anything. Ever. *The man who made me. My world, my hero, my everything.*

Deuce rarely confided in anyone—not even Chew—about his fear of being gunned down. It was something that first arose in him at a young age and then it never went away. Rather, it was exacerbated by the constant active shooter drills he partook in during his school years. But all throughout his life up until this moment, he had never seen a bullet in action. No, the prophecy would come to fruition with his father, Philipp Largo.

Finally, Donovan's classic "Atlantis" comes to an end, and Elon Musk's voice fills the night.

"Good evening. Elon Musk here," he begins, his voice booming throughout the Mission. "I would like to take a few moments of your time tonight before we flip the calendar to a new year, a new decade. Technology and innovation have brought us so far as a species and a civilization. In such a short amount of time, we conquered problems that our forebearers deemed unsolvable. The negative impacts of a carbon-fueled economy mostly reversed as nuclear fusion powers most of our planet. Look no further than the Amazon tripling since the turn of the century, carbon dioxide emissions returning to preindustrial levels, hundreds of formerly endangered species now thriving." He pauses and looks to all corners of the crowd, his eyes squinted, his lips pursed. All eyes are on him, no one seems to be making a sound. He takes a deep breath and continues, "On the home front, costs of living plummeted to levels not seen in a century. We're able to spend more time with loved ones, at study, on travel, and at leisure, thanks to the global alliance containing and harnessing the powers of AGI. We went to fucking Mars and back."

Entranced by Musk's words, the crowd continues to listen attentively, as he speaks of humanity's triumphs and the challenges overcome. But then, his tone shifts, addressing a lingering, unresolved issue as personal to Deuce and Chew as any.

"But one problem that this country has never tackled is the riddle of the gun. It continues to be an enormous concern for parents, for lawmakers, and for us all. We lost countless thousands to unnecessary gun violence in my lifetime. And we know a solution is not easy, for if it were, we would have aced it by now. We all know that. Our constitutionally defined freedoms are irrevocable, and this particular debate has raged for decades. So today, I want to showcase a breakthrough. For the past several years, a team of experts from my organization were working behind the scenes with the world's leading gun manufacturers. I would like to shine a light on our progress to a live audience here in one of my favorite cities on Earth. Alexander, if you please!"

Musk's announcement sets off a chain of events that both confounds and captivates the crowd. His image disappears into the blank façade of the towering structure. A solitary man in jeans and a black leather jacket comes storming out of the building's front entrance. He is carrying a gun. With a quick glance, Deuce discerns that it is a high-powered rifle. The crowd erupts in panic. The drones that were illuminating the night's impromptu show lock in on the gunman. People by the dozens are screaming and blowing past both Deuce and Chew. All in total terror. Their darkest fears coming to life right in front of them. But neither Deuce nor Chew are rattled in the least. They both know Musk is up to something and that they are quite possibly witnessing history, but why the others do not grasp this maybe they will never know. After a few long seconds of sheer horror stemming from the crowd, Musk's image reappears on the building.

The collective scream of the mob is deafening. Bodies collide, push, scatter. Shoes skid against pavement. A drink crashes to the ground, its glass splintering onto the pavement beneath the stampede of fleeing feet. Someone shoves Deuce from behind, nearly knocking him off balance, but he twists through the chaos, keeping his footing. The drones above shift positions in an instant, their red tracking lights locking onto the man with the rifle.

And then—just as suddenly as it began—something changes. A hesitation ripples through the multitudes, people tripping over their own frantic momentum. Their panic stalls, replaced by confusion. Deuce watches it all unfold in real-time—one terrified scream cutting off mid-breath, another morphing into a shaky exhale. Some people stop running entirely, their wide eyes darting from the armed man to the sky above.

Then he sees it. Musk is back on the screen. A single image, motionless, eerily calm. His expression doesn't match the madness below—It's composed, expectant, as if all this is going exactly as planned. The crowd doesn't know whether to keep running or stand still. A school of fish weaving through the current.

Deuce and Chew are right in the middle of it, getting pushed in every direction. Deuce locks eyes with an attractive, dark-haired woman who appears to be his age as she gets walloped from behind a few paces, but dozens of bodies, away. She is about to hit the ground, violently, and at risk of being trampled by the mob. Deuce bobs and spins through the action like an all-American running back and pulls her from the fray just in time. Before he can say anything, she is yanked away by some cyberpunk-looking chick with big, fearsome eyes. Deuce loses them in the insanity for a moment, but not for long.

They took refuge on a park bench that abuts a building hanging outside the commotion by mere feet. The cyberpunk squeezes her cute friend like she saved her life. The cute one leans back, eyes closed. Her friend finds Deuce in the crowd and lips a thank you. Deuce nods. There is a continual hiss in the air. Police sirens are wailing in the distance, finally closing in on the scene.

As Elon Musk pops back up on the screen, he attempts to address and calm the crowd. Deuce didn't notice it before, but now that he's somewhat closer and not distracted by a million maddening thoughts, he surmises something else amiss. Elon Musk looks younger than he did when he was forty. He can't process anything Musk is saying, something about how this new tech supposedly works. His head spins wildly trying to comprehend the look of the guy coming from the projection. The hysteria temporarily halts while the throngs of people look back up at his image and listen to his message with intent and awe. Deuce shakes it off, grabs Chew by the elbow and leads them over to the bench. He wants to be sure the gal he met eyes with a moment ago is unharmed by the hysteria.

CHAPTER TWENTY-FOUR

CONFLUENCE

A fully automated first-floor diner serves as their shelter from the storm. Four strangers—no longer just strangers—sit across from each other beneath the harsh wash of industrial lighting, the air between them dense with adrenaline and unanswered questions. The air crackles with static from abandoned speakers, fragments of Musk's voice distorting through unseen audio feeds. A low hum from surveillance drones hovers beyond the edge of perception, their presence a ghostly echo of the chaos that erupted minutes earlier. The electric charge of the crowd's hysteria remains, as if the very air hasn't caught up to reality. The afterimage is burned into Deuce's senses. Across from him, the dark-haired girl grips the table's edge, her knuckles balanced against the vinyl. She's trying to steady herself. A slight tremor runs through her fingers. Her friend, the one with the cropped, jet-black hoodie and sharp, restless eyes, squirms in her seat like a caged animal, her leg bouncing beneath the table. She looks like she's ready to bolt at any second. The only thing keeping them here is the coffee Deuce insisted on. He needed something to compose himself—something hot, something normal. Chew mentioned how she reminded him of Noodle from Gorillaz, just before they all took their seat.

"It was all an orchestrated stunt," Chew says, his voice carrying the same easy confidence that had gotten him into—and out of—trouble since they were kids. He leans forward in the booth, his hemp jacket crinkling slightly, dark jeans casually slung over his athletic frame. The women across from them are a contrast in energy—one coiled and restless, her arms crossed like she's already decided she'd rather be anywhere else; the other still catching her breath, hands curled around the edge of the table like she needs the solid wood to steady herself.

Deuce exhales, dragging his fingers over the polished chrome surface. The place feels like a paradox—retro as hell, yet completely automated. No cooks, no waitstaff, just gleaming machines that glide between booths, refilling coffee cups and wiping down tables with mechanical precision. By the entrance, two squat cleaning bots whir softly as they polish the glass doors, their circular sensors blazing bright red light. Through the windows, the streets still glow with the aftermath of Musk's spectacle, but the chaos has begun to settle.

"Musk wanted to make a big splash with some new AI he's recently developed," Chew says, reading info from his Leaf. "Supposedly it can disable firearms that are identified in public from a remote source in less than a second."

Deuce barely hears the words as his mind churns through the events outside. The madness, the sudden hush, Musk's eerie, youthful face plastered on the building like some kind of digital deity. And then the gunman. The panic. The swarm of bodies fleeing. But was it all a ruse?

He forces himself back to the present, his gaze and concentration moving to the dark-haired young woman sitting across from him. She's striking in a way that sneaks up on you, the kind of beauty that lingers long after you look away. Dark, wavy hair falls effortlessly over one shoulder, framing high cheekbones, full lips, and deep, knowing eyes—eyes that remind him of sun-warmed amber, catching the dim light in ways that make them impossible to ignore. There's a timelessness to her—something unpolished yet elegant, like a half-forgotten painting suddenly rediscovered. She's listening carefully, her lips pressed together in thought, fingers still wrapped around the edge of the table. She's still undoubtedly rattled from what happened outside, but beneath that, something else emanates—not fear, but composure and strength. A sharp mind working through the variables.

The other woman, the one with the punk energy and a presence like a coiled wire, isn't looking at him at all. She's eyeballing Chew, top to bottom. Deuce catches the beam of her gaze, the way her sharp eyes trace his posture, his expressions, like she's waiting to decide if he's worth listening to. Chew, in return, exudes an effortless cool, leaning back in the booth like he's exactly where he's supposed to be. But Deuce knows better. Knows him all too well. There is a hint of something off about him now. It's in the way he keeps glancing toward the window, toward the city still pulsating outside, like he's expecting something—like he's waiting for the night to twist in another impossible direction. Something about this whole evening has them all unsettled. Deuce turns away from the booth, pressing his hands flat against the table, grounding himself to the cool surface. He can't afford to get lost in it. Not yet.

"Says here there will be a full report tomorrow," Chew continues, reading rapidly as he scrolls through his Leaf's display. "City of San Francisco might press charges for inciting a riot. Musk claims he'll take the hit if it means making the new year and beyond mass-shooting free."

Deuce exhales slowly, his grip tightening around the ceramic mug in his hands. If only this had been around five years ago. The thought lands like a punch to the ribs. If Musk figured this tech out earlier, maybe Philipp Largo would still be here. Maybe his father's blood wouldn't have been mopped off some Midwestern sidewalk.

He forces himself to swallow the thought down before it can spiral. The last thing he needs is to unravel in front of strangers. But even as his mind tries to push forward, one detail from the night keeps clawing its way back: Musk looked young. Way too young. It wasn't a trick of the light or a distortion in the projection. Deuce knows what he saw—Musk looked like he was in his late thirties, early forties at most. Not the man pushing eighty who he is. The realization burrows deep, a quiet alarm ringing at the base of his skull. What the hell is going on?

Across from him, the woman looks directly into his eyes, leaning forward. "You saved me," she says, her voice steady, though there's an undercurrent of something unreadable beneath the words.

Deuce lifts his gaze to meet hers. She's stunning in a way that catches him off guard—olive skin, long dark-auburn waves, eyes the color of honey warmed by sunlight. Mediterranean, he thinks. She's his age, maybe a year younger, but there's something in the way she carries herself—like someone who's had to fight for everything.

"Seems like Musk is back to being a maniac again without Sam Harris to help guide him . . . I could've been stomped to death. Thank you, thank you, thank you." A small, wry smile tugs at the corner of her lips, but it doesn't quite erase the tension in her posture. "My name is Charisma. Charisma Sinclair."

Her name hangs in the air. It tugs at something, a faint thread of familiarity that Deuce can't quite place. But before he can chase the thought down, she keeps going.

"I can't believe this was my first real encounter with *the* Elon Musk when I was . . ." Her voice drifts off, her expression hesitant with something unspoken. Then she shakes it off, giving a small, dismissive wave. "Never mind. I shouldn't go down that rabbit hole right now." She steadies her gaze on him. "What's your name?"

Deuce hesitates for half a beat before answering. "Dante," he says. "But everyone calls me Deuce."

Charisma tilts her head, studying him in a way that makes his skin feel a little too tight. Then she smiles, slow and deliberate. "Well, I'm not everyone, am I?" She leans in slightly, her voice dipping lower. "Dante is a fabulous name. I think I'll call you that."

The way she says it—it's not a question. It's a decision. Something unexpected stirs in his chest. It's been a long time since anyone really saw him. Not just as the guy whose father was murdered. Not just as the ex-athlete who never quite made it. Just . . . him.

He doesn't trust himself to say anything, so he nods. Then Charisma's gaze glides past him, toward Chew, who's been unnervingly quiet for the last several minutes. Deuce knows that look in his best friend's eyes. He's seen it a thousand times. Chew is scanning—not just Charisma, but the situation, the angles, the implications. His best friend isn't just the charismatic, smooth-talking, good-looking guy that people assume he is. No, Chew is always calculating. And right now, Deuce can tell—he's put something together.

"Dang, Deuce, before you blurted that out, I had all but forgotten your real name!" Chew looks over to Charisma and slyly grins, before adding: "You're absolutely right, Charisma. Dante is a fabulous name. He got the nickname Deuce because the guy was a stud on the mound. Had the best curveball of his generation. And Deuce sounds way better than *old number two*."

Charisma looks at Deuce and giggles, lowering her head for a moment. Some of the tension in her shoulders eases, her trembling fades. Her body relaxes, like she's finding her footing again. But then, her eyes dart back up to him, and there's something different in her gaze—assessing, curious. Like she's realizing that, of the two of them, she isn't the one most shaken.

"So, Dante, you weren't the one who was almost trampled to death," she says. "Why do you look like you saw a ghost?"

The question lands like a stone in his gut. It has been more than a year since he last spoke about it. Before that? More than two. He buried it deep, locking it away in a part of himself that he had no intention of visiting again. But tonight—this city, Musk's spectacle, the impossible tech—It dredged everything back up. His heart pounds almost like a bomb in his chest. The weight of it, the sheer force of the past clawing its way back to the surface, is suffocating. Chew knows. He always has. But even Chew doesn't realize what's coming next.

"My dad was murdered," Deuce says. The words come out flat, hollow. "Shot to death in a mass public shooting. It happened near our hometown in the Midwest."

The diner seems to shrink around him, the booth's vinyl pressing against his back, the scent of fresh coffee clinging to the air. He exhales sharply, forcing himself to keep going.

"I was getting ready to play in what would've been my final series as a minor league ballplayer. Right here. In San Francisco." The irony of it tastes bitter on his tongue. "My dad had this big plan. Although he couldn't make the game I was scheduled to pitch, he was still bringing a bunch of friends and family for the remainder of the series. The whole weekend was supposed to be a celebration. Never had I looked forward to something more in my entire life.

For real. But instead, I ended up flying back home to put him in the ground."

The silence at the table is thick, stretching long enough for Deuce to feel the weight of all three of them listening intently. He keeps his gaze on the scratched-up table surface, unwilling to meet their eyes. Charisma doesn't say anything right away. He can feel her staring, the words forming and dying on her lips before she finally bites them back. No empty condolences. No meaningless platitudes. Just silence. But it's not an uncomfortable silence. It's something else entirely.

Chew rubs his eyes for a prolonged spell, widening them as soon as he takes his hands away from his face. Deuce doesn't look up, but he recognizes the familiar signs in his friend's posture—the subtle tension in his shoulders, the way his body language conveys both astonishment and a hint of grief. He's seen it in his friend before, signaling that Chew is deep in thought, processing everything that's unfolding. Despite the silence, Deuce can sense the weight of the moment pressing on both of them, the tacit understanding that tonight's revelations stirred something profound within his friend.

"Dante, or Deuce . . . I, I just can't—" Charisma finally starts, but he cuts her off before she can finish.

The floodgates are open now, and there's no stopping it. "My dad was a giant," Deuce continues, voice steadier now, but no less raw. "Or at least he would've been. He was well on his way. Culture, literature, politics . . . as a leading epistemologist, he was into it all. His finger was on the pulse of everything, always joking that he was trying to put his thumb on the scale."

The words pour out of him, unfiltered, unchecked. For the first time in years, he isn't just acknowledging his father's death—he's confronting what it meant. What the world lost. What *he* lost. First had come the expected: Grief so enormous it felt like it could swallow him whole. An abyss of sadness, an agony that dulled only with time and exhaustion. Then came the suppression. The shutting down. The refusal to acknowledge, to speak, to remember. Because the truth was, remembering hurt worse than forgetting.

But now, sitting here, with Charisma's eyes locked on his, with Chew listening but letting him speak, with the remnants of Musk's stunt still hovering outside—Deuce feels something warm and inviting blossom. He keeps talking. And for the first time in five years, the words don't choke him.

Chew had always been there. Practically raised alongside Deuce by Philipp Largo, slipping into the Largo household like a second son. Deuce remembered how easily he fit into their rhythm—how often his friend stayed for dinner, camped out for entire weekends, joined in all the debates like he earned his seat at the table. With Chew's own parents mostly absent, Philipp had stepped into the void, not formally, but in all the ways that mattered.

Deuce knew all of this, even if they never talked about it. He always felt it—the way Chew hung back sometimes when they were younger, like he wasn't sure if he was truly allowed to claim Philipp as a mentor the way Deuce did. But Deuce never saw him as an outsider. Not really. In their teenage years, when Philipp's profile was rising and his time grew scarce, they both learned to hold onto the moments they got with him, treating his words like gold.

If the *Time & Space* program sparked an entire generation's thirst for knowledge, then Philipp was the accelerant. One afternoon with him could ignite an entire future. And Chew had been right there beside Deuce, soaking it in. Though— hearing Deuce *say it*—to strangers, no less—Chew looks stunned. Deuce sees it in his expression, the way his posture changes. His friend isn't just listening; he's *feeling* this.

And it isn't just Chew. The table has gone silent, the weight of Deuce's words pressing down on all of them. He exhales slowly, trying to keep himself steady. The suppression, the years of silence, the way he locked every thought of his father away like some archived file never meant to be opened again—It's unraveling. He can *feel* it.

"He was only halfway through a first draft," Deuce continues, voice low, the words spilling out before he can stop them. "Scribbles, mostly. But I've read it over a dozen times. It had the feeling of becoming his masterpiece. His definitive work."

Across the table, Charisma watches him, her amber eyes conveying total understanding. Her expression unnerves him—not pity, but something close to it. Recognition, maybe.

"And that was when he was killed?" she asks, voice barely above a whisper.

Deuce nods. She doesn't push him to explain. Instead, she seems to be processing it herself, drawing her own connections. He can almost *see* the thoughts forming behind her gaze.

She runs a hand through her hair and in the process steals a glance at her friend before looking back at Deuce.

"I can't imagine," she says finally. "And I don't mean that in the bullshit way people say when they don't know what else to offer. I mean it *literally*. I can't imagine."

Something about the way she says it—the quiet sincerity of it—makes Deuce's throat tighten. He swallows hard and forces himself to keep going.

"It was like the thirtieth mass shooting already that year," he says, staring at the table. "Easter weekend. The media kept talking about how we were *trending* in a positive direction. Like somehow fewer mass shootings was a win worth celebrating." He lets out a bitter laugh. "Only the US of A would pat itself on the back for a stat like that." He drags a hand through his hair, forcing himself to push forward. "Twenty-eight people killed. Tristan Harris, my dad . . . a dozen others whose names were barely mentioned in the news cycle. But Dad—he didn't die right away. He made it to the hospital." Deuce's voice wavers, and he grips his coffee cup like it's the only thing keeping him tethered.

"The real agony of that day? They pronounced him dead." He exhales, shaking his head. "Chew was the one to break the news to me while I was in the bullpen, moments from taking the mound at the Oracle II. Everything after that was a complete blur before we made it east, two time zones away. The scramble to the hospital was like something out of a Tarantino film. And then—minutes after we arrived—a nurse came sprinting out of the operating room. She whispered something to the doctor, and just like that, he was *alive again.* A faint pulse. A mistake, an oversight, whatever the hell you want to call it. But he was *alive.*"

Deuce stares down at his hands, remembering the way his fingers had clenched into his jeans, nails digging into his thighs as he tried to make sense of the messages coming through his phone that day.

"He fought like hell for eight days," he says, voice barely audible now. "Eight days before death eventually claimed him."

The table remains still. No one rushes to fill the silence. No one utters some weak attempt at comfort. For the first time in five years, Deuce has *said it.* Given the nightmare a voice.

There is no more holding back. Tears slip down Deuce's face, unchecked, and for the first time in ages, yet he doesn't care. His shoulders rise and fall with the weight of his grief, his hands clenched into loose fists on the table. Across from him, Charisma watches, her amber eyes reflecting something he can't quite name—empathy, curiosity, something deeper.

Beside him, Chew breathes rapidly, his own composure cracking. He leans in, pressing his forehead against Deuce's shoulder for a second before straightening again. He had been there when it happened. *He* was the one who made the call, his voice cracking as he told Deuce the unthinkable—*Philipp Largo is gone.* Then, following their arrival, the impossible reversal. A frantic nurse, a whispered message, the sudden scramble in the ER. Hope had flared, wild and reckless, only to collapse under the weight of reality eight agonizing days later.

Deuce forces himself to breathe, to keep talking, to push through the knots in his chest. He looks at the others, one by one, letting the words come. "You mentioned Sam Harris earlier," he says, voice low, rough. "There was no one more influential in helping steer the ship out of the Terrible Twenties. Reclaiming the sane center, taking us back to a nation of logic and reason. My dad was in the thick of it with him. Challenging the extremes . . . on both sides."

His fingers tighten around the cooling ceramic of his coffee cup. "They were about bridging divides. Standing up against the rising tide of blind nationalism and calling out the suffocating political correctness and other absurdities from the opposite side. They fought to keep rational, fearless conversations alive. My dad . . . he had this way of cutting through the noise. Bringing clarity where there was chaos. And the ability to have a thoughtful conversation no matter one's stripe or creed." Deuce exhales, his breath unsteady. "And then, everything shattered."

The words settle between them. Charisma's inviting expression, her fingers lightly tapping the edge of the table, waiting.

"The media spun it their way," Deuce continues. "Called the shooter some hardcore Trump fanatic. But the truth? It was less complicated or even political. He was an incel—angry, isolated, spiraling. He didn't kill my dad because of his politics. He did it because he blamed men like him—men with power, intelligence, influence—for everything he wasn't."

The table falls silent. Not awkwardly so, but weighted with the depth of what's been said. Chew bobs in his seat, running a hand over his mouth. He knew most of this. But to hear it now, to feel the impact of it all over again—it never gets easier.

"The MAGA massacre," Mulva mutters suddenly, breaking the quiet. She shakes her head. "Shit, yeah. I remember that."

Charisma shoots her a look before refocusing on Deuce. There's something unreadable in her expression now, like she's turning something over in her mind. "What became of his book?" she asks. The words slip out quickly, almost like she regrets them the second they land.

Deuce doesn't answer immediately. His gaze drops to the table, his jaw tightening. He forces himself to shrug, but the motion feels hollow. "It's been five years," he says. "I always meant to get it finished. I told myself I would. Found some editors, went through the motions for a while. Then I . . . stopped. And in doing so I failed him."

Chew turns sharply toward him, shaking his head. "That's bullshit, man. You didn't *fail* him."

Deuce lets out a hollow chuckle, his eyes settling on Charisma's. There's something so comforting about her gaze, something steady. He swallows hard. "I did. It's the *one* thing I could've done for him. And I didn't get it done."

The table lapses into quiet again. Not heavy with regret, but something softer, more introspective. Charisma leans back, watching him, studying him like she's committing him to memory. Beside him, Chew exhales slowly, his posture finally loosening. Deuce doesn't need to look at him to know what he's thinking—that this, *all of this*, is a breakthrough. That it took five years, but here they are.

Mulva, who was silent for longer than seems natural, crosses her arms and smirks faintly. "Well, this just got a whole lot more interesting."

Deuce activates his Leaf, paying the tab with a seamless

motion. The act feels almost absurd, settling him in the small, mundane details of reality after everything that was said. The year is almost over. The decade slipping into history. Outside, the streets are thick with law enforcement—cops, detectives, and surveillance drones combing through the aftermath of Musk's spectacle. Blue and red lights strobe across damp pavement, illuminating faces of bewildered onlookers hanging out at the edges of the scene. Investigators huddle in tense clusters, parsing through whatever occurred. Midnight and New Year's is still a day away, but time feels strange, stretched, suspended.

Inside, none of them move. The weight of the night settles over them, unspoken yet understood. For now, they remain seated at the booth, at the confluence of something bigger than themselves.

CHAPTER TWENTY-FIVE

SO LATE WE GET SO SMART

Charisma couldn't shake the thought—could she have done anything to save her mother, Carmen? The weight of this question intensifies after hearing Deuce's revelation about his perceived failure following his father's grisly death. While Deuce's dad succumbed to a hail of bullets in a mass shooting, Carmen lost herself largely due to the cultural upheaval of the Terrible Twenties. Witnessing her mother's descent into depression following the tragedy in Juarez, Charisma now reflects on whether she could have been more empathetic, charitable, forgiving, and patient. She was none of these things when Carmen needed her most. In her formative years, she watched her mother's strength wither away, unable to comprehend how someone so dynamic could transform into a frail and lifeless figure.

Charisma and Deuce, the same age or perhaps a year apart, share remarkably similar stories. Their meeting during Elon Musk's peculiar stunt adds an extra layer of surrealism to their connection. Despite the chaos in the Mission District and her flawed plan to unleash Mulva, Charisma can't pull her attention away from Deuce. The way he speaks, the quiet certainty in his voice, tugs at something deep inside her. She wasn't prepared for this—not tonight, not after everything—but here he is, and here she is, leaning in, drawn to him despite herself. She is torn between the desire to make amends with her past and the eagerness to get to know him better. Deuce's voice, deep, welcoming, and inviting, adds another component to his allure. She finds herself drawn into his story, curious about his origins and fascinated by the protective aura he exudes.

Charisma traces the rim of her coffee cup, its heat lingering against her fingertips as she watches Deuce. Outside, the bright glow from a nearby sign spills through the diner's window, painting streaks of color across the table. She shifts, stretching her legs beneath the booth, then meets his gaze. "Was your father the one who got you into Sam Harris?" she asks, her voice softer now, curiosity settling in.

"For sure," he says without hesitation. "I don't think they were super close, but they definitely knew each other and were working toward executing the same mission. I never had the chance to meet him. I remember Dad saying that when Sam and others of his ilk became as cool and popular as rock stars and super stars of sport, society began turning away from the maladies that plagued it for much of the twenty-first century. And of course, the *Time & Space* program had a lot to do with that as well."

Charisma smiles wide. She can't feel the pit in her stomach making her ill at-ease since they arrived in San Francisco. The sinister specter brought on by the letter she received from Samantha and her former company are held at bay. She feels like her old self in his presence. It's so relieving, like a massive weight being released from her neck. Sam has been her own personal north star for years. Having spent the past hour with Deuce, she's not surprised to learn that Sam has had an impact on him as well.

"Deuce, you had everything taken from you by madness. I have to ask: was revenge something that drove you at any part following your father's tragic demise?"

While she's curious to know, she's asking for personal reasons. She feels disgusted with herself for even considering violent retribution. She knows it's never the answer. Still though, that fire still burns and her hatred for what Samantha did to her rages fiercely.

"My dad talked all the time," Deuce starts off with a weary smile, nudging his pal Chew. "I mean that in the kindest way possible. He spent so much time with me, with us, while we were growing up. Around every corner there was a lesson, an insight, a pearl of wisdom. Although I'm not a fan of anything that came after *Jedi*, watching those original *Star Wars* movies with him and this guy right here are some of my favorite early memories. I bring this up because, well, any time I close my eyes and quiet my mind he's there. Like my own personal Obi-Wan Kenobi. His killer will never know freedom again. And just about everything my dad fought and advocated so passionately for during his time on this planet happened, or is moving in the right direction. Having him on my shoulder everyday, in that way, well . . . I'm certain he wouldn't want me wasting any time on vengeance. He always used to say that only by attempting harmony can it be achieved." Deuce pauses to reflect and looks over at Chew. His friend has a tear in his eye, but a slight smile on his face. "But . . . I can do a whole heck of a lot better in honoring his memory. My pal Chew organized this trip out here to our old favorite city to visit. It starts here in San Francisco in a way."

Charisma is absolutely smitten now and cannot take her eyes off Deuce. She takes a sip from her coffee, ready to hear from and learn more about this haunted, beautiful young man. This Dante Largo. But she decides to be proactive and inquire if they have anything in particular lined up for the final day of the decade.

"So, what do you guys have planned for New Year's?" she asks.

"There was never really a plan," Chew says before Deuce can open his mouth. "I just wanted to get this guy back out here and see what may come. It's been quite the journey thus far and we haven't even hit the twenty-four-hour marker."

At Chew's response, Mulva's eyes gleam with mischief. She leans closer into the middle of the table, her voice layered with a conspiratorial undertone. "Hey, it just turned New Year's Eve. One final day of 2049. What do you say we all go out with a bang?" Mulva suggests, a sparkling glint in her eye. Charisma turns sharply and gives her a look that propounds she's pleading with her whacky friend not to screw things up. "I have a few tablets of T-3000," she continues, smiling ear-to-ear and breathing ultra heavy. "Have you guys ever heard of it?" She looks at them expectantly, an air of excitement surrounding her proposition.

Her question hangs tantalizingly in the air for a few moments. Deuce exchanges a cautious glance with Chew. *What on earth are they thinking now?* Charisma closes her eyes for a brief second to consider the potential bomb that dropped. How could she be surprised in the least? This is Mulva Warfarin after all. Charisma's breath catches in her throat. A thin wire of anticipation coils in her stomach, tension and exhilaration twined so tightly she can't tell where one ends and the other begins. Mulva's words hang between them, electric, reckless—irresistible. Charisma knows what this is. A test. A provocation. A goddamn hand grenade lobbed into the quiet, intimate gravity of this moment.

Part of her wants to say yes. She imagines the night unfurling before her, brilliant lights of all sorts streaking through the city, music sinking into her bones, Deuce at her side, his voice a tether as the world distorts and expands. The thought is intoxicating. She barely knows him, but something about him—his grief, his quiet strength, the way he looks at her like he sees more than she's willing to show—stirs something deep, something long dormant. What would it feel like to let go? To stop calculating, stop anticipating, stop worrying about the past clawing at her heels and the future bearing down like an avalanche?

But then, panic surges. *Mulva, what the hell are you doing?* Charisma doesn't dare look at the guys. Is Deuce repulsed? Offended? Amused? The thought of losing this fragile, magnetic connection before it even has a chance to take root terrifies her. She sneaks a glance at him, heart pounding. His expression is unreadable, somewhere between intrigued and cautious.

Chew tilts his head, studying Mulva like an equation already solved. Charisma can't tell if he's entertained or unimpressed. He's the wildcard—unpredictable, unreadable. And if Chew walks, if he laughs it off and pulls Deuce with him, then whatever spark ignited between her and Deuce might be snuffed out before it has the chance to burn.

The diner, with its low hum of machinery, and lights dimming at the turn of midnight reflecting faintly off its stainless-steel counters, feels like a liminal space—caught between past and future, hesitation and recklessness. Time slows, elongates, distorts. Outside, the world is still reeling from Musk's spectacle, the city thrumming with late-night mania and flashing lights, but here, in this booth, it's just the four of them, the weight of a decision pressing down like an unspoken dare.

Charisma swallows. She must choose, now. Indulgence or control? The past or the future? Fear or freedom? Her fingers graze the edge of her cup, condensation pooling beneath her fingertips. She licks her lips, exhales slowly, then lifts her eyes to meet Deuce's.

"Well," she murmurs, voice softer than she intended, "what do you guys think?"

CHAPTER TWENTY-SIX

DEATH IS SO FINAL

Charisma's question lingers in the air like a spark from a dying firework—"What do you guys think?" The words barely left her mouth, but already she wishes she could snatch them back and tuck them away for a less fragile moment. Around their table, the diner buzzes faintly with aging light fixtures and the low mechanical shuffle of service bots wiping down booths. Outside, flashing reds and blues from the police convoy cast rippling shadows across the windowpane, the residual effects of Elon Musk's stunt still echoing in the distance—sirens rising, drones overhead, detectives and officers pacing the sidewalks.

Across from her, Deuce's eyes remain fixed on the small plastic bag on the table. The T-3000 tablets shimmer under the overhead light like tiny relics from a forbidden ritual. Chew leans back in the booth, half-smirking, half skeptical. And beside her, Mulva nearly vibrates with excitement, her legs bouncing in time with some rhythm only she can hear.

"Relax," Mulva says, her voice husky with anticipation. "They're straight from the lab. Clean, pure bliss, fellas." She shakes the plastic bag and stirs in her seat, grinning from ear to ear.

Charisma forces a smile, her thoughts tangled and taut, a sharp contrast to Mulva's whimsical and reckless attitude. This decision, fueled by a potent cocktail of fear and excitement, could be the key to an unforgettable night or the gateway to unforeseen and iniquitous consequences. The betrayal surrounding Loopd>In still so fresh and raw, but Charisma is titillated at the notion of spending the remaining few hours of this decade with the haunted but charming young man sitting across from her while under the influence of potent psychedelics.

"It's been years . . ." Charisma says, her voice barely audible above the din, each word now carrying the weight of her past and the fragile hope for a brighter future that could start now.

Mulva's grin widens, her eyes gleaming with excitement. "So, we're doing this?!" she asks, her voice laced with a thrill. "This city at night will be a whole new experience. We'll see it through a different set of eyes."

"Curious," Deuce says. "Were you planning to take this stuff before you met the two of us or did what just went down in the Mission trigger you into such a proposition?" His query, laden with implications, hangs heavily in the air as all four sets of eyes dart back and forth across at one other.

Charisma hesitates, her internal battle evident. She doesn't want to make the wrong move or say the wrong thing to turn off Deuce. Her mind races, caught in a storm of conflicting emotions. Fear gnaws at her heart. Doubt too. The idea of violence, once a potent cocktail of rage and despair, now feels repulsive. She's terrified of jeopardizing this connection with Deuce, his heroics, kindness, and curiosity feel like the complete opposite to the darkness she carries. She yearns to tell him the truth, to share the burden of betrayal and the longing for justice. But another fear holds her back. What if they don't believe her? Samantha meticulously erased her from Loopd>In's history, leaving only hard questions and the gnawing suspicion that her memories are mere delusions. The thought of their disbelief feels like another betrayal, another blow to her already fragile self. In the moment, Charisma is paralyzed, caught between two conflicting desires. Should she remain silent, protecting this fragile bond with Deuce, or risk everything by revealing the truth? As she looks into his questioning eyes, a spark of determination ignites within her.

"We came to San Francisco for a revenge mission," she declares, her voice surprisingly steady despite the emotional turmoil within. "But meeting you two . . . well, I must admit, it's changed everything for me . . ."

Chew leans forward, his devilish charm momentarily replaced by a seriousness that surprises Charisma. "Revenge against whom?" he asks, his voice carrying genuine interest.

Charisma looks at both of them, her eyes filled with a newfound clarity. "This won't be easy for me. It's been the most difficult month of my life. But after hearing Deuce's tale, I can ante up."

As she speaks, the story of Loopd>In unfolds. Charisma, with a calm resolve, details her revolutionary VR–CID-A fusion technology that would become the product that both guys experienced on their maiden HyperLoop voyage hours before. She explains how she took the CID-A breakthrough of the early 2040s and merged it into the advancing world of virtual reality software. That was the fun part. Articulating what came next is terribly painful for Charisma, but she keeps her composure and explains the treachery of Samantha Ravensby, the ultimate betrayal that ripped her world apart. She speaks of Loopd>In's true potential to revolutionize mental health treatment and her dream of making it accessible to everyone. She also confesses how they originally came to San

Francisco for vengeance.

"Was it a kill mission?" Chew asks. "Were you two set to take out this Samantha Ravensby chick, for real? How were you going to do it?" There's no judgment behind Chew's words, only intrigue and inquisitiveness.

Charisma feels Mulva glance her way. She knows her friend well enough to read the hesitation in her body—the slight shift in posture, the way her lips part like she might speak up, but doesn't. She's waiting. Allowing Charisma to be the one to answer.

Silence lingers until finally . . .

"Say, you guys said you were from the Midwest, right? How did you make the trek out to California?" Charisma is all smiles again, changing the subject by redirecting entirely.

"We took the HyperLoop from St. Louis," Deuce responds. Instantly Charisma's insides have a makeover like she's been dressed up to attend the Oscars. She's beaming, sits straight up with her shoulders back, exuding the kind of confidence she portrayed whenever pitching investors or seeking partners for Loopd>In. "It was the experience of a lifetime. We got here in under two hours. And what we got to do while on board? Wow! Well, I've never seen anything like it."

"That's right," Chew jumps in. "As incredible as the HyperLoop experience was, the VR on board could give you a powerful enough orgasm to cripple you! For real."

"Let me take this one," Deuce says, cutting in before Chew can go further. His tone isn't rude or dismissive, just firm and deliberate. Charisma senses something change in him, like a line was drawn and he's decided not to budge. There's a new weight in his voice now, one she hasn't heard until this moment. "Anyway," he continues, turning back to face Charisma and Mulva, "what they provided to all passengers on board was exceptional. And it wasn't just the VR. A compound came with it. Isolated CID-A. What you told us about, right?"

"Yeah," Charisma says. "That was mine . . . The key cog in Loopd>In." She smiles modestly and looks down. The whole saga rushes past her eyes as if her life were on fast forward. Chew and Deuce look at each other briefly, mouths closed and lips pursed, then dart right back to her. "The plan was to customize the user's experience with a combination of the CID-A capsule, our VR software, and the speed of the HyperLoop. You could pick any story from our catalogue and be a part of it the way you visualized in your mind, or as close as possible. The deal with Musk and the HyperLoop was to serve as the pilot, but I planned to get it on every form of commercial travel in a few years. Well, it'll probably happen now, as you can tell."

"This is the multibillion-dollar business you're referring to then? You're saying that you are the originator of Loopd>In?" Deuce's tone is measured, but something in his eyes—wide and searching—tells Charisma he's caught off guard. Maybe even intrigued. She feels his gaze on her, not just with disbelief, but with hope. He wants to trust her—she can sense it—and that possibility makes her heart ache. But she also knows the next step: the activation of his Leaf, the impulse to fact-check, to look her up. And sure enough, she sees the microhesitation in his posture, the subtle twitch of his fingers. She beats him to it.

"You won't find my name tied to the company in any way," Charisma says, sitting up even straighter and catching the faint shift in Deuce's posture—a tell that he's thinking about checking his Leaf. She gets ahead of it. "My business partner found a way to completely eradicate my history and involvement. It was sinister. She got her claws into me semiearly and must've plotted her move right from the jump." As she speaks, she watches his expression closely. There's no malice, no outright skepticism, but something quiet and unsettled behind his eyes. It stings more than she expected. She's given him reason to doubt her—hasn't she?

"What she did was punishable by death," says Mulva, leaning back and extending her shoulders for a prolonged stretch. "At least in my book. And a very painful death too, if it were up to me."

"So, the two of you weren't fooling around?" Deuce asks. "You're as serious as a heart attack?"

"We must sound like fiendish fools." Charisma leans toward Deuce and covers his hands as they sit on the edge of the table. Their eyes are locked. "Madness. Complete madness. I still can't believe I allowed it to happen. Samantha Ravensby took everything from me. She pulled the rug out from underneath me when I didn't even know I was standing on a rug. And now Loopd>In is hers and whatever it shall soon evolve into."

"And you were going to kill this woman? That was your plan?" Deuce's tone is uneven, but Charisma senses the weight behind it. She studies him—his jaw tight, his stare steady but unreadable now. Her heart lurches. Has she lost him? She can't tell if he's judging her, trying to understand, or quietly backing away from the insane thing she admitted. She wants to reach out for his hand again, to lock them both in the connection that sparked earlier. But she holds still, afraid that any sudden move might shatter whatever fragile trust remains between them. Did she come on too strong? Say too much? But it is the truth, and hiding it would've felt far worse. She watches his eyes—not cold, not cruel, but deep in thought—and tells herself to breathe. Whatever happens next, at least she was brave enough to say it out loud.

"That's still what I'd like to do," Mulva reinforces. Her smile emphasizes her intentions—unapologetic and fierce.

"But there's no way in hell you'd get away with it," Chew chimes in. "Surveillance is everywhere. The two of you don't seem like you were on a suicide mission."

"I was going to say that getting away with it wasn't part of the plan," Mulva responds. "At least not for me. I was ready to go out in a final blaze of glory, pretty boy." Mulva gives Chew a wink.

Charisma breaks her eye contact from Deuce and looks down. She is embarrassed, ashamed. Hearing all of it out loud makes it seem even more ludicrous. What was she thinking? "We were still working out the details," Mulva continues, "when we arrived here. The closer we got, the colder Charisma's feet got. Now they're nothing more than blocks of ice."

"That's fair," says Charisma. "As it neared the eleventh hour and our target came into focus, my senses came back to me. She might've taken everything I worked so hard to build and the massive fortunes it will produce, but exacting revenge of this sort isn't worth my life nor my friend's. It's not worth our freedom either. Death is so final, whereas life is so full of possibilities. No matter how bad a hand you've been dealt."

"A GoT reference? That's our fav." Deuce says, showing off his widest smile yet. Charisma is not surprised he's a fan. He's as sharp as he is cute.

"Why yes, it is," she says. "I still use them all the time. It was the best story ever told."

"I agree," says Deuce. "Our grandparents had the Beatles. Our parents had *Thrones*. I'm hopeful our cultural zeitgeist hasn't emerged yet. Kind of bleak out there on that front, especially since the best band on the planet is almost seventy. Goes to show AI doesn't make everything better."

"Why am I not surprised?" says Charisma, looking into Deuce's eyes once again. This entire conversation was one wild roller coaster ride of emotion. Even though it's late and one of the most maddening days of her life, Charisma is not tired. She wants to stay in his presence. She wants to learn more about him. She doesn't want this night to end.

"Fuck it," she continues. Mulva perks up in her seat, looking back and forth between Deuce and Chew. "Let's take some of what Mulva is packing. What say you boys? Wander around this city through psychedelic eyes and see where it leads us? If nothing else take a wild stroll down the ol' Kingsroad." Charisma's Westerosi accent is stupendous and all four share a laugh.

In the electric atmosphere hovering over their table in the diner, Charisma's bold proposal hangs in the air, doubling down on a daring invitation to an unknown adventure.

"Adventure is why we came here," Deuce says, looking over to his friend while putting his arm around him. Chew nods in agreement, his stalwart energy unmistakable.

"San Francisco through a psychedelic lens? On the final day of the 40s?! Count me in!" Chew declares.

Charisma senses the subtle change in Deuce's expression—the way his mouth curves ever so slightly, like the idea is lighting something up inside him. She can feel it in her chest, too. That low reverberation of anticipation. Not nerves exactly, but something adjacent. Possibility.

Chew, of course, is now grinning like he's about to jump off a rooftop just to see what happens. Even Mulva—Mulva!—looks halfway to euphoric. Charisma catches the glint in her friend's eyes. *God, when was the last time we both looked this free?*

When Deuce stands and offers her a hand, something clicks into place. Not destiny or fate or any of that nonsense, but something very real. Something earned. The kind of moment you only get when you finally stop running away from your past and start moving toward whatever's next.

The door slides open. Cold, fresh air rushes in, full of sirens and uncertainty and a city catching its breath. Charisma steps out last, her fingers tingling from Deuce's touch. What's waiting for them out there? She's beyond relieved the acidic pit in her stomach went away, given way to excitement and hope.

CHAPTER TWENTY-SEVEN

DARK WINGS, DARK WORDS

Chew watches as Deuce and Charisma walk ahead, their figures barely discernible against the impressive expanse of Ocean Beach. The salty air stings his nostrils, and the sand squishes satisfyingly between his toes. The rhythm of the crashing waves provides a constant wall of sound, a soothing counterpoint to the distant, muted glow of the city behind him. After being taxied by a driverless Tesla in less than fifteen minutes, they arrived.

He grins, the kind of grin that feels foreign to his face, like an old friend he hadn't realized he missed. For the first time in what feels like forever, the world doesn't feel so heavy. Deuce is laughing again, mixing it up with someone new in a way he used to do like clockwork. The plan—the whole damned idea of coming back to San Francisco to bury ghosts and start something fresh—it actually feels like it's working! The air is crisp, the ocean a steady lullaby, and they're about to dive into a night that promises weirdness, wonder, and maybe the ultimate catharsis that Chew has sought for so long. For a brief, buoyant second, he lets himself believe in the magic of it all.

"You don't have to worry, you know?" Mulva leans into him, her voice a low, husky whisper. A mischievous glint dances in her eyes as she elbows him playfully in the side. "The tab you took," she continues, her lips curling into a smirk. "It's a placebo. No need to worry about blasting off into the cosmos."

Chew slows his pace and shoots her a look, one eyebrow arched in surprise. "Placebos?" he repeats, his voice colored with disbelief and amusement. "That doesn't sound like your style at all."

Mulva shrugs, her eyes playfully gleaming up at him. "It seemed like a good idea at the time. Those two are clearly hitting it off, and you seemed like you wouldn't be averse to having a little fun. Besides, no one really drinks any more, so I figured a magical trip could be an excellent bonding experience."

But then, her expression shifts, and a brief flicker of seriousness replaces the playful façade. "The truth is," she says, her voice dropping back to a whisper, "if my friend up there took real T-3000 while out here, without professional supervision, she'd lose it. Her mind would snap and be obliterated into a million pieces."

Chew stops walking, his gaze locking on hers. A wave of curiosity washes over him, replacing his initial amusement. He's certain there's way more to this story after hearing Charisma's tale about Loopd>In. And that fox of a CEO who's now running the show playing the part of the uber-villain? He knows a hidden narrative awaits unraveling.

"There's something happening between Deuce and her," he says, his voice soft but firm. "And I can't help feeling like something bigger is at play. Please, Mulva, tell me what you know. Deuce is an orphan. He's a survivor. He can handle anything you throw at him."

A sigh escapes Mulva's lips. She looks out toward the horizon, where the immeasurable, starless sky is swallowed by the darkness, pierced by the distant, glimmer of the city. The waves crash against the shore, and she appears both sad and reticent as she looks up at Chew.

"You're right," she says finally, her voice laced with a hint of resignation. "There is a story here, Chew. A story that begins and ends with Samantha Ravensby."

The revelation that the tablets were placebos hits Chew like a rogue wave, washing away the light-headedness and replacing it with a cold, unsettling dread. The playful banter between him and Mulva feels like a lifetime ago, a cruel mirage that masked the potential harsh reality unfolding before him. Charisma's story, with its fantastical elements and veiled truths, planted seeds of doubt in Chew's mind—outlandish claims woven with pain—but Mulva's quiet warning reframes everything. This is no longer a quirky tale. It's a fault line, and Chew can feel it shifting beneath his feet. Was Charisma really a visionary—brilliant, wronged, and misunderstood? Or was she clinging to a story crafted to make sense of a breakdown no one else could see? And what about this Mulva chick standing next to him in the sand? Was she the loyal friend doing her best to protect someone on the edge, or something else entirely—someone with her own agenda, pulling strings under the guise of sisterhood?

Chew steals a glance at Deuce from a few yards away, his friend lost in the depths of laughter and conversation with Charisma. Chew's mind spins with tangled questions, each one colliding with the next. Mulva's reveal pulled the ground out from beneath him, and with Deuce steps ahead and seemingly lost in Charisma's orbit, Chew feels the weight of uncertainty pressing in on all sides. Standing there, with the ocean's rhythm in the background, he's struck by the parallels between this night and the one five years ago. The same city that once bore witness to his and Deuce's unimaginable loss hosts a new, complex dilemma. The irony isn't lost on Chew; here they are again in San Francisco, at a crossroads that could define their future. Well, at least Deuce's.

His thoughts drift entirely toward his best friend, who seems captivated by Charisma. Chew can't help but feel protective, his instincts on high alert. He knows Deuce's history better than anyone, the pain he's endured, and the walls built to safeguard his heart. The idea of Deuce falling for someone who might be unbalanced, especially here, in this city laden with their shared sorrow, unsettles Chew. An enormous part of him wants to believe Charisma, to trust this connection could be something good, possibly even something extraordinary for Deuce.

He can't quite get past Mulva's admission, however. His natural skepticism kicks in, mulling over her words. Is Charisma's story about Loopd>In a fabrication, a delusion? Or could there be a sliver of truth in it? Chew knows the tech world can be ruthless, filled with betrayals and underhanded tactics. Could Samantha Ravensby be the villain in Charisma's story, or is it a convenient narrative to mask something else? He is anything but certain.

Chew wants to support his friend, to be there for him as always. But he can't shake the feeling that they're treading on dangerous ground. The weight of responsibility feels heavy on his shoulders. How should he navigate this? How does he protect Deuce without suffocating the possibility for something genuine?

"Mulva, I promise, you can trust me," Chew says, his hand gently wrapping around hers. His eyes shift to Deuce and Charisma, silhouetted against the ocean, their conversation masked by the steady rush of waves. "Just tell me what's really going on. No riddles. No half-truths. If there's something coming, something we need to be ready for—I need to know."

Mulva studies him for a beat, then gives a tired smile and lowers herself into the sand with a slow, deliberate grace. Chew follows, sitting beside her, but his attention remains fixed on the shoreline. The surf eats at the distance between them and their friends, and with every wave, he feels the urgency tightening.

He doesn't know if he's about to learn the truth—or peel back another layer of mystery—but either way, he's made up his mind. Whatever the cost, whatever the fallout, he'll protect Deuce from another loss. Even if it means losing something himself.

CHAPTER TWENTY-EIGHT

GOD BLESS THE GOBLIN

An electric taxi buzzes overhead, a fleeting spark against the now moonlit canvas of the night sky. Deuce watches it disappear behind the clouds covering the city, the awe of technological marvels never failing to ignite a spark within him. He turns to Charisma, their figures bathed in the soft glow of the moon as they stand on the beach, the rhythmic crash of waves a constant thrum against the backdrop of their hushed conversation.

"Flying taxis," says Deuce. "Never gets old."

Charisma nods, but something is tight and uneasy about the way she does it—like her mind is still caught back in the Mission. Her shoulders remain slightly hunched, as if bracing against a brutal wind that isn't there, and her arms are folded tightly across her chest like she's still clutching on to something she can't let go of. He thinks back to the chaos Musk stirred up earlier, and how close it all came to going sideways. It didn't feel like progress. Not in the way Musk framed it to the crowd and in his following public statement. The whole ordeal felt more like a haunting throwback to everything civilization was supposed to have outgrown.

"It's difficult for me to be critical, Deuce," she says, turning to face him. Mulva and Chew are out of earshot, but she whispers as if she's surrounded by voyeurs. "He's helped change the world for the better a thousand times over. But I remember reading what he was like prior to Sam Harris getting involved with his enterprise. Seems to me there's no way this would've happened if Sam was around and in his ear."

Harris had passed away a year prior. For over two decades he served as Musk's primary advisor, a partnership many saw as the catalyst to springing America past the Terrible Twenties.

"Ha, you mean Musk recklessly trying to show off this new tech to help avoid mass shootings?"

"I'm sorry if that came off as insensitive," Charisma says without pause. "I know gun violence hasn't impacted me in the way it has for you. We could've been killed back there. And people like Elon Musk, like Samantha Ravensby . . . they seem to be able to get away with anything and everything these days. I don't think that happens with Sam around, you know? At least in Elon's case."

"Don't be sorry, Charisma," Deuce says. "That was beyond crazy what went down in the Mission. But I'm not worried about Elon Musk. It's not like he's going to forget and forego everything he learned from Sam. At least I hope not."

Deuce turns back to Chew and Mulva who remain a few yards away. He can see Chew's face now that the moon has settled away from the clouds. *God knows what he's up to with that wild one.*

"I'm curious, Charisma. You must've gotten to know Musk at least a little since your product is now featured on the HyperLoop." He looks straight up into the night sky and pauses briefly for effect. "Of all his accomplishments—"

"I didn't know him," Charisma says. "All that was done behind the scenes. I wasn't privy to any of it." She sidles right up to him and gently puts her arm around his back. "But as amazing as the HyperLoop is and what it will do for global connectivity, everyone alive knows what they were doing and where they were when twelve humans took a single step in unison onto red soil."

Deuce doesn't respond right away, leaving Charisma's response hanging in the crisp air of late December against the backdrop of the soothing tide mere steps away from their feet. He senses a surge about to overtake him, believing the tablet he ingested minutes ago is starting to kick into full gear.

"What is it?" Charisma asks. "I'm sorry I cut you off, but that's what you were asking, right? Was that the wrong answer?"

"Certainly not. You're right. Amid everything else, the Marvel on Mars was the seminal moment for a generation. I was sitting with that guy over there," Deuce pauses again as he points to his friend with a sly grin, "on the floor in my living room. My dad hosted a party for all his friends and our neighbors. But . . ."

He drifts off momentarily, his thoughts turning back to his dad. He was only a few miles away from where he stands now when he first learned the horrific news. He continues to relive it, the cascading emotions of torment and tears. But his mind is strong, and he doesn't allow himself to go down that tunnel of torture. He comes back to the moment.

"It was something Dad was a part of that stands out when it comes to Musk's crowning achievements. One he didn't get much credit for."

"Who?" Charisma asks. "Your dad or Elon?"

"Both, actually," Deuce says, kicking up some sand and casting his gaze to the ocean's waters. "My dad was one of the early architects of what became known as the *Time & Space* program. He and dozens of others like his friend Tristan Harris were the ones who first proposed and later advocated for its nationwide implementation. Them and of course the Four Horsemen, well really only Dawkins and Sam since Hitch and Dennett had passed away by then. But it never would've come together without Musk pushing for the new tax levy to support it. Once he got involved and committed to supporting it . . . well, I'm sure you're keenly aware of what happened."

"That's incredible, but I must say after getting to know you tonight . . . I'm really not that surprised. Wow, I, I . . ."

"What is it, Charisma?"

She takes a moment before speaking again, easing back into his arms like she's settling into something familiar. Deuce holds her gently, watching as her face lights up—not just from the moon's glow, but from whatever memory surfaced.

"Our class took to calling it the 'Cosmic Connection.' Our teacher was absolutely world class. Mr. Cody. He taught the subject matter with such a grace and ease that it pulled everyone in from day one and never let go. The impact it had, Deuce. My god, the impact. For me, I never looked back. From the very first session I wanted to become a scientist. Or an engineer. Or both. But it was so much more than that. It inspired everyone in my class. It changed the paradigm. Once everyone, and I mean just about everyone, had a firm appreciation for our place in the cosmos . . . For the uniqueness and preciousness of life . . . Well, the ridiculousness of our parents' generation melted away, didn't it?"

The central tenet of the program was always clear: ignite a sense of awe and wonder in every child in every school across the country. And not just through textbooks or rote memorization. For two weeks each year, starting in second grade, America's public school system paused its usual rhythm to immerse students in the cosmic perspective—time, Earth, and humanity laid bare through distilled teachings of thinkers like Dawkins, Hawking, Sagan, and

Harari. But even with a rock-solid plan rooted in logic and reason and billionaires like Musk advocating for a special tax to pay for it, none of it would've come to fruition had it not been for a miracle of its own. Deuce couldn't believe it when his dad first told him the story. The irony never stopped being surreal.

"It almost died on the vine," his dad said. "The most fervent detractors called it an atheist fever dream. A leftist indoctrination campaign. Said it was anti-American, anti-God, anti-everything our country stood for." But then, somehow, the tide turned.

It was none other than Donald Trump who made it happen, in the final months of his extraordinary life. Deuce never got used to that part. His father—Philipp Largo—loathed the man during his presidency. Called him the Orange Goblin almost exclusively. Railed against and ridiculed his presidency in essays, guest columns, and on his podcast. Philipp Largo adamantly believed the MAGA movement was one of the most destructive forces of American civic life in the twenty-first century.

It was near the end of Trump's life when Largo and his cohort were trying to make the *Time & Space* program a reality. And it was Trump, more so than anyone else, who convinced conservative leadership of the day that the program wasn't a threat to faith—but a pathway toward deepening it. He argued, in his own indomitable way, that understanding the scope of creation didn't pull people away from God, it drew them closer.

"He told them it would be like pointing a telescope at the divine," Deuce says looking deeply into Charisma's eyes, over the wash of the waves, and the amalgam of sound emanating from the heart of the city. "I'm not sure if he really believed that or if it was Musk who convinced him once they repaired their relationship. But no matter what happened behind close doors, it was unquestionably Donald Trump who got the Red Team on board. And from there . . ."

Charisma looks up at him, nodding slowly, like she's pulling a half-buried memory into the light. "I remember that now. That phrase. 'God Bless You, Mr. Trump.' It was everywhere for a hot second."

Deuce grins faintly, closing his eyes and seeing his dad's face in the aftermath of the program's federal approval. "Yeah, that was my dad. Couldn't believe he said it, that he was the one who coined that term, especially considering how he felt about the man beforehand. I remember him referring to it as 'grace in space.' The ultimate *close* by a man he once thought irredeemable."

Charisma moves closer to him, her voice soft. "And then he never got credit for it."

Deuce's smile fades. "No. Tristan Harris got headlines, and deservedly so. Many others too. But my dad? Barely a footnote. That's why I said I failed him back at the diner. Had I done everything I could to get his book out, it might've been different." He turns to her, eyes gleaming, heart racing at an all time high. "But besides all that, you know what the real proof of the program's success is?"

Charisma tilts her head, curious.

"You," he says. "You are. You described exactly what it was supposed to do—change the way we see ourselves, our world, and our place in it. You're the walking embodiment of everything my dad hoped it would accomplish."

Charisma goes quiet, visibly moved. And Deuce feels something shift inside him—a weight long carried, now shared.

"So, my knight in shining armor is the son of the father of the *Time & Space* program. This is surreal."

"You can say that again, Charisma," Deuce says. "He didn't get to see its full impact. But I like to think he'd be super proud of what it's become."

Deuce knows their conversation will continue to rise and fall like the tide—there's still so much more to uncover about each other. But for now, all that matters is this moment: moonlight above them, sand beneath them, and the sense that something long buried is beginning to break the surface. They're no longer wanderers in the night—they're inheritors of something unfinished, something vital. He doesn't want to lose that feeling. Doesn't want to lose her. Without another word, he spins Charisma around and pulls her gently down into the sand, eyes locking with hers as if they've known each other through a thousand lifetimes. Then, with the surf singing in the distance and the ghosts of the past beginning to fade, they kiss—fiercely and fully—as if the world were about to end, and love was the only truth that mattered.

CHAPTER TWENTY-NINE

FOR THE LOVE OF THE GAME

Chew gazes at the distant figures of Deuce and Charisma, their silhouettes barely distinguishable against the backdrop of Ocean Beach. The rhythmic crash of waves provides a soothing undertone to his thoughts, which are awash with a keen remembrance and concern. He contemplates the unfolding events of the night. Standing beside Mulva, he's struck by the irony of returning to the same city where he learned of Philipp Largo's death, now possibly watching his best friend fall for someone who might be entangled in her own complex delusions.

Mulva, seemingly reading his thoughts, remarks, "And I changed my name to spite my dad," she says, laughing a little too hard, like it's no big deal. "He was a *Seinfeld* fanatic, a fool, a fiend, and a shitty father. So I thought I'd put it back in his face. It's always about making a statement, sending a message, ya know?"

Chew watches her, unsure whether she's joking or confessing. There's no mystery here—She's telling him exactly who she is. Fierce. Unfiltered. And clearly still carrying around the weight of that old wound. This is all an amusing side note, but Chew's mind stays fixed on what really matters—Deuce, and the strange uncertainty hovering over everything tonight. He doesn't know what to believe, or his next move.

"So, she was never really in charge of Loopd>In?" Chew asks Mulva, seeking confirmation of his suspicions. "Is that what you're saying?"

Mulva, pacing the shoreline, pauses to toss a pebble into the waves. "I've only heard bits and pieces, as I've said, Chew. But it's pretty clear to me that Samantha's cease-and-desist letter was the breaking point for Charisma. She told me Samantha stole everything—Loopd>In, her original tech, and consequently her future. And part of me wants to believe it." Mulva pauses, her tone dipping just below the surf. "But the whole thing . . . it's grand. A little too grand. A burgeoning tech empire ripped away. A global VR revolution masterminded by someone no one's ever heard of? I don't know, I'm not saying she *couldn't* do all these things, she's the most brilliant and inspired human I've ever known, but that's not saying too much coming from the likes of me. I guess what I'm saying is that there are gaps in her story. Things that don't line up."

Chew sways back and forth in the sand, steps away from the Pacific, eyes narrowing like he's bracing for impact. "And since that letter landed? She's been spiraling—or that's what you noticed?" His voice isn't accusatory, but it's sharp, laced with the quiet calculation of a man who's seen too many minds crack and bend under pressure. "Because either this woman built the future and got robbed, or she's lost in a delusion convincing enough to pull us all in, most especially my man Deuce."

Mulva turns to face him, the wind catching a few loose strands of her hair. Her jaw tightens, then she exhales through her nose—slow, steady, like she's settling into something she's carried too long. When she speaks again, there's no flippancy, no shield. Just the bare edge of truth. "She's struggling. But aren't we all, in our own ways? We all suffer from the human condition." Her voice softens. "There's strength in acknowledging our battles. But make no mistake: Charisma Sinclair is also brilliant. What I know of Samantha Ravensby, she's much more on the nefarious side."

Chew appreciates Mulva's candor. He wants to believe her story, to help the situation in any way that he can. Her straightforwardness, coupled with fierce loyalty, is compelling. He smiles, finding solace in her presence.

"How far back have Charisma's struggles gone?" he asks, genuinely interested in understanding more.

Mulva's gaze drifts to the horizon. "Since her mother's breakdown. Carmen Sinclair was once a force to be reckoned with—until she wasn't. Charisma wanted nothing more than to redeem her mother, somehow, someway. She pushed herself to the brink for years. Then she snapped, way worse than me. Mental health doesn't discriminate, Chew. You strike me as someone who's seen that up close, especially after hearing what your best friend is going through. You know damned well how rough the turf is out there."

Chew nods, his mind reflecting back to Deuce's dad. To one lesson he gleaned from the man in particular, articulated for the masses through an essay titled "For the Love of the Game." It had always resonated deeply for Chew, especially when life's challenges and hurdles became salient. Largo's words about 'life being a game, but we can't see the clock' echo in his thoughts. 'We're free to make the game as exciting and interesting as we can dream. That we can discover new games no one has thought of yet.' Has this thinking harmed Charisma?. And how far has Deuce actually fallen for her during their time together on the beach?

"You've been a steadfast friend to Charisma through all this," Chew remarks, admiring her unwavering, albeit unconventional, support. He remains curious about the entire ordeal, never one to believe in coincidence, having homed in on Samantha Ravensby earlier in the day, arbitrarily, now her specter clouding over the two ladies he met during the madness in the Mission.

Mulva chuckles lightly. "I've always had a special place in my heart for cripples, bastards, and broken things."

"Classic," Chew responds. Mulva moves closer to the water's edge, gently tossing stones into the tide. Her form is wretched, but her distance is impressive. "I wonder," Chew says, inching closer to her a soft step in the sand at a time, "had you ever heard of Philipp Largo prior to tonight?"

"No, but I remember the MAGA massacre. Clear as day. That's so awful Deuce's dad died like that."

"We didn't come out here to mess around on the HyperLoop or escape the holidays," his voice firmer now, more grounded in conviction. "I led the charge. I brought us here for him. Deuce hasn't stepped foot anywhere near this city since the day his life got split into before and after. I figured maybe, just maybe, if we came back, if he saw something new in a place that used to haunt him, he might start to let some of that weight go. He's been living like a shadow of himself ever since his dad was murdered. Wouldn't talk about it. Not with me, not with anyone. What happened tonight back at that diner . . . that wasn't just him opening up. That was Deuce taking his first deep breath in five years."

"And now you're concerned that he has opened up and might be falling in love with a crazy person?"

"I'm not judging. I'm—"

"You're fine, hotshot," Mulva says, breaking away from tossing stones and turning to face Chew. "My, my, would you look at that?" She takes a hold of him by the back of his head and points his direction to Charisma and Deuce who are now lying on the sand together in a full embrace. As the dawn approaches, Chew feels a renewed sense of clarity. The ghosts of the past, the pain of loss, seem to recede once he witnesses Deuce and Charisma together on the sand. They've been replaced by a real sense of hope and possibility. He glances at Mulva, grateful for her company and the unexpected journey of this night.

"Whatever the future holds for them," he says, "I believe wholeheartedly in the resilience of the human spirit. Maybe they're both exactly what they need for each other."

Mulva smiles her widest smile of the evening, her eyes reflecting the first light of day. "In the end, that's all we have—our spirit and the connections we make along the way."

The two sit in silence as the first brushstrokes of morning stretch across the horizon, painting the sky in soft, surreal hues. Chew leans back into the sand, his head resting against Mulva's knee, unsure if the shimmering streaks above are the sunrise, the tablet, or exhaustion folding in on itself. He looks over to Deuce and Charisma in the distance, tangled in the kind of embrace that feels like it belongs to a storybook or a hallucination. For the first time in years, he doesn't try to figure it all out. He lets it be—this moment, this mess, this possibility that maybe the broken ones aren't doomed, rewiring in real time. The wind kicks up slightly, salt and memory on the air. Whatever truth lies buried in this night, he knows one thing for sure: he came here to help Deuce heal. And for the first time in five long years . . . it looks like he might have.

CHAPTER THIRTY

DOES GOD LOVE HIS CHILDREN?

It's a few minutes before six in the morning on the final day of the decade, and Samantha Ravensby is all alone in her downtown San Francisco office. There is no place she would rather be. Her wide corner spot overlooks the Bay in a way that allows her to see it in its totality, save for the darkness or fog. On any given day when she allows herself a breath and a moment of reflection and quiet, she's able to watch ships come and go for miles perched in her mighty corporate tower. This isn't *work* for her though, and it hasn't been for years. Not since she took control of Loopd>In, being the one who steered the ship and eventually put all the pieces together to create a truly transformative piece of razor's edge technology. Her office is her throne, and she has no qualms with spending over eighty hours a week here. Or when she wasn't at the Nexus like the better part of last year. But it's this office that so much more effectively serves as her command center from which she orchestrates her vision for the future—a future she ardently believes can redefine humanity's trajectory as the second half of the century beckons.

Her journey was marked by an array of triumphs and setbacks. For every loss endured, her victories have shone brighter, fueling her conviction that she stands on the precipice of monumental change. With Loopd>In, she didn't just invent another piece of technology. She crafted a key to unlock new realms of human experience and potential, inspired by the likes of Musk and Jobs. Driven by a relentless pursuit of success instilled in her by her late father and a natural affinity for advanced technology and problem-solving, Samantha embodies the spirit of the mid-twenty-first-century entrepreneurial warrior.

In the solitude of her office—her kingdom—she reflects not just on the path that brought her here, but on the journey ahead. The dawn of a new decade holds the promise of her greatest achievement, a culmination of years of dedication that could offer untold benefits to humanity. However, Samantha is acutely aware of the challenges that lie in wait: doubters, rivals, Luddites, and the unpredictable twists of fate that always accompany great endeavors. Despite the obstacles, her resolve remains unshaken. As the city awakens below, she readies herself with a few moments of silent meditation.

This morning, this final dawn of the decade, there are plenty of tactical things to do, boxes to check. Year-end financials need to be closed out. Several internal and external memos to compose and send to senior staff, customers, and partners. But none of that is taking up space in her mind right now. The real reason she is here at this hour, on what is a holiday for just about everyone else, is that she did not want to take the incoming call any other place. After one flash on her retinal Leaf, she quiets her mind and answers.

"Darius, right on time, as always. How are you?"

She doesn't know precisely where he is as his tracking feature is blocked. Samantha finds this oddly curious, but chooses not to press him on his exact whereabouts.

"Happy New Year, Samantha."

"We still have eighteen hours left of these fabulous 40s."

"Not where I am."

She uses the scan feature on the Leaf to see if it can pick up his location. Still no dice.

"Have you spoken with your boss since yesterday?"

He huffs into his speaker and clears his throat before answering "Not at all."

"Quite the spectacle he put on here in my hometown," she says. "But who on Earth would expect anything less from that man?"

"Elon went totally dark following the events in San Francisco. No one has heard from him. He's off the grid."

Samantha is even more curious now, but also doesn't want to go down that rabbit hole too far. Elon Musk is most definitely fine, probably better than ever. She needs to get specific information from this call, not wander about into matters in which she has no skin in the game.

"Maybe he's trying to enjoy the New Year somewhere without any noise," Samantha says to lift the conversation. "I'd say he deserves to do that every now and then."

"I assume you saw everything. It was in your own backyard, as you stated."

"Yeah, me and ten billion other people. He sure knows how to grab the audience's attention better than anyone."

"He pulled this one off on his own. No one on the inner circle knew anything about it."

"Did you know your eighty-year-old boss looks like he should be carded if he tried to purchase booze? Christ!"

"Seventy-eight. He's not eighty yet," he corrects.

"Whatever, you know what I mean. Pretty drastic change since the last time anyone saw him publicly. Kind of hurt his messaging and what he was supposedly trying to accomplish, if you don't mind me saying."

"I'm afraid I don't know what you mean," Darius hisses. Samantha catches a glimpse of herself in the reflection of a framed picture that sits behind her desk. She has slowly swiveled around twice since answering Darius's call. The picture is of a sunset over the Andaman Sea. In the far distance Samantha is swimming past the surf, smiling wide in the throes of a perfectly captured backstroke as her hair is submerged in the ocean waters. The sun is a reddish orange sphere of light and life behind her outstretched left paw. It's such an awesome photo that several have inquired over the past twenty years since it was taken as to whether it was the work of a clever photoshop artist or AI. She recalls being happy in that moment. Happy, hopeful, and still quite youthful. Although she doesn't feel anything close to resembling youthful this morning, she's still quite happy and hopeful. And she still looks youthful thanks to her latest CRISPR therapy although it can't help everything with seventy-year-old bones.

"Oh, come now, Darius," she says, spinning quickly again in her seat so that she can rest her elbows in the middle of her massive mahogany desk. "Your boss is eighty going on thirty. We all know he subscribes to the notion of *Homo Deus*. It doesn't take a genius to realize he's found a way for CRISPR to work for him. Way more people are freaking out about how young he looked rather than the actual spectacle that took place. The public is starting to realize that we're not far away from man becoming God." She holds back a laugh, knowing how well this new tech really works. Fortunately for her, no one in her current life really knew her back when, and so has no context for how effectively it has de-aged Samantha.

"How unfortunate," says Darius. "I'm sure that was not his intent."

"But I thought you weren't in the know regarding last night's foray into solving gun violence and mass shootings."

"I said we didn't know it was coming. Or that it would be executed as such. But anyone who knows Elon—or has read any of the dozens of books written about him—knows how embarrassed he is that such incidents are still so prevalent in society. Especially after everything else accomplished these past few decades."

As Darius speaks, Samantha's gaze drifts momentarily toward the city below, its early morning lights flickering awake. *Embarrassed? Anyone who's truly awake and aware is embarrassed.* Despite the advancements, the gleaming skyscrapers that surround her, and the seamless tech integrating into daily life, the core problems—violence, ignorance, human folly—remain unerringly stubborn. Are we really progressing, or dressing up the same old world in new tech? *That's why my solution is so elegant . . .*

"Well, I'm not sure what answer he proposed last night, but that's not the reason you're calling me, is it, Darius?"

She stares into the layers of the city below and processes the conversation, her thoughts synchronized with the subtle movements of her eyes, which navigate the virtual interface of the Leaf effortlessly. *Tech is merely a tool, after all.* The realization solidifies like one of her many mantras. *We wield it either to build or to destroy; to veil our issues or to confront them squarely.* She always championed the latter, but doubts, unwelcome as always, intrude upon her certainty.

"Not necessarily, Ms. Ravensby. These matters are interrelated. Your tech is groundbreaking and serves a purpose, sure. But we're still not quite sure if it will do more harm than good in the end."

Darius touches on a truth, she concedes silently. Even Elon's most grandiose schemes, like all visionary projects, cast long, intricate shadows. But isn't that the essence of all human endeavors? Imperfect, yet perpetually striving for something beyond the present. She steadies her breaths, thinking fast and slow, like a chess master poised to make a critical move, staunchly aware that each word can change the dynamics of this delicate game of influence and negotiation.

"Boy, Darius—you are quite contentious these days. I guess it's tough with your boss man being a total wild card again. No longer being on that . . . what did you say? Inner circle? Yeah, that must've been a wicked little kick in the gut for you."

Samantha does not have a good feel for where this conversation is heading so she attempts to jam him before he can get off the line of scrimmage. Darius opened the door for her by divulging he's no longer a close confidant of Musk, corroborating what was reported all over every legitimate news and media outlet: Ever since Elon Musk's guru passed, he's more eccentric than ever. Poking a guy like Darius Simonmontha will go one of two ways for her, and she's no longer concerned with the overall conversation going south. She gets the sense that a lecture on the dangers of merging virtual reality technology with components of psychotropic compounds will be forthcoming. The last thing she wants this morning is a discourse on this particular challenge from a stooge like Darius.

"Elon is not the same. We all know that. But who is whenever they lose their own personal Yoda?"

Samantha snorts aloud, an old habit she tried to break since she identified it as a personal weakness back in her teens. It's difficult in this moment, however. The absurdity of comparing that little green doll to Sam Harris is too much to control before her amusement comes out sounding pig-like. Most pundits and much of the public attribute Musk's true ascent to his relationship with Harris. When the Making Sense podcaster started making sense for Musk. When he became his meditative and emotional compass, sometime in his late fifties. Musk took things to the next level for his mission and for mankind. While this is the general consensus, Samantha never bought in.

"You're right, and I'm sorry," Samantha says before Darius can continue. "I thought it was humorous when mentally comparing the two side-by-side." That and Samantha preprogrammed her Leaf to flash an image when her mind requested the comparison. "I was an enormous fan of Harris in my own right," she lies, her voice steady and convincing.

Inside, however, a wave of contempt rolls through her. Samantha harbors a deep-seated aversion to Harris's assertions that humans lack free will. *How was he ever taken seriously?* The idea that human actions are nothing more than the result of chemical reactions in the brain strikes her as not only scientifically reductionist but also fundamentally defeatist. *If we don't have free will, how can anyone claim to be a creator, an innovator, or a change-maker?* This question, sharp as a sword in her mind, cuts through any semblance of respect she might have harbored for the man. For Samantha, who built her career and life making decisive, strategic, and sometimes ruthless choices, the notion that these were not truly her own decisions is both absurd and offensive. This belief alone should have disqualified Harris from being a voice of reason in any public debate, let alone an advisor to visionaries like Elon Musk. *To think that such a man had that kind of influence on one of the greatest minds of our time . . .* The thought irritates her, a sharp pebble in her shoe, unbearable and inescapable.

"If you really listened to Sam Harris then you would be as cautious with your fusion of these technologies as we are. Most especially combining psychedelics with where VR is today. There's still so much we don't know."

Samantha hesitates to reply while not allowing herself to let out an agitated sigh. *This fool probably doesn't understand the Stoned Ape Theory as accepted science.* She doesn't want to get back on the defensive, however, and she sure as hell is not in the mood for a lecture. Nearly a half minute of awkward silence passes before Darius continues. "We're not far away from a time when people can just dip out of reality entirely and live in a virtual world. Loopd>In is only going to accelerate that. Accelerate and exacerbate the coming paradox. Ask yourself this, Ms. Ravensby: Do you really, truly want to be the one out front on this? And, by proxy, Elon Musk as well? Everything he accomplished could be wiped away if he were to be viewed as the one responsible for humanity retreating into a netherworld of our own making. Have you thought about this at all, Ms. Ravensby, or do you simply want to make your fortune and seize your fame?"

"We're providing people with an unforgettable and life-altering experience," Samantha snaps back, no longer able to bite her tongue and play the game with this fool. "The tech is here, and it's coming to the masses one way or another. The sustained speed of the HyperLoop is a crucial component currently in creating that experience—We both know that. But we're less than five years, maybe much sooner, away from being able to replicate that in any module. It'd be a shame for you to miss out due to unwarranted trepidation. It surprises me that Mr. Musk surrounds himself with such Luddites."

"Unwarranted? Ms. Ravensby, we're at the doorstep of a world in which over ninety percent of the population will be effectively useless when it comes to the workforce. Where do you think these billions will turn when they have no daily purpose, hmm?"

"Then let's finalize a long-term partnership and figure out the best path forward. Together."

"No, I'm afraid you only want to expand your product throughout our travel and logistics solutions for your own fiscal gain. I personally believe that your product is one of the most dangerous out there today. And I certainly don't want to be responsible for creating billions of sleeping zombies."

"Yeah, well, your boss thinks differently. He—"

"Don't presume to think you know my boss at all when you've met him once for a few fleeting moments. Ms. Ravensby, our discussion today is at an end. We will fulfill our contractual obligation and run Loopd>In within selected pods throughout the first quarter of 2050. We'll convene in three months. Good day."

"Wait!" Samantha yells. "Please wait one more minute. This is unrelated. Yesterday two young men entered my building here in downtown San Francisco. They were not authorized, nor did they have an appointment. One of my security robots got a clear retinal scan. One of them was Philipp Largo's son. Does any of this mean anything to you, or might you know something that could be connected?"

"Not a thing. I guess I wasn't even aware that he had a son. I haven't thought about Mr. Largo for years, not since his violent and untimely death. Now is that all, Ms. Ravensby?"

His condescension exudes more than anything across the connection. Samantha fantasizes about snapping him in half and tossing him into the Bay. She wonders how much Musk really knows these days. This simian twit is holding up the expansion of Loopd>In because he's intimidated by its potential. And he has the gall to demean her? He's not even smart enough to understand it's no coincidence about Largo's son being here. Samantha verified he came by way of the HyperLoop. So, in all probability he was one of the first commercial users of Loopd>In. If he's anything like his father then he's adroitly aware that Loopd>In will become the same kind of game changer that retinal Leafs, automated driving, and therapeutic psilocybin were for the masses. By a magnitude of one hundred or more. If only she didn't have to maneuver around such fools to make it happen.

She wastes no more time with Darius, but rather ends the call abruptly. Using her Leaf, it takes her less than ten seconds to track down Dante Largo's contact information. She's not sure what she should say to this kid now. She thinks about Philipp Largo. There was never a man quite like him that came into her life. She thinks about his unpublished book, as she pops up from her seat and walks over to stand directly in front of her office window, which overlooks the mesmerizing Bay. The sun returned, and a myriad of colors cover the prism of her entire view. Light blues and brilliantly faded pastels comprise the magnificent Californian sky.

Reflecting on the first time she met Philipp Largo, Samantha feels a wave of nostalgia wash over her. It was after one of his influential TED Talks on her campus. She was immersed in grad school, a period of her life where every new idea felt like it could spawn a revolution. Largo had captivated her, not just with his vision, but with his unwavering optimism and commitment to societal advancement. Initially, she found the concept of the *Time & Space* program somewhat whimsical, but a lengthy conversation with Largo over beers at the campus pub changed her perspective. He spoke of igniting a spark of curiosity in the youth, a flame so potent that it would be hard to extinguish throughout their lifetime. Samantha realizes now, looking out over the Bay, that Largo's vision has been unfolding for over a decade, shaping a generation. He was certainly on to something. *And still no one remembers him. Because of me.*

The memos and financial closeouts can wait. Her curiosity is piqued and her attention is fully focused on finding out why Philipp Largo's progeny briefly entered her building, then darted out almost immediately. It's like he and his companion were on the run from something. She uses her Leaf again, this time to track down his whereabouts. It takes her less than a minute. But the device informs her of much more. When she learns who he is with, she feels drugged like entering the first stage of a surreal and nightmarish trip. Her head feels as heavy as a fully loaded suitcase, packed with bricks and concrete blocks. She slumps back down in her chair and tries to regain her composure using a series of breathing and meditative techniques so that she can wisely contemplate her next move. Again, doing her best to think fast and slow. Coincidence rarely holds up to scrutiny. Samantha knows this is shaping up to be one hell of a day, and everything is a clock. *How in the hell do Philipp Largo's son and Charisma Sinclair know each other*?

CHAPTER THIRTY-ONE

CALL THE BANNERS

"You give me grief about thieving women from you, and yet when you have one practically giftwrapped, you don't take a swing. I don't get it." Chew chomps on his gum with exaggerated gusto, mimicking a caricature of a yesteryear hillbilly chewing tobacco. His tone is playful yet probing, the twang in his voice adding a layer of irony, while his aim is clear: to needle a response, any response, from his friend.

But Deuce remains contemplative, his gaze fixed upward, captivated by the hotel lobby's dome. The ceiling swirls with an array of pastels—soft pinks, muted blues, and gentle lavenders—that blend into an abstract image reminiscent of so many others he remembers with lucidity as a youngster whenever coming to visit this city with his father and oftentimes with Chew. He can tell his friend is a bit peeved and probably suffering from sleep deprivation, but after receiving the message, there's no time for rest now.

"You can learn so much about a woman when you get naked with them," Chew continues. "Sometimes I wonder if you ever listen to me."

"Knock it off," Deuce snaps, his voice steeped in both irritation and amusement, yet he does not break his gaze from the dome. Around them, the hotel buzzes with a flurry of constant activity, the air filled with the comings and goings of guests, all greeted by the eerily lifelike humanoid robot concierge staff, their movements fluid and their facial expressions uncannily genuine. These robots are so convincing that many could effortlessly pass the Turing test. It's a striking scene of the times—No human staff in sight at midday of New Year's Eve in one of the busiest hotels on the West Coast.

"It wasn't the right time," Deuce says, his voice trailing off as he begins to walk toward the hotel exit, Chew following close behind. The marble floor underfoot reflects the light of the hotel's lobby, casting ephemeral shadows that dance around their steps. "Besides, I needed actual rest if we're serious about ending this decade with a bang. And . . ." He pauses, a sly smile creeping across his face, the kind reserved for when he knows he has a piece of news that will unsettle Chew. "I got a message that changes things. We're about to have additional company soon."

Chew stumbles to a halt, blinking like he misheard. His eyebrows shoot up, and without a word, he lets his gum fall into the trash can beside the exit—like his brain ejected it out of sheer disbelief. "Additional company? Who?"

As they step outside under the hotel entrance's black canopy, the morning sun meets the towering skyline and creates a series of long shadows on the pavement. A cool breeze carries the distant sounds of the waking city. Deuce continues, his voice tinged with both urgency and fatigue. "When we went into the lobby of that skyscraper yesterday, before the chaos in the Mission District, we were recognized. Well, I was. Samantha Ravensby herself reached out to me directly. She—"

"Hold on a second. Do you mean that Ravensby chick who stole your girlfriend's business?!"

Deuce shakes his head, the weight of sleeplessness starting to hit him hard even with the adrenaline stemming from what's to come when they meet Samantha. He hasn't slept at all in over twenty-four hours and it's behavior like this from Chew that tends to grate on him most. "There's so much wrong with that statement, I won't even start. But yes, Samantha Ravensby. And before you jump to conclusions, she wants to meet because . . . she knew dad."

The revelation hits Chew like a thunderbolt, eyes blinking erratically for a few moments as the shock in Deuce's revelation is fully absorbed. "Serendipity has a way of revealing intent when you dig deep enough," he says, eyeballing his friend with a serious and sharp look. Although Chew is exhausted too, there's no way either is going to get any rest until this impromptu meeting happens. There are so many questions, so much happenstance, it's starting to feel like a fever dream. The universe rarely stumbles blindly.

Deuce nods solemnly, his tone ultra resolute like it was back in the day when he took the mound. "Spot on there, my friend. I need your powers of charm and cunning to deduce some stuff, namely if it's her or Charisma who's telling the truth. And, I'd sure like to know how she knew Dad."

"This is right in my wheelhouse, pal. Lead the way."

They step out from the canopy, emerging into the bright morning light. The city's noises bubble up around them, a background hum that seems distant as they each get lost in a sea of thought. The intricate web of connections—Samantha Ravensby's sudden interest, her unknown ties to Deuce's dad, and Charisma Sinclair's enigmatic past—creates a vortex of uncertainty that challenges their longstanding skepticism about fate and coincidences.

Deuce glances at Chew, feeling a familiar sense of solidarity. Chew, with his quick wit and unwavering loyalty, has always been his anchor in tumultuous times. As they stand on the brink of potential revelations and momentous insights, Deuce finds his usual dismissal of 'everything happens for a reason' being tested. The confluence of events, too intricate to be mere chance, gnaws at his rational mind.

"I've always thought that coincidences were just that—coincidences, nothing else," Deuce muses aloud, his eyes scanning the bustling street as the city awakens with a vibrancy so visceral Deuce can taste it in the air. This final holiday of the year . . . of the decade. "But all this . . . it's like pieces falling into place in the most bizarre way. And I didn't even realize we were putting a complex puzzle together until a few moments ago."

Chew, usually quick to brush off any notion of destiny or preordained meaning as well, nods in agreement, his playful demeanor subdued by the weight of the conversation and what's soon to come. "It's quite strange, isn't it? You know me better than anyone: I've never been one for belief in fate, but . . . this entire situation . . . It's like we're being pulled by a herculean current that we can't see."

Deuce closes his eyes for a moment and focuses on everything that's gone down, using an old mindfulness practice his father taught him years ago. He's trying to see the strings, the connections. The revelation that Samantha Ravensby knew Philipp Largo, intertwined with the mystery of Charisma Sinclair's claims about Loopd>In, creates a labyrinth too intricate to be mere chance. Chew's beach walk with Mulva, revealing possible delusions of Charisma, adds another layer of complexity, pushing him to question everything since arriving in San Francisco.

Deuce's gaze drifts to the horizon, where the rise of the new day lifts the remnants of the Bay's fog, revealing the sprawling cityscape city—a visual metaphor for their unknown journey ahead. “It’s as if we’re part of a narrative that’s been written without our knowledge. Cogs in the wheel of a simulation, perhaps. Ravensby’s connection to my dad, all things Charisma . . . It’s hard to keep dismissing it as a random chain of events.”

Chew gives a resigned sigh, his usual bravado replaced by introspection. “There has to be a reason for all these connections, Deuce. Let’s find out how she knew your pop. Then we can dance around the whole Loopd>In/Charisma thing when the opportunity presents itself. Whatever this is, whatever ties all these threads together, we’re going to unravel it. Together. Where are we meeting her?”

“Right here, man. This hotel’s lobby. She should be arriving any time now. That’s why we’re forgoing sleep. I want to get to the bottom of this and then we’ll get some shuteye. Party with the ladies after the sun goes down.”

“Well then,” Chew responds, a spark igniting in his eyes. “It’s game day. You’ve always been best when the light shines brightest, my man. Let’s do this.”

Their friendship has been the one solid thing in Deuce’s life. He trusted Chew with his life a million times over. There’s no one he’d rather be in a foxhole with and certainly no one better to engage the likes of Samantha Ravensby and get her to spill the intel. The final hours of the decade stretch before them, a canvas to be painted with truths and revelations. In this moment of uncertainty, one thing remains clear: they are in this together, ready to face whatever destiny has in store.

CHAPTER THIRTY-TWO

A DAY ON THE COSMIC CALENDAR

In the subdued light of their hotel room off Haight Street, Mulva lounges on the bed, her eyes darting across the glow of the retinal Leaf display. She's borrowing it from Charisma, the first time she's used one. The breaking news streams in a vivid cascade of bright colors: "San Francisco Charges Elon Musk with Inciting a Riot." She chuckles at the absurdity, and dark amusement highlights her tone. "Typical Musk bullshit," she mutters, shaking her head. "I'm sure he'll get away with it."

Charisma gazes forlornly out the window at the cityscape bathed in morning light. The bustling street below seems a world away as she's ensnared in her own tumultuous thoughts. The news about Musk barely scratches the surface of her consciousness. Charisma is yearning for Deuce, craving the comfort of his voice, the solidity he brings amid the chaos of her life. It felt like they parted ways abruptly on the beach, but she's hopeful they'll meet up later to celebrate the New Year together.

Mulva tries to snap her back to reality. "Charisma, come on. It's all good. We'll see those boys soon."

"It's not that, it's . . . I made my struggles sound so significant. Compared to Deuce, they seem so trivial. His father, his loss . . . I feel so . . . insignificant . . . a complete fool."

The early morning ambiance of San Francisco and the energy emanating from the streets at this hour, the very final day of this decade, stand in stark contrast to what's going on inside Charisma. She feels like she's already screwed it up and chances are she won't even see Deuce again. It's a hollowness like she went through following her purge from Loopd>In. The pit in her stomach returned as quickly as it dissipated earlier when she was still in Deuce's presence.

Mulva reaches out, her hand resting reassuringly on Charisma's shoulder. "Don't do this to yourself. Please, not now. You both found each other for a reason. Let's see where it goes. And if nothing else, let's have a blast with those guys tonight."

Charisma turns from the window, her stare lost in the distance, not quite meeting Mulva's. She sits on the edge of the bed and a pang of realization crosses her face, a mixture of awe and a deep, resonant understanding. "It's surreal, knowing Deuce's dad had a hand in shaping the *Time & Space* program," she says, her voice tinged with reverence. "I know what it did it for me . . . It didn't just light the spark. It kindled a firestorm of curiosity and passion driving me ever since. It's part of who I am, embedded within my DNA, and it's the light guiding me through my darkest days."

Mulva edges closer. She leans in, like she's trying to hold some of the weight Charisma has been carrying. "I know it feels like the world is against us so often," she says, her voice a gentle anchor for a change. "But think back to Mr. Cody, remember? Our very own cosmic sherpa, guiding us through the mysteries of the universe with grace and enthusiasm that made everything seem possible."

Charisma lets out a small laugh, a brief respite of warmth lighting up her features. "Our gateway to the cosmos," she says, the nickname they had affectionately coined for their beloved teacher. "Experiencing that program for the first time, with him as the guide, was like being given a key to unlock the universe." She pauses, her eyes glinting with the vivid memory of a defining moment. "I'll never forget the day he rolled out that life-sized poster, a sprawling canvas that stretched across the classroom wall. It was a visual chronology of the known universe, all of its 13.8 billion years condensed into a single 'cosmic calendar.' Each month represented over a *billion* years, each day nearly forty million years, and every single moment of human history was just a fleeting blip at the very edge of the December 31 marker."

Charisma's voice grows tender as she recalls the awe that swept through the room that day. "He pointed to the various epochs with his laser pointer, tracing the slow dance of cosmic evolution—from the Big Bang, through the formation of stars and galaxies, to the rise of life on Earth. He narrated the story of the universe as if he were letting us in on the secrets of time itself. And he always answered our barrage of questions with such patience and insight, making me believe there wasn't a single mystery we couldn't unravel together. Even now, I go back to those lessons. The context especially. I can't believe I even thought about using you to help me kill Samantha. That's not the right move. It never was. There's another way."

She begins to pace all over the room, trying to recall every bit of their conversation from the diner to the beach. "To think," she says, her voice thick with emotion, on the verge of tears, "Deuce's father was instrumental in creating something that's touched millions of lives, including ours. And then, to lose him and Tristan Harris in such a horrific way . . ." she trails off, the enormity of Deuce's loss enveloping her in a silent, somber cloud. She falls back onto the bed abruptly, the thoughts fastening her to the spot, her hands clasped as if in prayer or in an attempt to hold herself together.

Mulva extends her support with a tenderness that belies her usually tough and raw exterior. "We've all got our demons, Charisma. Your pain, your fight, it's valid. Important. You know this, girl." Her voice, usually so full of fire, is a soothing balm, acknowledging the shared scars they both carry. She pulls Charisma back up to her sitting position on the bed.

Charisma smiles at her friend and closes her eyes. She attempts to lose herself in the memories of Mr. Cody's classroom, where the seeds of her lifelong quest were sown. But this pleasant remembrance doesn't last long as she's suddenly jolted back to the present by a hard shake from Mulva and her urgent tone that follows: "Charisma, holy shit. Listen to me. I got a message from Chew . . . Deuce and him, they're walking into a meeting with Samantha Ravensby as we speak. What in the holy fuck?"

The news hits Charisma like a dagger to the heart, her body tensing, then releasing a raw, visceral scream of frustration as she leaps to her feet and rushes toward the room's back wall. Her scream echoes through the room and feels like it shakes the entire hotel, a sound so fierce and laden with rage that Mulva recoils slightly, her own resolve shaken by the intensity of Charisma's reaction.

The moment hangs between them as they stare silently and unblinkingly at each other, charged with energy and emotion, as Charisma tries to grapple with the betrayal and the pain of knowing that Deuce, someone she's come to care for deeply, is now unwittingly entangled with the woman she loathes above all others. Her own personal Lex Luthor. Mulva stares at her intently, concern and determination in her eyes. "We'll get through this," she murmurs, more to herself than Charisma. "Together."

Charisma screams a second time, her face flushed bright red as the feeling pours out of her and rips through the air, raw and animal, echoing throughout the room like the cry of something severely wounded but not broken. When it finally tears out of her completely, she doubles over, clutching her knees, chest heaving with every breath as if her body is trying to shake loose the panic and fury. Mulva covers her mouth with both hands in the form of a cup. Charisma slowly straightens. Her eyes burn now, not with fear, but something colder, sharper. She turns to Mulva, her voice low and steady. “Let’s move. Now. Time to take this woman head on, once and for all.”

CHAPTER THIRTY-THREE

MAKING SENSE PART I

"She should be arriving any time, right?" Chew asks, his tone laced with his typical eagerness, but also carrying a hint of apprehension, like a child on the edge of a thrilling yet uncertain adventure. They are cocooned in the stillness of the now foggy San Francisco morning, the final hours of the decade ticking by with a gray, ethereal blanket now draping the city. They tucked themselves away in an alley, an oasis of serenity amid the urban buzz, the smooth pavement beneath their feet reflecting the misty skies hovering over the great city. Two murals depicting a menacing dragon and gigantic elephant bookend the columns of the alley. The artwork is nothing short of world class. LEDs are hung in rows all up and down with several businesses sharing the alley and using it for seating when the temperatures are right and the inside crowds overflow. Not today, however, with the temp stuck in the upper 40s.

Deuce, deep in thought, barely registers Chew's question, his eyes fixed on the enigmatic, foggy blanket hovering above. "I'm not sure," he says, his gaze shifting from the murals to the bustling hotel lobby across the street. He's drawn to the fluidity of the crowd, each person their own story, oblivious to the roller coaster he's been on since he set foot in town. "I told her to meet me in the hotel bar as soon as it opens. But I want to gauge her the moment she steps in— check if she's got company or not. That's why we're in this alley."

"Did you say anything about me? Does she know I'll be with you?" Chew's curiosity is evident in his shifting expressions. Deuce can't help but laugh at his friend's unchanging nature, always the seeker of thrill and romance. "Relax," he says. "You'll get your introduction. Let's keep this smooth, alright? I need your A game, now more than ever."

The city's year-end energy, the bizarre events they witnessed, and the impending meeting with Samantha Ravensby, coalesce into a surreal atmosphere that hangs heavily around them. Chew pops a bubblegum flavored gummy he packed before their departure. Deuce shakes his head. "What did I just say? A game, man! I don't need you all whacked out."

"Relax, Deuce. This is nothing. It'll help me keep it together, if nothing else. You know I know what I'm doing."

And there's that wide grin he's adorned to get him into and out of countless situations since their youth. Deuce knows he needn't worry. There's never been anyone near as reliable as his best friend. As he's about to offer Chew a compliment, his thoughts are interrupted by a roar coming from the heavens. It's as loud as an old-school locomotive running at full speed through a whistle stop. The roar dissipates to a loud purr for about a minute then goes away entirely. Deuce can tell it's coming from overhead, but the density of the morning's fog clouds his vision. Whatever it was, it wasn't around for long. He checks the time. Samantha should be here any minute.

He lets out a sigh and steps a foot outside the alley, taking in the sites of the streetscape, the trees perfectly trimmed covered in bright white LED lights, their beds tidily prepped and made. Music comes in all directions and everyone he sees come and go is happy, supremely joyous at the turn of the year, smiles and laughs as prevalent as the low-hanging clouds drifting throughout the Bay. It wasn't too long ago when San Francisco was written off. Destined to fall into a spiral of calamity and misery of which she'd never recover. Prophets of doom could be found on just about every publication, platform, and street corner around the time he was born, those Terrible Twenties. Now, not so much. For the past decade or more, San Francisco reclaimed her spot as a crown jewel of the American West and showed once again that dismissing her as a dystopian hellscape is as silly and shortsighted as throwing away a diamond because it's covered in dirt.

A message comes through Deuce's Leaf—Samantha Ravensby is already at the hotel bar. His plan to observe her arrival is foiled. His heart races as he realizes the gravity of the moment—a face-to-face with the woman intricately linked to Charisma and mysteriously somehow to his late father.

"Let's go," Deuce urges, grabbing Chew beneath his elbow as he bolts into motion, his strides long and unyielding, like a man chasing down fate. His jaw is tight, shoulders squared, each step hitting the pavement with purpose. He knows they're about to walk a tightrope. The connections between Charisma, Samantha, and his father are too entangled to be coincidence. Something larger, potentially dangerous, is unfolding.

"Wait, what's our play here?" Chew asks? "We need to be on the same page. Are you leading this? Do you want me to flirt with her? Or if you want me to keep quiet, I can . . ."

"We're about to find out how she knew dad," Deuce interrupts. "And what it is that she wants. Let's start there. I'm not even sure

I'm going to bring up anything about Charisma or Loopd>In. Let's just see where it goes. I wonder how long she's been in there," he says as they both reenter the lobby. "And if she brought any company with her." He grinds his teeth. They were thrown into this chess game without a clear strategy, but he's ready to make his move.

"Alright, my man," Chew says, as they are back in the lobby surrounded by guests and the hotel's robotic, humanoid service staff. "You do your thing and find out what you're looking for. I got your back all the way."

They walk hurriedly, together in stride, through the lobby and make the turn toward the hotel's bar. There she is, donning a skintight purple crop top and feathery black shawl draped over her toned, muscled shoulders. She's even more attractive in person than any of her digital portraits or online avatars.

"From the looks of it, you must be Philipp Largo's son, I presume." Samantha Ravensby's gaze falls on Deuce as he walks into the bar alongside Chew. As soon as she asks, her attention shifts toward Chew and her eyes light up while she eyes him top to bottom.

"I'm Dante Largo, but you can call me Deuce. This is my friend, Chew." Standing right next to Chew, Deuce is slightly overshadowed by his buddy's magnetic and imposing presence.

"A pleasure to meet you both," she says with both warmth and subtle intrigue. Deuce and Chew take their seats at a roundtable across from Samantha. At this early hour, they're the bar's only patrons.

The bar holds a quiet, waiting stillness. Every surface appears to catch the early light like static on chrome. Frosted glass panels diffuse the winter sun, casting a pearlescent sheet across velvet stools and brushed steel accents. There's a quiet precision to everything—as if the place has been expecting them for years. Low-hanging brass chandeliers radiate a warm, muted light across the rich mahogany counters, the surfaces polished to a mirror-like gloss that reflects the array of crystal decanters and glassware lined meticulously behind the bar. The air is tinged with the faint aroma of aged wood and lingering spices, a hint of cardamom perhaps, mixed with the subtle undertones of bourbon and old leather, evoking a sense of the storied past this place holds.

Art deco elements, from the geometric patterns etched into the bar stools to the ornate, gilded frames of the wall paintings, speak to a bygone era of glamour and opulence. Soft jazz music, barely audible, drifts through the room, the slow saxophone solos weaving through the still air, adding a layer of acoustical velvet to the ambiance.

"Deuce, first of all, I want to start off by apologizing. I should've reached out to you far sooner. Your father . . . he was a hero of mine in several ways." The quietness of the bar, combined with the intimate setting, creates a bubble around their table, making their conversation feel both secluded and intensely focal. The world outside continues to slowly wake on the holiday, but inside this bar, time seems to slow down, amplifying each word, each glance, as if history itself is paying attention to their exchange.

Deuce does not respond immediately, lowering his eyes from Samantha's direct gaze. "He was that to many," Chew says. Deuce knows Chew doesn't like awkward silences and was bound to speak up. He wants to get as much out of Samantha as possible, although his intuition is telling him that she can't be trusted.

Samantha moves her gaze over to Chew for a pointed moment, then looks back to Deuce. "You're not over this death, are you? How could you be? He was such . . ." She trails off, but doesn't break eye contact with Deuce. She lets out a long sigh and says, "It was one of the worst days of my life, too."

"Samantha—" Deuce says, as a waist-high android server shaped like a large water jug with wheels approaches their table. Samantha shoos it away with an open hand and he continues. "I appreciate your sympathies, but I assure you I'm fine. I am curious as to how well you knew him and how you knew him."

She smiles, leans back in her chair, and crosses her legs the opposite way she's had them during this encounter. "To be honest with you, Deuce, I kind of stalked him. He gave a TED Talk at the University of Virginia. I was getting my master's there at the time. After his talk—which I found to be mostly riveting—I sought him out on campus and talked him into having drinks with me at a local pub."

Deuce glances over at Chew. He nods back at Samantha and she continues.

"Let's just say the guy was far more charming and inspiring one-on-one than he was on stage." Deuce doesn't appreciate the look on her face as those words come out, subtly hinting at something romantic and possibly sexual. "Your father wasn't at all pretentious. He had no ulterior motives. He simply thought that . . ." As she trails off, Chew jumps in.

"Turn a generation of kids into space boys and girls and the consequences will be mighty and they will be good," Chew says, grinning ear-to-ear. It never gets old for Deuce when Chew hits the mark with an old Phillip Largo quote.

"Something like that, yes. I'd describe it differently, but that works. A generation of space boys and girls. That's you now, right? The new generation all grown-up and come of age. Our beloved little UnPluggers." She smiles wide at Chew with her eyes piercing into him like a wildcat ready to pounce. When she licks her upper teeth for a brief moment Deuce can feel the steam coming off Chew.

Oh Lord. *Here we go.* "Yeah, dad was sure big into that. He—"

"Big?" Samantha interrupts. "Deuce, you do realize none of that happens without your father? I know that he's largely been forgotten by the masses, but surely you're aware of his involvement with . . ."

Chew pipes in again for his friend with a sharp edge in his voice. "Lady, you don't think we know all this? It was Philipp Largo, this guy's pop, who put Musk and Sam Harris together. He was the catalyst for everything that came after that. Please, we're not in need of a history lesson."

Samantha smirks and shakes her head. She motions the android server back over to their table and orders an espresso martini. "My treat, fellas. What's your poison?" Both Deuce and Chew order spicy Bloody Marys and nothing else.

"It amuses me how much credit you get for the progress and positivity ensconced in our culture. In a sad irony, Philipp Largo hardly gets any." Something in the way she says it makes Deuce think that she's proud of it, his dad being left to the dustbin of history.

"The truth is Samantha, I—we—didn't know everything. I was tied up trying to make the big leagues and Chew here has been an integral part of the McWhorter Foundation since high school. There was a stretch of time before his death where we didn't see each other all that much."

"Funny," she responds. "I would've guessed it to be the other way around. Your friend here certainly looks like he could be a professional athlete." She winks at Chew and it's as if the temperature in the bar instantly goes up ten degrees. "Kidding aside, do you know how it was that Philipp Largo bridged that gulf? It's a stretch to say that the Musk-Harris relationship was, how'd you say it? The catalyst for all that came after . . ." She trails off with a laugh. Although Deuce is picking up some serious sinisterly vibes, there's no denying her sex appeal. He's worried Chew won't be able to contain himself if she's any more suggestive.

"To be honest, I was never a fan of Sam Harris, but when you look at it objectively there's no arguing how much he helped Elon when he was brought on as an advisor."

"How do you know all this?" Deuce asks. "How close were you?"

"To Elon? Never that close. I've only met him a handful of times. But I was very close to your father for a time. Until we had a falling out. But that's neither here nor there. Back around the time we all thought the world was going to come unglued, the Terrible Twenties or whatever the latest twit in journalism refers to them as, Elon Musk was turning into his own father. And he hated his father, Errol, for several legitimate reasons. Legend has it that your dad arranged a trip of sorts, with both Harris and Musk. Psilocybin. Magic mushrooms in nature. He joked to me that if Bill Maher could sit down and have dinner with Donald Trump, then Sam and Elon could at least attempt to fix the contentiousness that bloomed in the wake of COVID. They used to be friends. By the mid-2020s they hated each other. Your father was on a mission to alleviate partisanship between great thinkers. To him, there was no better place to start than with Sam and Elon. He had the perfect window once the Trump administration announced it was going to deem Christianity as the official religion of the United States. He knew that would finally be a bridge too far for Musk. He took his chance and got them both together for a walk in the woods under the spell of psychedelics. I never heard the specifics, but everyone is aware of the outcome."

Deuce is on the edge of his seat. This woman, while exuding a Cersei Lannister type of energy, has no reason to lie to him. Chew must be on edge as well as he's already finished his Bloody Mary.

"You didn't know any of this?" she asks, smiling and lightly shaking her glass with her right arm outstretched. "Astonishing," she says to herself. "Not even his own son." She sits back in her seat in a relaxed fashion, exhaling, and shaking her head. "I'm guessing you didn't know about his last book."

"That I did know," Deuce says. "He didn't have the chance to get it completed. I was planning to do it, but . . ." He trails off, meekly, not knowing what to say next. He doesn't want to come off as weak in front of this woman, but he's struggling to come up with an excuse as to why he didn't get the job done.

"So, you've read it?" Samantha asks. "I wasn't aware there were any copies out there."

"Just scribbles. It was a reflection of the twenties mostly, from what I recall. Dad hated how everything had become so ridiculously polarized. I remember him saying it was the height of absurdity that we could deflect asteroids, launch the James Webb, and communicate with whales, but as a society we couldn't agree on plain election results or treat political opponents with any semblance of respect."

"Are you aware of the title?" Her eyes light up again, eyebrows raised a full inch.

Deuce shakes his head and looks over to Chew. He sits up, puts his drink down, and chimes in. "Lady, wait a minute. How do you know all of this? You can't be that much older than we are," Chew says, exuding his personal charm as he reaches out to touch Samantha's hand.

"Ha! Lucky for you, you're a pretty fool. I'm only a few months away from turning seventy-one."

Chew pulls his hand back and looks over to Deuce before shouting, "No way, Samantha! Forty-five, tops! C'mon, what do you take us for?"

She stretches her arms behind her head and once again looks relaxed. Deuce is taken with how easily she can move between states of being: loose to imposing as quickly and easily as a passing thought. "I see everybody's talking about Elon's little stunt last night," she says, breaking eye contact, gazing up to the ceiling.

"Yeah, we were there!" Chew exclaims.

"They're not really talking about his sophomoric attempt to

quell public gun violence, are they?" In the next breath she instructs their robot server to bring a fresh round of drinks.

"So, what are you trying to say?" Deuce asks, nudging his friend underneath the table. "That you and Musk found the same fountain of youth?"

A group of five enter the bar for a brief moment, before turning around and exiting as quickly as they came. Samantha and the boys continue to have the place to themselves.

"You didn't think we'd stand idly by and allow CRISPR and our other brilliant biotech of the day to only cure and prevent disease, did you?" Her rhetorical question is chilling. Deuce is tracking with her and gets a sense of what's coming next. "These powers we now possess. Call them whatever you wish, they'll destroy all of us if we let anyone and everyone use them. You must understand this, right?"

Their drinks are delivered by the same server. Samantha sucks half her martini glass down in a single gulp. Neither of the guys touch theirs initially as she continues.

"Tell me, what do you know of *Homo Deus*, Deuce Largo?"

"We were just talking about this the other day, weren't we, Chew? It's the next logical step in evolution, right Samantha?" Deuce plays coy, again trying to see if she'll divulge more if he continues to go along.

"Don't fuck with me, Deuce. You won't like me when I'm vexed."

"Not at all. I wouldn't dare. Just answering your intriguing question as straightforward as I can." He takes a sip of his drink, realizing he wants to go back a step.

"Hold on. Before we get all heavy into *Homo Deus*, I'd like to know if you were aware of the title to my dad's unpublished book. You asked if we knew a moment ago."

She takes another drink, this one more of a sip, and sighs exhaustively. She bobs her head down, back, and side-to-side as if working out a kink of great tightness. "Of course I knew, Deuce. Why do you think I asked? It's called *God Bless You, Mr. Trump*. Written by a man who referred to him as the Orange Goblin. How's that for irony?"

Deuce thinks back to his conversation with Charisma a few hours ago on the beach. It makes sense, yet something stirs inside Deuce. How does she know so much more about this than he does?

"I get the sense that you were in love with my father," he says, coming off strong and cold, however desperate to know more. Deuce is no longer in the mood for games or subtlety. Chew gives him an approving wink and nod.

"You're so naïve. Even more so than your father. I have no response to that. Go on and believe whatever you'd like. But for today, I do have other pressing matters. I asked you about *Homo Deus* because I wanted to glean whether you realized the movement's significance. Its necessity and importance for the future of everyone. And, truth be told, I asked because I know how the two of you got here. You were some of the first passengers to ride the HyperLoop. And some of the very first to experience my product during your journey."

"As in Loopd>In?" Chew asks, jumping back into the discussion. "Is it really *your* product?"

Samantha puts her glass down and seethes. Her temperament changes instantly with a glare that could kill. Deuce's heart skips a beat. He's not certain how dangerous this woman is, but he's worried he's about to find out."

"The two of you went to my company's headquarters yesterday. Why would you think that as the CEO of Loopd>In, it's not my product? What on earth would give you that idea? Let me guess . . . Was it Charisma Sinclair who planted that wicked little seed in your two little nitwit brains?"

CHAPTER THIRTY-FOUR

MAKING SENSE PART II

Her name alone springing from Samantha's lips sends a shiver down Deuce's spine. With his right foot he taps Chew's left. Before Samantha can say any more, he answers her with a feigned smile.

"Your condescension aside, we met her under the wildest set of circumstances in which I've met anyone—Last night in the Mission right as Musk was pulling his stunt. I hear your city is pressing charges against him for inciting a riot."

She purses her lips and leans in toward Deuce. "You're telling me that you didn't know her before? Hadn't known her at all previously?"

"That's right. She almost got trampled when the crowd went into a frenzy. We helped them out of the fray. Then we enjoyed one helluva story about Loopd>In while we got to know each other over coffee."

"Ha," Samantha snorts, but offers no other response. Deuce senses apprehension and a bit of dread grows across her face. Worry was not a look she wore earlier.

"It was hers, wasn't it?" Chew asks, puffing out his chest, lowering his left eyebrow in an over-the-top fashion. In the next instant, Samantha snaps back.

"Now listen here, you little shits," Samantha hisses like a cobra ready to strike. "Loopd>In is *mine*. The concept. The fusion of technologies. And the execution. I steered the ship. If she remained in control the entire enterprise would've cratered. That bitch is totally delusional if she told you otherwise."

"Is she?" Deuce asks, refusing to back down. "Must've hit pretty close to the mark to get you all riled up like this."

Samantha's eyes widen, her gaze seething across the table, but Deuce is confident that there's a there, there when it comes to Charisma's involvement and what Samantha is refusing to disclose.

"Look, Samantha, there's no reason to get hostile," Deuce says, attempting to diffuse the tension. "Like I've said, I didn't know either one of you existed twenty-four hours ago. But what I do know is that the experience while traveling here on the HyperLoop was like no other. If it's replicable outside the moving pods, no question it will be the latest tech that transforms the world."

Samantha relaxes from her attack position and slumps back in her chair, letting out a prolonged sigh. "I've heard that a lot lately," she says, taking a drink from her martini glass. "Both sides of the coin. The truth is . . . it's so *necessary*. It has to happen. And happen soon." Samantha sips her drink again, looking back and forth between the guys.

Who knows what's truly going on in her mind, something from menacing to unhinged. "What has to happen?" Deuce asks. "*Homo Deus*? You're on board with what all that entails?"

"Broad statement, but the short answer is yes," she says while in the next breath requesting a round of ice waters. Their android takes the order and moves along in a few seconds without interrupting. "But what's not debatable is that we need the masses to plug back in. Fully this time. Enjoy the virtual world in bliss while we finish the job."

This is precisely what Chew brought up back at the space bar the night before they left. It's what his father warned him about as well. The uber-elitists of this new age wouldn't be satisfied being in the 1 percent when it came to wealth. They wouldn't be satisfied with mega-influence over elected officials or control over markets, energy, development. That would all be small potatoes for them. No, they would strive to *evolve*, to transform into a higher class of species. One that saw humanity, *Homo sapiens* as an also-ran. They'd use twisted logic and wicked rationale to justify their means and ends. Like 'escaping the Great Filter.' Deuce didn't need any further proof or conjecture. Like he so often was, his father's forecast was spot on. And this dangerous future was already here.

"I'm tracking with you," Deuce says. "And I think that's heinous. Who gives you the right to play God?"

"Ha! That's precisely what I argued about with your father. For all his merits and charm, he could still be quite the fool. Sorry, not a fool per se, but somewhat of a naive eternal optimist. And in his case, fatally."

Deuce exchanges a look with Chew, shaking his head slightly. He's heard enough. "We came here, Samantha, because this place—once our favorite city to visit in our youth—became synonymous with ghosts and demons. Here, a few miles away, I learned of the MAGA massacre and my father's murder. I was supposed to play a ball game at Oracle II. Instead, it became the worst day of my life. We came here this time, we thought, to put all that mess behind us. Me especially. But now I realize that was all window dressing. A catalyst perhaps, but nothing more than ancillary theatrics to the true rub. I can't believe that I'm saying this, but it has to be fate. Some kind of cosmic destiny that my caveman-like brain can't quite comprehend."

"What, like the architect behind the screen? Some old, white, loquacious fellow dialing up all the buttons?" Nothing but condescension exudes from Samantha's retort.

"If examples from Hollywood help you, sure, fine," Deuce continues. "But I know in my bones this cannot all be happenstance. There must be other more powerful forces at play."

Deuce sits forward and crosses his hands as if in prayer. He closes his eyes briefly, trying to summon all the wisdom and courage his father tried to pass along to him during their brief time together. "Dad warned us about people like you. An elitist class taking over coupled with the rise of all this hyper-tech. That you'd use mantras like 'evolving into *Homo Deus*'s or 'Escaping the Great Filter' as your alibi, to do and get away with anything."

Samantha pounces. "Your father would be disgusted. You sound like every other UnPlugger—self-righteous, naïve. And let me guess . . . you're high or fucked up on psychedelics, or both, aren't you?"

The table falls silent. The android server brings her next round, same as the first. The guys decline a second drink. Deuce's mind swirls with how he should respond. He's not intimidated in the least. He's confident that she bought into his 'fate brought us here' diatribe, having spun that to cool her down, giving him a better chance of extracting more authentic intel.

"You know, Samantha, I don't know the truth about you and if you were really friends with my dad. Whether or not you heisted Loopd>In from that sweet young woman we met last night. But I do know this: The folks who helped get us here, guys like Sam Harris, my father . . . they'd be repelled by people like you."

"That's a laugh, Deuce," Samantha says and leans across the table, patronizingly patting him on the cheek. "The fact is that the death of Sam Harris might've been the best thing to happen to humanity in some time. Musk is no longer tethered to Luddite ideologies and misguided morality that will hold us back."

Her response makes him want to puke, but before he can respond, none other than Charisma and Mulva burst through the bar's main entrance. In the next instant he sees the gun.

CHAPTER THIRTY-FIVE

THE DEVIL YOU KNOW

In the morning light of the hotel lobby's bar, Charisma feels as if she's stepping into a slow-motion nightmare. The opulent surroundings, with their polished marble floors and the soft, sinister glow of ornate chandeliers, form a chilling backdrop to the unfolding drama. Clad in a fitted black leather jacket that hugs her like armor, she moves forward with a deliberate grace that belies the tumult of her emotions. The jacket, paired with dark trousers, gives her a striking, almost warrior-like appearance, echoing the dark resolve that settled over her. Beside her, Mulva's presence in her jet-black hoodie mirrors Charisma's ensemble, both prepared for confrontation, united in their purpose.

Every heartbeat pounds in her ears like thunder, mirroring the tumult of her emotions. Why now, why here? Her heart is a cacophony of emotions—pain, confusion, and unbridled fury—all swirling into a storm she can barely contain. She's gripped by a sense of betrayal as she sees Deuce, the one who stirred her soul from its long slumber, engaged in easy conversation with Samantha Ravensby, the architect of her ruin.

Mulva is a pillar of dark resolve. Her whispered words cut through the haze of Charisma's thoughts, sharp and clear. "What now, Wonder Woman? Do you really need to see any more?" Her voice carries the weight of unspoken battles, of loyalty that knows no bounds.

Charisma's eyes dart around, paranoid that Samantha's minions might lurk in the shadows. "She must be following us," she whispers, the thought unsettling her core. It's the only explanation that makes sense of this twisted theater.

The sight of Samantha casually touching Deuce's face, as if staking a claim, sends a jolt of raw, primal anger through Charisma. Rage courses through her veins, a burning desire to right the wrongs, to reclaim what was hers, and to protect what little she has left. Samantha Ravensby has been a menace haunting her life, and now, it seems, she's set her sights on Deuce.

For a fleeting moment, her mind is transported back to the day when her mother called her from Juarez, informing her about the horror that had taken place in the Mexican border city. She sounded nothing like Carmen on the phone and, for Charisma, Carmen never came back. She saw her mother, once vigorous and unbreakable, reduced to a shell by a tragedy she was unable to prevent. The memory was a blade, slicing through the years to remind her of the vow she made amid the ruins of the past; never again to stand by, helpless and defeated.

In that instant, Charisma's resolve hardens like steel tempered in fire. She understands, with a clarity that cuts through the fog of her rage, that this confrontation is more than a personal vendetta; it's a chance to redefine her legacy, to fight back against forces that sought to diminish and control her. She refuses to be a bystander in her own life, haunted by the cloud of failure and depression that claimed her mother.

"Give me that thing," Charisma demands, her words dripping with desperation and determination. She knows Mulva is armed, always prepared for a fight. The weapon feels foreign yet familiar in her grasp, a tool for justice and destruction.

Mulva's smile is grim, a silent acknowledgment of the path they're about to tread. Charisma can feel her presence like a shadow as they move through the lobby, an unstoppable force driven by years of pent-up fury. They cross the threshold like a thrown gauntlet. The quiet elegance of the bar cracks beneath their entrance. Samantha turns first, her smile freezing mid-sentence. Deuce rises halfway out of his seat, eyes wide, caught between recognition and alarm. Chew stiffens beside him. Charisma moves like she's being pulled by something primal and inevitable. Her only focus is the woman who orchestrated her downfall. The weight of the pistol in her hand is a harsh reminder of the gravity of her decision. This moment isn't merely about vengeance. It's a crucible, testing the essence of who Charisma Sinclair is and who she's willing to become in her fight against the devil she knows all too well.

CHAPTER THIRTY-SIX

BLOOD ON THE TRACKS

Deuce's mind flashes back to his father's musings on an old pop culture debate: Did Han shoot first? His father saw it as a prime example of how a small change could redefine a character's entire arc. In this harrowing moment, there is no ambiguity. In the tense silence that follows Charisma and Mulva's bold entrance, Samantha's hand twitches. Just slightly. But Deuce catches it. Before he can react, she moves. It's not a dramatic flourish—no shouting, no warning. Only a precise, practiced flick of her wrist. Smooth and silent. Her shawl falls open like a stage curtain, and from beneath it, she draws a weapon of her own. It is unlike anything Deuce has ever seen. Sleek. Angular. Matte black. Less like a gun and more like a piece of avant-garde sculpture, defying traditional expectations with its fluid, almost organic contours. Its surface, a deep, unreflective black, seems to swallow light, giving it an almost phantom presence in her hand. The weapon makes no sound, no cocking mechanism, no hiss of pressure release, not even a digital chirp. Just a faint shimmer along its surface, as if the very air around it recognizes what's coming. Deuce strains to hear something, anything, but the silence is absolute. It feels wrong, dread engulfs him. Like the moment before a lightning strike—charged, still, and inevitable.

As Samanta raises the weapon, the subtle glimmer of light traces its edges, the only indication of its deadly purpose. There's no flash. No recoil. Not even a whisper of air. Only a ripple—like heat rising off asphalt—briefly distorting the space between Samantha and the girls. A movement so subtle it could be missed in a blink.

Then they seize—Charisma first, her body tensing, eyes widening. She starts to move, but it's too late. Deuce sees her muscles lock, her weight shift slightly, as if her instinct were to shield Mulva, or strike out, or shout. He'll never know which. Mulva jerks in unison, caught mid-step, her jaw clenched, shoulders squared. She looks ready to leap across the room, a silent war cry coiled behind her eyes, but she never gets the chance.

They collapse together. The sound is soft but final—two bodies folding in on themselves, limbs tangled as they hit the floor. Blood spills out fast, a spreading halo on the tile. Deuce can't look away. His brain short-circuits. He was expecting a bang, a flash, something loud and unmistakable. This . . . is worse. The silence makes it feel clinical. Efficient and inhuman. He doesn't know what to do with what he just saw. The stillness of their forms on the floor—their limbs tangled, lifeless. Charisma's face is turned slightly toward him, her mouth parted as if a scream was cut short. One hand is curled into a fist, the other stretched out, fingers twitching once, then going still. Her eyes, half-lidden, are locked open in a gaze that's both accusatory and afraid. And Mulva . . . God, Mulva looked like she was fighting even as she fell. But it's Charisma's expression that brands itself into Deuce's mind. The last thing she ever showed the world: a frozen blend of fury and disbelief, locked into her features like a mask that never had time to fall away.

Deuce erupts. "What in the holy fuck!" He struggles to comprehend Samantha's cold, unemotional demeanor. Chew collapses into his chair, his face a portrait of shock and terror.

Samantha's voice cuts through the air, disturbingly calm, "I didn't want it to come to this. But I couldn't take any risks with those two." Her words hover over Deuce, as emotionless as her expression.

The scene quickly morphs into surreal efficiency as androids swarm the area, sanitizing the aftermath with robotic precision. Deuce looks on, paralyzed, as the grotesquerie of their situation begins to sink in. Samantha is in total control of this situation and has been from the jump. She guides them out of the bar and into the lobby, her composure unshaken. Patrol cars arrive, but there's absolutely no urgency. The officers' movements are casual, almost disinterested. Fear and confusion consume Deuce, his stomach feels as if it's been filled with a nitric acid while Chew remains mute.

Samantha converses briefly with the officers. Deuce has no idea who or what alerted them, but they seem to be following her orders. His stomach becomes even more acidic, his knees weak. He has to catch himself lest he fall to the ground. Samantha casually saunters back over to them and offers a detached apology. "I'm sorry you saw that. I couldn't let them threaten us, or worse." Her tone suggests a minor inconvenience rather than a life-altering event.

Deuce, knowing that he and Chew could be next, summons his courage as best he can in the moment. "You're a monster! They didn't have to die." His voice trembles with rage and despair. His hands shake like he's losing control of their movement and he feels like he's on the verge of vomiting violently.

"They were dangerous, Deuce," Samantha insists, her voice still eerily calm. "They were delusional, lost in their VR fantasies, claiming I stole Loopd>In."

Skepticism gnaws at Deuce. Samantha's narrative feels too crafted, too dismissive. She was scared about what they were set to reveal, wasn't she? But he, too, is frightened that in this moment this woman is capable of anything.

"What in the holy fuck," Deuce repeats with a whisper, his voice barely audible over the sound of his racing heart. He watches as the gun Charisma held is collected by a droid, his mind reeling, as it motors away, around the corner and out of sight.

"C'mon, let's get some air," Samantha suggests, her voice regaining its earlier energy. She leads them out, navigating the lobby with an eerie calmness. Deuce follows with Chew right behind, his mind still clouded with shock, fear, and exhaustion.

Outside, Samantha speaks briefly with more arriving officers, her words lost in the city's New Year's Eve day buzz. When she turns back to Deuce and Chew, her face is unreadable, almost stoic-like. "I'm really sorry you had to witness that, but again . . . I wasn't going to risk anything. Not with those two. The police were fully briefed on the situation. No need for either of you to speak to them. They said they have what they need and don't require a statement."

"You're evil," Deuce snaps. "You could have easily neutralized them without killing them. What, do you control the cops too?"

Samantha rolls her eyes dismissively and starts strutting away. Deuce, driven by a primal fear, but also an insatiable need for answers, follows.

"Those two were far too dangerous not to be dealt with effectively," Samantha begins, but Deuce cuts her off.

"They told us you stole Loopd>In. Is that why you killed them? To hide the truth?"

Samantha's expression hardens. "You don't understand a God damned thing. Your father . . . He wouldn't be proud that his son was such a simpleton."

Deuce, undeterred, counters, "You think you're above everything, don't you? Playing God, achieving *Homo Deus* at any cost?"

Samantha's response is cold. "Those two were an imminent threat. You saw the gun and the look in their eyes. And as for Loopd>In, I created it. I put it all together. Period. Full stop. Charisma Sinclair's claims were pure delusion, fueled by VR and irresponsible use of psychedelics. She was nothing without me. Loopd>In would have never seen the light of day."

"But why push a product that exacerbates the issue?" Deuce questions, his skepticism growing with each second.

"It's absolutely necessary. We're about to deal with tens of millions comprising an entirely *Useless Class.* Loopd>In will keep them occupied while we work toward . . . *evolving.* And toward achieving Sagan's dream of reaching the stars. Just like you boys were taught in school, right?" Her smile is as devilish as a fox slipping unnoticed through the henhouse. Deuce and Chew exchange a glance, realizing the magnitude of Samantha's words and vision. Philipp Largo's warning coming to dark fruition.

Deuce stumbles a step, his shoe slipping briefly on the slick tile before he regains his footing. The temperature dropped in the last hour since they were outside last, the chill of the morning air hitting him like a slap in the face, but it didn't clear the fog. Beside him, Chew keeps pace, his jaw clenched, eyes darting, barely breathing. Samantha strides ahead, unbothered. Deuce speeds up, closing the distance. "You think you can manipulate, and even kill, your way into this . . . status, don't you? And then attempt to zombify-America?"

Samantha smirks. "You're young, and not too enlightened, disappointingly. You certainly don't see the larger picture." Her smirk lingers and she appears like a jungle cat ready to pounce and devour either of them in a flash. Both Deuce and Chew are unnerved. "Our time together today is at an end. And I don't think

I want to see either one of you in the future. Don't let me catch you around here again," she says. "Probably a good thing your father isn't around anymore. He would be most displeased with such a pitiful excuse for a son." She stares at Deuce like she's contemplating another move then turns, stepping away from them and moving elegantly back toward the hotel lobby's grand entrance. Deuce watches Samantha disappear from view, the sudden, but familiar roar of an engine breaks the silence, drawing their attention upwards. The unmistakable silhouette of an aerocar cuts through the San Franciscan fog, roaring powerfully as it ascends into the sky. Deuce realizes this was how she was able to beat them to the meeting spot. *We were the bait.* She used us to lure Charisma into her trap . . .

As the horrific reality of the situation settles, Deuce and Chew stand frozen. Deuce's shock wanes and gives way into a profound sadness. Chew's face is covered in sweat conveying horror and a deep sadness, his usually buoyant demeanor extinguished by the double-murder they witnessed. "God, Deuce . . . I . . . I was the one who messaged Mulva. If I hadn't—" Chew's voice cracks, the guilt wringing in his words.

Deuce, his heart a wild maelstrom, places a firm hand on Chew's shoulder, steadying them both against the sway of their emotions. "Chew, look at me," he commands, his voice equal parts sorrow and steel. "They were going to find us anyway. You know the tech, the surveillance everyone has at their disposal. This is not on you, so don't allow your mind to stay there. You understand me?"

But Chew's gaze is distant, haunted. "We were just getting to know them . . . Charisma, she was . . ." His words cannot encapsulate the whirlwind of a connection cut brutally short.

Deuce nods, his jaw clenched tight as he forces back the tide of his own anguish. "I know. And now we owe it to them. That bitch might've drawn first blood, but she doesn't know what she's up against."

"I don't think there's any point in talking to those 'cops,'" Chew says, nodding back to the hotel's main entrance where they've all gathered.

"Not at all," Deuce responds. "They're clearly in her pocket. Let's get the hell out of here."

As they stride away from the dark tableau back into the uncertain light of day, Deuce's mind whirls with the gravity of their new reality. He can't help but wonder about his father's true sentiments regarding Samantha Ravensby. Had his dad ever mentioned her in passing, a shadow in his personal network of visionaries, pioneers, and all sorts of other characters? Deuce can't recall a single instance, which only deepens the mystery. Nothing she said earlier can be trusted, but he's still confident there was a connection. *Why on earth would Dad ever associate himself with such a vile human?*

"You think she'll have us followed?" Chew's voice quivers slightly. "I wouldn't be surprised if she has this entire block and the hotel bugged."

"Everything is on the table with her. We must be cautious," Deuce replies, his eyes scanning their surroundings. The weight of Samantha's perceived omnipotence looms over them, eerie and foreboding.

"Are you sure you're ready to take on someone this powerful?" Chew's concern is palpable.

"Absolutely," Deuce says, his determination unwavering. "In a way, I've been looking for a fight like this since dad died." He pauses and looks up to the sky, lips pursed eyes squinting. "I know I ran away and hid for so long following his death. I know I could've done so much better. It's so awful it's taken a jolt like this to . . ." He looks his best friend directly in the eye and continues. "I'm ready to re-ignite that pact Dad and I made years ago. But this time the daily overdrive is going to have a singular focus. She really thinks she can kill two people with no repercussions? Zombify America, or the world, and then waltz off into immortality? Not without some good old-fashioned resistance, by-God. Chew, she's the perfect adversary for a couple guys like us. This might not have been the plan coming out here, but you better believe that I have a mission now."

Chew nods and puts his hand on Deuce's shoulder. "We had one damned fine teacher, buddy. The absolute best. I do know that without a doubt."

Deuce steps back and takes a moment, allowing the cacophony of the city to fade into a backdrop for his introspection. Images of his father blaze through his mind—a flood of wisdom, laughter, and unconditional love. "Perspective and context," he muses aloud, echoing the foundational teachings that were imparted to them. "Dad always had this uncanny ability to weave every lesson back to those principles. To remind us of our incredible fortune to be alive in this era. That no matter how bad things might be in the moment, hour, day, or year . . . we've all hit the cosmic jackpot being alive in this place and in this time."

As they turn the corner and leave the scene for good, the momentousness of what lies ahead settles in. Celebrating the final day of the decade is a distant thought now. Retribution is top of mind. Their new friends died violently at the hands of someone who represents the seeds of this new elite class striving for a distorted vision of immortality.

"Sometimes the most effective forms of innovation and problem-solving simply require recovering what was lost," Deuce says, his pace quick and determined, Chew keeping up with him step for step in the heart of downtown San Francisco.

"What's that?" Chew asks.

"Another one of dad's favorite adages," Deuce says. "Our next move is to find Charisma's mom."

"I'm with ya 100 percent. Always and all the way, my man."

"I know you are, buddy," Deuce says, stopping for a red light at an intersection in the bustling city center. "There are no other men like you, Chew. Only you."

To be continued . . .

The Time & Space program referenced throughout God Bless You, Mr. Trump was passed with bipartisan support in 2030 and implemented across the majority of public schools by 2033. It was funded through a voluntary tax on the wealthiest 0.1 percent of Americans. Of the nearly 200,000 households who qualified, more than 90 percent opted in. What follows is a recovered transmission from the private archives of Philipp Largo, sent anonymously to the Wall Street Journal on the first day of 2050.

"Groovy Nordy" by Philipp Largo

The crimson embers danced and swirled in the bonfire, casting restless shadows on the dunes of Santa Rosa Beach. Winter break stretched out before us, a welcoming emptiness of recharging, promising lazy mornings and sun-kissed afternoons. As the Gulf Coast sparkled and awed with every gentle wave, my attention wasn't on the rhythm of the ocean or the warmth of the flames. It was on Nordy, my colossal suitemate, his silhouette a titan against the stardusted night.

Nordy, the behemoth defensive lineman with a beard like tangled midnight and hands capable of crushing coconuts, was, despite his imposing exterior, way more philosophy than fists. Off the field he carried a surprising gentleness—and a curiosity he rarely voiced. But that night, as the ocean breeze teased through his thick mane and a book about science trumping religion buzzed in his mind, something inside him cracked open.

The catalyst? Richard Dawkins' *The God Delusion*, a book that shook my own foundations weeks prior. But Nordy, not known for his literary pursuits, devoured my enthusiastic summaries like a neutron star consuming gas. And under the boundless Florida sky, with the Milky Way stretched above like a long trail of cosmic sugar, the conversation ignited.

Time and space, those abstract giants, became tangible toys in our hands. We marveled at the Milky Way's hundred billion stars, a number so mind-blowing it sent Nordy pacing the sand, roaring, "No way, man! How can we know this?! I always knew the universe was *big*, but this is . . . I can't even begin to wrap my head around it. It's making my mind hurt thinking about that kind of size for even a second." Every answer I offered—from the wonders of Hubble to the revelation of spectroscopy and the precision of carbon dating—was like tossing logs into a growing fire inside him.

And then, as the sun dipped low, painting the sky in hues of tangerine and indigo, that fire became something else entirely. Nordy returned from his beachside rant, eyes lit with intensity. "Dude," he boomed, "it's like an atom bomb of wonder dropped into my skull. I . . . I need to know more."

I recalled that very feeling myself, years prior. Reading the right books—maybe not at the right time, but devouring them nevertheless. The age of our planet and the known universe. The ever-expanding size of the cosmos. Our brief but extraordinary time here, on planet Earth. The staggering explosion in human ingenuity over the past few decades relative to the tens of thousands of years that came before. All these pieces of knowledge stacked atop one another like stones on a sacred path, pointing toward something essential. A feeling and tacit understanding of how we're at once so incredibly tiny and insignificant—but also rare and astonishing beyond measure.

A week later, back on campus, Nordy barged through our adjoining bathroom doors as he often did, this time grinning ear-to-ear and clutching a half-dozen books: Sagan, Dawkins, Hawking. "That night on the beach set my brain on fire," he declared. "It's all I've been thinking about. These gents shall serve as my guide now."

And in that moment, under the fluorescent lights of our dorm hallway, another surge lit up inside me. What if everyone—not just a college buddy like Nordy—could experience this kind of awakening? What ripple effects would it have on humanity? On our fragile blue dot adrift in the cosmic sea?

That week, fueled by Nordy's enthusiasm, Sagan's poetic musings, and my own yearning to share the magic of existence with every soul under the same sky, the seed was sown. It was a dream born not out of curriculum standards or education reform—but from the simple, profound belief that awe changes people.

The *Time & Space* program was conceived not just as an educational initiative, but as a cultural movement—designed to ignite curiosity and imagination on a mass scale. It was about helping people, especially young minds, connect to the immensity of the cosmos, to understand the singular chance of being alive and sentient, and to be moved by that recognition. But above everything, it was to hammer home the most vital message of all: the rarity and sanctity of life. And that no matter your age, race, gender, creed, political affiliation, or sexual orientation, *we're all in this thing together.*

Nordy's journey—from the trenches of football to the galaxies overhead—remains one of the most important transformations I've ever witnessed. His story, rooted in pure and unpretentious curiosity, showed what's possible when a mind is sparked at the right time. He reminded me that the human spirit, when properly lit, is capable of absorbing the immenseness of the universe without feeling crushed by it.

His awakening became the emotional blueprint for the program. And his response—that fevered, reverent hunger to know more—affirmed that wonder isn't reserved for poets or physicists. It's in everyone, waiting to be activated.

As I reflect on those early days—the bonfire, the crashing waves, the wild questions shouted into the wind, and the birth of what would become a national movement—I feel nothing but gratitude. Because it wasn't policy or funding or academic pedigree that gave this idea its start. It was friendship. It was starlight. It was beer and a beach and questions without answers.

And it was one very groovy goliath, pacing the shoreline, roaring at the heavens, demanding to understand his place in it all.

If we can ignite that kind of hunger in just one person—just one—we can start a chain reaction that alters the trajectory of our entire species. Not with fire or fury, but with awe. With curiosity. With perspective.

That night on the sand showed me what was possible. And it's why, to this day, I believe the best kind of revolution doesn't begin with a bang—but with a quiet conversation under the stars . . .

ACKNOWLEDGEMENTS

This book started with a conversation. Followed by a challenge. Back in December 2017, my good friend William Pattison and I were discussing future cities—places where we could meet for a weekend or two in the coming year. He lives in New Jersey; I live in Cedar Rapids. But instead of locking down anything specific, the discussion drifted to what future travel might someday look like for the average American. He challenged me to write a story where momentous leaps in technology drastically bring down the cost and improve the efficiency of travel for ordinary folks.

That was all it took.

The concept lit a fire. It touched on so many aspects of life that have long fascinated me—none more than humanity's greater story. Where do we come from, and where are we going? Within a few weeks, writing most nights, the tale evolved into something much more.

I've been deeply influenced by modern thinkers, historians, and scientists like Carl Sagan, Sam Harris, Yuval Noah Harari,

Jennifer Doudna, and Stephen Hawking. Their work planted a seed: *What if our collective future was shaped by minds like them—rather than politicians, influencers, or pop icons? What if society at large could see the world through their lens?*

Steven Pinker's *Enlightenment Now* became the perfect companion as these ideas crystallized in early 2018. To my mind, there's no book that more clearly articulates why—despite our constant turmoil and cultural friction—we're living in *by far* the best era in human history to be alive. Thank you, Dr. Pinker, for offering the world that perspective.

And while I'm on the topic of thank-yous, a special one to Bill Maher. Through his weekly show, I've been introduced to many of the minds that helped shape this book. He may be the only one still genuinely trying to have conversations with both sides—a rarity in these divided times. Thanks, Bill. I hope my Friday nights remain *Real Time* for years to come.

After nearly four years of solitary progress, I was ready to share the work. On a February Friday in 2022, four of my fellow bibliophile friends met me at a local restaurant, armed with notes and red pens, ready to discuss where the story stood. To Kenyon Thorp, Ellen Seyfer, Clarissa Koch, and Laura Thomas: That evening remains one of my all-time favorites. Your candor, preparation, and generosity made all the difference in shaping what this book would become.

I'd also like to thank Jason "Wild Card" Blue, who documented the discussion while sipping Jameson neat—and Judge Nicholas Scott, who reviewed an early draft and didn't hold back. Gentlemen, your honesty helped me course-correct at a critical moment. Thank you both.

After much restructuring, I knew I still needed help—real help. And that's where Brie Shouppe enters. Through a mutual connection (her wonderful mother, Julie Kraft), Brie learned about the project and what I was trying to do. Since November 2022, she's been part editor, part marketer, part strategist, and part counselor—and a trusted friend. Brie, I know it sounds cliché, but I truly wouldn't have gotten here without you. Thank you, a million times over. I hope this is just the first of many creative journeys we take on together.

Once I secured a publishing deal with Indigo River, I still had work to do to elevate the manuscript. That's where David Remy came in. Over eight months of thoughtful collaboration, David helped me refine the story's structure, deepen the characters, and sharpen the edges. David, you're the finest editor I've worked with in over 25 years of writing. Thank you for your wisdom, your patience, and your precision.

To Noella Simmons—thank you for your careful, thoughtful copy editing of the final manuscript. Your eye for language and rhythm made the final stretch far smoother and stronger. And to my good friend Matt "Jimmy" Like, who eagle-eyed the final, final version and helped correct the last batch of lingering inconsistencies and errors—you were clutch in the eleventh hour. Thank you for stepping in and elevating the work one last time.

I've had the privilege of traveling from Berlin to Bangkok since graduating college in 2003. Along the way, I've met so many remarkable people—but no one, *no one*, is a better human being than my mom. And I say that as objectively as I can. She's a selfless saint and a terrific teacher without peer. She read a late draft in the summer of 2024 and, as always, told me exactly what I needed to hear. Thanks, Mom. You've always been there when it mattered most.

And finally, to my wife, Sarah. Thank you for putting up with all the emotions, obsessions, and peculiarities that come with the writer's life. I know it's not easy some days. There's no one I'd rather orbit the sun with at 67,000 miles per hour. You are my ultimate copilot, and my best friend on this beautiful, fragile, fertile pale blue dot.

ABOUT THE AUTHOR

Jesse Thoeming is a writer whose work explores the intersection of humanity, progress, and imagination. Originally from southern Illinois, where he grew up in the shadow of the Gateway Arch, he has lived and worked in Cedar Rapids, Iowa, for over two decades. His essays and commentary have appeared in numerous local and regional publications, and his debut novel, *The Brown Bottle Squeeze*, earned praise for its narrative voice and depth of character. *God Bless You, Mr. Trump* marks the beginning of a bold speculative trilogy set in the near future.

When he's not writing or traveling the country and world with his wife, Sarah, Jesse finds his balance on open-air trails—hiking, biking, and thinking deeply about where we've been—and where we might be going next.

www.ingramcontent.com/pod-product-compliance
Lightning Source LLC
LaVergne TN
LVHW091034080826
845145LV00002B/492

* 9 7 8 1 9 6 9 9 3 5 1 6 9 *